DEAD GAME

Keith Calder is an itinerant gunsmith and shooting instructor. He is also a rascal with a total disregard for the law, a skilled and dedicated poacher of birds of both varieties.

Calder is a guest at a shoot in the Scottish Borders when one of the syndicate members dies—apparently by accident, but a bullet is found in his body.

Calder has a personal interest in the case, which deepens when the brother of his current girlfriend is arrested and charged with the murder. Calder begins to makes his own enquiries but he and Molly find themselves in danger . . .

DEAD GAME

Gerald Hammond

First published 1979
by
Macmillan London Ltd

This edition 2004 by BBC Audiobooks Ltd
published by arrangement with
the author

ISBN 0 7540 8660 7

British Library Cataloguing in Publication Data available

Printed and bound in Great Britain by
Antony Rowe Ltd., Chippenham, Wiltshire

I have tried very hard to create characters who bear no resemblance to any real persons. If any unlucky combination of name, place, description, profession and/or other factors causes embarrassment to anyone, I can only offer to buy them lunch while I apologise. (This invitation is, of course, as fictitious as the characters.)

G.H.

CHAPTER 1

The ambulance jounced away down the track behind the fire-engine, followed in its turn by a short and sad procession of cars. The two big vehicles lurched straight ahead, while the cars felt their way carefully between the ruts and pot-holes like Rangers fans among Celtic supporters.

Two vehicles remained on the patch of turf where the track ended at a gate to a field of stubble. The van was brown with green panels. It was not camouflaged, but it settled back into its surroundings, modest and unassuming, while the police Land Rover, orange on white, dominated the scenery as if on point-duty.

The uniformed inspector of police looked round at the creased and folded countryside, with moors above and fields around and the red-brown froth of tree-tops foaming in the valleys below, all glowing in the late afternoon autumn sunshine. The inspector had the long, moody face of the true Celt. He came from Lewis, and the comparative lushness of this lowland country still surprised him and left him ill at ease. He sighed, turned to the van, knocked curtly and climbed inside. The sergeant who followed him in was a local man, hefty and rubicund.

Despite a number of obvious modifications the outside of the van betrayed its origin as a mobile bank, but internally the front half at least bore more resemblance to a modern cabin cruiser. The driver's and passenger's seats had been replaced by swivel armchairs which were now unlocked and turned to face the flapped table bolted to the centre of the floorspace. A settee or bunk ran along the offside wall. A partition cut off the rear half of the interior, and along this was a compact galley. In the near corner, beside a door to the rear half, stood a unit in which a small television set and an amateur-band radio were conspicuous. Incongruously, a smell like peat-smoke was in the air, competing with the smell of cooking. The inspector thought that it smelled like the croft he grew up in.

From a basket under the table a black Labrador bitch raised her head and tensed, but she relaxed on a word from her master although her eyes were alert.

Keith Calder, who was drying glasses at the sink, deliberately finished his work and put the glasses away in a fiddled mahogany rack. He was a handsome man in a black-haired, gipsyish way, and this, he knew, was a disadvantage in his dealings with other men. His build was that of an athlete.

Calder hung up his cloth and only then acknowledged the presence of the two policemen, although in that confined space only an insensate object could have missed them.

'Now, Mr Calder,' the inspector said. 'I've kept you waiting, but at least you could wait in comfort.'

Keith Calder nodded. 'Sit down,' he said. The inspector and the sergeant took the armchairs, but Keith sat at the end of the bunk where he could monitor the progress of a panful of meat. 'I'd have been here making a meal, anyway,' he said.

The policeman nodded. 'I'm Inspector Munro,' he said, 'and this is Sergeant Ritchie. I'm not needing to tell you what it's about. We've taken short statements from the others and let them away home. They were cold and shocked.'

'And important?'

'Aye, they're not the sort of folk to offend lightly,' the inspector admitted. 'I'll get their full statements the morn.'

'But tonight it's my turn.'

'I left you to last, Mr Calder, because you had a fine, warm place to wait in, with food and a dram and a change of clothing.' The inspector looked around him. 'That's a fine smell. Pheasant, is it?'

Keith Calder raised his eyebrows. 'How would it be pheasant on the first day of the season?'

'I was thinking that it might be one of today's.'

'A pheasant is not worth the eating without hanging. Partridges, man. I'm making a game stew – two partridges and a rabbit. You'd be welcome to share it when it's ready.'

'No, thank you.'

8

'As you like. A dram, then?'

'Not on duty.' Nor any other time, his tone suggested.

'Too bad.' Keith poured a tot for himself from a Johnny Walker bottle and winked at the sergeant.

'You will not be drinking too much of that if you are driving, I hope,' said the inspector. 'I would not like to be interviewing you again so soon. Now, I will just ask you a few questions. Sergeant Ritchie will be making notes, so do not go too fast for him. Later, we will have a statement typed up for you to sign.'

'Fair enough. There's to be a fiscal enquiry?'

'That's for the fiscal himself to decide, but I wouldn't doubt it. Now, your full name?'

'Keith Donald Calder.'

'Age?'

'Over twenty-one.'

'Thirty-seven,' said the sergeant.

'I'm not quite thirty-six,' Calder said.

Inspector Munro smiled faintly. 'Address?'

'No fixed abode. This is my home. This van.'

The inspector grunted. 'There is no need to be thrawn, Mr Calder,' he said. 'I am not after you for any offence just now. But I need an address where I can reach you. Otherwise, if we put you down as a vagrant, I'll have to keep you under my hand until the need for your evidence is past.'

Keith Calder shrugged. 'I can always be reached through my sister. She acts as my secretary and *poste restante*, and I'm in touch with her by phone or radio at least once a day. Put care of Mrs Elsie McKinness.' He spelt out a Perthshire address.

'Ah. That's how we got the message through the Dundee police?'

'Not quite.' Calder nodded at the radio. 'My sister listens for me twice a day, and takes messages between times. But I couldn't raise her this time, so I got through to somebody else. I have a licence to transmit.'

'I never doubted it,' the inspector said patiently. 'Your occupation?'

'Itinerant gunsmith and shooting instructor.'

'And dealer?'

'To a limited extent.'

'Right. Now, would you tell us in your own words about the events of today.'

Calder hesitated. 'I've a pretty thorough memory for anything that I noticed at the time. Do you want every tiny detail.'

Inspector Munro made a gesture of uncertainty. 'That is just the trouble, Mr Calder. We don't know yet what we're investigating. Very likely it will turn out to be a big nothing – as far as the law is concerned, but not for himself of course. On the other hand, if it turns out to be a matter for us, then we'll need every detail. So just tell us about the day, if you will, and I'll tell you if you're saying too much or too little. But take as long as you like.'

Calder looked into space for a moment, his grey-green eyes pensive. 'Several weeks ago,' he said at last, 'I was invited by Sir Peter Hay to come on today's shoot. I've been asked before, and always accept if I can. Sir Peter owns most of the land around here, and he's a member of the local syndicate. I gathered that several of the syndicate members wanted to make up a party for opening day – this is the first of October, in case you hadn't noticed, and pheasant shooting opens today. Only three of the members could get away, as it's mid-week. As a result it was rather a mixed bag of guests, not all of them local. Some of them had come a fair way.

'We met at the farm-house, a dozen people altogether including myself. I'd met most of them before, either here or on other shoots, or as clients. In fact I think I'd done work for most of them at one time or another, and I'm re-stocking Sir Peter's best gun for him just now.'

'Did they all seem to know each other?' asked the inspector.

'I couldn't say – I was almost the last arrival. I certainly didn't notice any introductions being made. But I did notice that there seemed to be some embarrassment – not needle, just a feeling that two or three of them shouldn't be talking to each other because of a court case or something.'

'Who were those?' the inspector asked.

'Offhand, I don't remember. Could it be important?'

'Probably not. Go on with the story of the day.'

'All right. Well, Hamish Thomson – the big chap with all the hair – he acts as gamekeeper although I don't think he's full-time, and he was organising the whole thing, but I think he was very much following the orders of Sir Peter, who heads the syndicate.'

'Why did you think that?'

'Because he seemed to avoid the best pheasant coverts. Understandable, with only three of the syndicate present – they'd want to leave plenty on the ground, but just give us enough sport for a worthwhile day. And he gave the syndicate members the easiest day of it, though to be fair he gave the older guests an easy time of it too, and left the uphill work and the hard going to the younger guests.'

'There were no beaters as such?'

Calder shook his head sadly. 'I'm afraid the kind of shoot that gets paid beaters is the perk of the rich, or of estates that charge the foreigners a packet to have half-tame birds driven over their heads. But you can still manage with a large party if you split it in half and organise it well.

'Hamish took us up to the top in the Land Rover and gave us a beat along the bit of moor, for grouse. He took the standing party up first and then came back for us athletes and took us to the other end, and we beat towards the butts. It wasn't very profitable, because the grouse season opened about seven weeks ago and the birds are getting pretty wily. Then we walked down through a small wood, supposed to be for pheasants but we only got three plus a blackcock and some pigeon. Then across the top pasture in a long line, picking up a few hares, and downhill again through another small wood. The seniors went to the bottom and stood while we drove down to them, and this time there were some pheasants all right.

'Game-bags were getting pretty heavy. Hamish walked up and fetched down the Land Rover and took the bag aboard and also the frailer brethren, but we of sterner stuff walked across the lower fields for hares again, although I could see a stream and bushes below us that were fairly hopping with pheasants.

'That brought us all to the barn at the top of this wood

– Oak Wood, they call it, though there are precious few oaks in it now. We ate our sandwiches in or around the barn, and Hamish had laid on coffee in a couple of big flasks, and some drinks.'

The inspector raised an eyebrow, and the sergeant looked up. 'Was much drink taken?'

'Not a lot, that I noticed. Most of us had a tin of beer with our lunch, and a dram to follow. And there was something different for Lady Hay. I certainly didn't notice anybody over-indulging, and they all seemed pretty steady afterwards. When there's been a boozy lunch you hear people shouting at each other to be careful.'

'Did they all stay together?'

'Lord, no!' The late sun which had glowed through the cabin and struck ruby lights off the surfaces was down now and Keith Calder reached up and switched on a pair of fluorescent lights. The roomlet brightened up. 'We moved about, went for a stroll so as not to stiffen up. Went round the back of the barn for a pee, Lady Hay being there. That sort of thing. But I didn't notice anybody being out of sight for more than a couple of minutes. And then some of the dog-owners got into an argument, and to settle it Hamish got a couple of rabbits out of the Land Rover and we did a little test in turn with Hamish judging and a pound each in the kitty. A double retrieve, one of them out of sight. Hebe won it for me,' he added with satisfaction, and hearing her name the bitch looked up and her tail gave a thump. 'Come to think of it, I picked up a fiver, so there must have been five of us in it.'

'And then?'

'Then Hamish loaded the aged and infirm into the Land Rover again and Sir Peter drove them round and back to the bottom of the wood, and on a whistle signal we started down.'

'What was the order of people at that time?' the inspector asked in his soft and careful West Highland diction.

Keith Calder grimaced in an effort of memory. 'Three of us with dogs went down the inside of the wood. David McNeill, the tall chap with the face like a parrot, he went down the middle. He's a councillor, somewhere around the

Forth, I think, and has something to do with the building industry. I was on his right, and on his left was Ron McLure, the man who died. I hardly knew him, but he was a heavily-built man with protruding teeth, and he had a strong Glasgow accent although he practised in Edinburgh. He was an architect, I think. But you probably know all this.'

'Never mind,' said Inspector Munro. 'Go on.'

'Outside the wood on our right, that's the west side, was Derek Weatherby, the stout, grey-haired man. He had his daughter Janet with him – the girl of about fifteen.'

'Was she shooting?'

'Oh, yes. She has her own twenty-bore which I stocked for her – a lot of my work's in guns for youngsters – and she's getting quite good. Anyway, her father's the farmer here, and a member of the syndicate.

'On the left flank, outside the wood on the eastern side, was Andrew Payne. I gather he has a factory, somewhere around Edinburgh. He's tallish, bald and expensively dressed, in case you've forgotten him, and he looks like a bloodhound with a lot on its mind. Hamish was further out on the same flank and a bit forward, because that's slightly the more downhill side. The wood runs down the hill but a bit diagonally, if you follow me. The birds try to slip out downhill, and Hamish was there to encourage them to follow the line of the wood down to the standing guns.

'We set off down Oak Wood – '

'Time?'

'About two-thirty.'

'And kept the same formation?'

'As far as we could. You've seen the place. It's nearly half a mile long by about sixty yards broad on average, wider in bits. Here and there are some deciduous trees of various sizes, and undergrowth of brambles and so on, and there are clearings where it's rocky and broken. But much of it has been re-planted forestry-style with conifers, and in those strips it's hellish hard going, all ridges and furrows, and since the furrows aren't quite at right-angles to the line of the wood you tend to squeeze up towards one end. It was hard going, as I said, and the midges were still out in strength, and where it's really thick you don't often see each other, so it was difficult to keep a straight line.'

'Would that not be getting dangerous?' the inspector asked.

'In those conditions, it's only safe to shoot overhead, and as far as I know that's what everybody did. He wasn't shot, was he?'

'We won't know that until after the post mortem.'

'No, I suppose not. Well, we worked down the length of the wood, downhill and slightly across the slope, all the way. We got a number of pheasants ourselves, but we flushed a whole lot and sent them down the hill, and it sounded like a small war at that end. I know I was carrying a brace and a large hare in my bag, and Weatherby and his lassie on my flank had done better. I heard plenty of shots on my left as well, but I don't know how they connected.

'At last we got to the bottom. I was pretty damn tired after that rough going. At the bottom, we were looking down from the top of the banking just above where we are now. The standing guns were in the field the other side of the track. From my left to right were Captain Hodges, the old sea-dog. He shoots as if he's steering a clipper. He's a fierce-looking little man, but I've had some dealings with him and he's as mild as they come really. He lives up in Fife somewhere. Then Mr Oxter, who makes me think of a rather large gnome, but in a flabby, pasty way. He's a solicitor, practising somewhere around Dundee, but I believe he's semi-retired now from something I heard him saying. Then Sir Peter, and Lady Hay next to him. And lastly, on the right of the line as I looked at it, William Hook. I believe he's another solicitor by training, but he's something very senior in one of the new local authorities. You wouldn't think it to look at him, though – he looks much more like a farmer than Weatherby does – all muscles and sunburn. Probably gymnasium and sun-lamp, but we can't all have open-air jobs.

'We were looking down from the top of the banking as I said. There was quite a scattering of pheasants on the stubble. Oxter and Lady Hay were working their dogs, and the rest of the standing party were picking-up by hand. Oxter's dog, I remember, was having the very devil of a job.

He was trying to retrieve a runner. He's only a small Cocker, and the runner was a cock almost as big as himself and a damned sight angrier.

'Then Sir Peter looked up and asked where McLure had got to.'

The inspector, who had been glaring at Keith's shelf of books as if betting himself that they were only there for show, roused himself and broke in. 'Now, stop just a minute,' he said. 'That was the first time that he was missed?'

'It was the first time that I noticed his absence or heard anyone else remark on it,' Keith said carefully.

'Was everyone else present and in their proper places?'

Keith Calder paused again, looking through the van's thin wall to conjure up again the scene as it had been. 'Yes, I'm sure of it,' he said at last. 'The standing party was all there, as I described it. Janet was chattering to her father on my right. McNeill on my left was mopping his forehead and shouting at his dog which is an ill-trained beast from a bad stock. Beyond him I could see Payne looking through his gun-barrels. And Hamish was already down on the track.'

'What happened next?'

'Sir Peter asked whether anyone had seen McLure. McNeill said not since we were about half-way down. Payne said he thought he'd seen him only a hundred yards back, but it might have been McNeill or me that he saw – we were all wearing those waterproof grey shooting-jackets and flap-less deerstalkers, so that it'd be easy to mistake us.

'That was about the last peaceful moment of the day. Captain Hodges, in that rather squeaky voice of his, said that he could see smoke coming from the wood.

'We left our guns and bags on the track with Lady Hay to watch over them, and the rest of us puffed our way up the east side of the wood. I'm probably the fittest of the lot, except maybe for Derek Weatherby, but I must admit I found it steeper going up than I had coming down. We could see a good blaze developing, and the thought in my mind was that McLure was a fool to stop and try to fight it alone instead of getting help.

'Derek and I were first on the scene with Janet on our heels and the rest arriving roughly in inverse order of age.

15

'An area about twenty yards square was blazing, with some smaller patches alight round about, probably where sparks had flown from the original blaze. And, by God, it was really burning. You know how dry it's been for weeks past. When we were up on the moor the heather had just smoked with dry pollen behind the dogs. It was mostly heather and grass and old leaves that were burning. Fortunately the area was bare and rocky in places or the whole wood might have caught. In the middle of the fire were two gorse-bushes, probably dead ones from the way they were blazing, and McLure's body was lying between the two bushes. His dog was going round and round the outside of the blaze, whimpering.

'William Hook wanted to dash into the flames and drag him out – who'd have thought the old perisher had the guts? But it was obviously too late. The body was actually burning. I didn't know that a person could catch fire like that.'

'Aye,' said the inspector. 'I've seen it before. The fat melts, you see, and the clothes acts like a wick in a candle.'

'So I saw. There was no saving McLure, so the first thing was to get the fire under control without anyone else getting hurt. Payne had a muckle great sheath-knife on him, so we cut branches to beat at the flames with.

'As soon as the fire seemed to be under control, I offered to run down and call the emergency services. Weatherby said his phone was out of order, and I said I would use my radio. I ran down here, told Lady Hay what was ado, and jogged along to the farm-house. I got on the radio there,' he nodded at it. 'My sister at Aberfeldy listens out for me twice a day, and I can sometimes raise her at other times but this wasn't one of them. So I managed to get on to a ham near Arbroath and asked him to pass on the messages for me.'

'What did you do then?'

'Brought the van along the track to here. Lady Hay had gone up to see that Sir Peter was all right, I suppose. The smoke was less evident, but that kind of fire can flare up again in a moment, so I guessed that the others were all standing by or dealing with small outbreaks. I thought somebody should be here to watch over all the guns and to tell

16

the emergency services where to go. So I stayed here, had a wash and changed out of my smoky clothes, and waited.'

'You didn't make any more calls?'

'No.' Calder looked at his watch and got up. He sampled his stew and turned out the gas under it, and then busied himself preparing a meal for the Labrador.

Inspector Munro recognised the hint without being flustered by it. 'We shan't keep you very much longer,' he said. 'But we saw the body after the fire had done its worst. You saw it before it was so badly burned. Did you see anything at all to suggest a cause of death?'

Keith Calder shook his head without turning round. He sprinkled meal on the meat and put the dog's dish down on the floor. The Labrador opened her eyes wide, but not another muscle moved. Calder turned round and leaned back against the sink. He was feeling nauseated by the memory of the burning corpse and the smell that had hung over the scene, but he would have joined the late McLure rather than let the inspector see his weakness.

'I saw nothing at all like that,' he said. 'But then, the body was smoking and we were kept about ten yards back by the flames. I took it that he'd probably fainted or had a heart attack while lighting that filthy pipe of his, and set the fire going that way. Did you find his pipe under the body?'

The inspector shook his head. 'It was beside him. But since the jacket was mostly burned away there was no saying whether it had been in his pocket.' He shifted his position uneasily, and his soft Stornaway lilt became more noticeable. 'It is a bit difficult. The medical examiner may find anything in him, from signs of a thrombosis to an ounce of shot. We cannot keep everyone here until the morn, and yet it would be foolish to let the evidence be scattered, just in case. First of all, it would be helpful to know your forthcoming movements. There may be more questions, you understand, when we know how the man died.'

Calder looked at his watch again, and switched on the radio. 'My sister should be coming on the air now,' he said. He returned the set to a frequency that was carefully marked with a painted arrow, and suddenly the van was filled with

17

the sound of a clock ticking, greatly magnified. He turned the volume down, but it was still like being an ant trapped in an alarm clock. 'It's her tuning signal,' Calder said. 'She puts the microphone down on the kitchen clock.'

The inspector made an impatient movement. 'Is it really necessary?'

'She keeps my up-to-date diary.'

In the background of the ticking could be heard, faintly, the sound of chickens. A pair of feet approached *crescendo*, there was a creaking of wicker as somebody sat, and then harsh, metallic sounds made them flinch as a distant microphone was lifted.

'Keith? Keith? Are you there, Keith?'

'I'm here, Elsie. Over.'

'Keith? Are you there?' Elsie's voice was plaintive.

'Elsie, you're still transmitting. Switch to receive. Over. Normal service will be resumed as soon as possible,' he added to the inspector, 'but she has to learn the way of the damn thing every time.'

'Keith? Are you there, Keith?'

'Switch over, Elsie. Take your thumb off the tit.' Calder raised his voice, as if somehow that would force her to hear him.

'Hullo, Keith. Are you there, Keith?'

'Bloody woman!' he exploded. 'Next time I'm up there, I swear I'll fit a radio-controlled electro-magnet, so that I can shoot a needle up through the seat of the chair every time she forgets to take her thumb off . . . Hullo, Elsie. Over.'

'I am sure you would not do such a thing, Keith. And if you call me "Bloody woman" on the air again you can find yourself a proper secretary and telephonist and radio operator. Are you all right, Keith? Over.'

'I'm fine, Elsie. I'm at Corner Farm, on Sir Peter Hay's shoot. Elsie, would you please read out my diary, from now into December? Over.'

Elsie read the diary while Keith filled in the gaps and amended his own copy. Some telephone numbers, for calling back, were passed. 'Keith,' she finished, 'I had that nice Mr Skelly on the phone from Arbroath. He said you'd been trying to reach me about an accident. It was not an accident to yourself was it, Keith?'

'Nothing at all like that, Elsie. It was nobody you know, and – '

'Keith, you must press the titty when you want to transmit, or else I can't hear you,' Elsie's voice said triumphantly.

Keith Calder finished the transmission a little red around the ears. He sat down and passed his diary to the sergeant.

'Here you are,' he said. 'The two speaking engagements, the coaching dates with the clubs and the field trial are firm and inflexible. The Saturday shoots I can miss but I don't want to. The other engagements I can shift, given a little notice.'

While the sergeant copied out the dates, the inspector looked over his shoulder. 'You're going north, then,' he said.

'Aye. I want to get round my clients up as far as Inverness and beyond, and back down the west coast, before the worst of the weather. If it looks like a hard winter I'll probably spend most of January and February around Dumfries or Galloway, catch up with a backlog of work, and then start round again.'

'But we can always reach you through your sister's phone number?'

'That's so.'

The sergeant returned the diary.

'You've been very helpful,' said the inspector. 'If you'll be giving us just a little more co-operation, then we'll be leaving you in peace. We'd just like to give your van a bittie search.'

'What in hell for?'

'If I was knowing that, Mr Calder, I would not be needing to search. We would not even be needing the post-mortem examination. By the time we get the report, all kinds of evidence could have been lost, destroyed or disposed of. The others didn't mind a search of their cars.'

'Maybe not,' said Calder. 'But this is my home. What if I object?'

The inspector's voice took on the coaxing tone special to the West Highlander. 'I'm sure you'll be reasonable, Mr Calder. You're a registered gun-dealer – '

'I'm sure that a man like yourself wouldn't threaten me,' Calder said softly.

'Certainly not,' said the inspector. 'Of course. I was just pointing out that we have the right to inspect your stock of guns, and compare it with your register, at any time. But, as I said, I'm sure you'll see reason. We may find that McLure did not die naturally, and if we were to be trying to make a case against somebody, then a positive statement on record of what I have just said to you and that you had refused to co-operate . . . well, it might be suggested that you had known how the mannie had died, and maybe that a little time was needed to get rid of evidence.'

Calder sighed, but a very acute observer might have noticed an amused glint in his eyes. 'Very well,' he said.

The sergeant searched the small cabin thoroughly but without flair, while the inspector contented himself with scrutinising the objects on view and asking occasional questions. Calder, as far as he could in the confined space, kept out of their way.

The driving-living-kitchen half of the van revealed nothing of interest, but when they moved past the tiny compartment that held the lavatory and shower into the workshop section, the inspector whistled. 'You could fight a minor war with what you have here,' he said. 'Are these all stock?'

'These six, with the labels on,' Calder said, 'are in for repair. In fact I've done five of them and I'll be dropping them off in the next few days. The ones racked horizontally above the others – two shotguns, two rifles and a drilling – are my own. The others are stock, mostly single-barrelled twelve-bores, because I specialise in the fitting of guns for boys – or girls – who still have a bit to grow, and then take them back as a trade-in for an adult's gun.'

The sergeant completed a meticulous search, making copious notes, but missed the secret compartment sandwiched between the external game-cupboard and the back of the lavatory.

They stepped down into a dark world outside, although the moon was starting to rise and the higher ground was already washed cold with its light. The inspector took a lamp and set off round the van, kneeling to peer underneath.

'What if he'd accepted that dram?' the sergeant whispered.

'He wouldn't. And if he had he'd not know the difference, that one, islander though he is.'

The inspector rejoined them, puffing slightly. 'You'll be around here tonight and tomorrow?' he asked.

'I'm with Sir Peter tomorrow morning. That's his Holland and Holland inside. It was built for his father before him, so it was high time it was refitted. After that I go north into Fife.'

The sergeant snorted. 'Tonight he'll be parked behind Newton Lauder town hall,' he said.

'I will, will I?'

'M'hm. Ronnie Fiddler's at home.'

'Fiddler?' said the inspector. 'Is that the shopkeeper, or Sir Peter's man.'

'He's Sir Peter's stalker and gillie. Divides his time between here and the Dawnapool estate. He has a pretty sister. When he's away and Mr Calder's hereabouts, the van's parked behind the cottage. But when Ronnie's at home, he won't have him near the place.'

'Ah, well,' said the inspector. 'I've heard about you, Mr Calder. And if I had a sister and she was pretty, I wouldn't let you in the house either.'

'Likely not,' said Calder. 'But if you had one, she wouldn't be. And if she was, she wouldn't be your sister.'

Pleased with his retort, Calder was smiling as he swung himself up into the van. The bitch watched him out of the corner of her eye. 'Take,' he said softly, and in a flick of the eye she was at her dish.

'We'll just bide a little, Hebe,' Calder said conversationally as he began his own meal. 'Just until the moon's well up, and we're sure our visitors are well away. There was a couple of runners left, and I think we'll just collect them before we go down to the town hall and see if anyone else comes calling. Better us than the foxes.'

He fetched his oil, wax and turpentine from the workshop, put a cassette into the machine, and sat down to polish a gunstock to the sound of Sibelius.

When the moon was bright, he moved. He let the van run

back a few feet, and got down with a spade. Where one of the front wheels had stood he unearthed a flat box and carefully filled the hole and trod it down. The box he stowed for the moment under the driver's seat.

Locking the van, he called the bitch and they went up the hill in search of the pricked birds, content in each other's company.

CHAPTER 2

The morning was fine. An overnight frost had lifted but had left its print behind. The last of the green leaves were now bronzed in the golden light, and there was little warmth in the strength of the sun.

The two men were too preoccupied to notice the scenery or the weather.

Sir Peter Hay lowered his Holland and Holland and dropped the barrels. The empty cartridge flipped over his shoulder and Keith Calder fielded it neatly. A wisp of smoke drifted away.

'I think we'd better stop now,' Sir Peter said. 'You've got me hitting about nine out of ten, which is better than I've ever done before.' Although born and bred a Scot, Sir Peter had the accent of an English aristocrat, which seemed at odds with the kilt which he habitually draped around his bony frame and his unruly tangle of grey hair.

Keith put down the thrower and removed the last clay pigeon from its jaw. 'You're sure? They've been pretty easy birds so far.'

Sir Peter whinnied with laughter. 'Quite hard enough! Give me any harder ones and I'll lose my new-found confidence again. You can come back and give me some more coaching in a few weeks after I've settled down. Must you really take it away again, just at the start of the season?' he asked wistfully.

'You've got another gun.'

'But I don't *like* my other gun.'

'Do you want to sell it, then?'

Sir Peter laughed again. 'No, thank you very much. It's a good enough gun, it just hasn't been fitted to me like this one. You can do that job for me, if you like.'

'Surely,' Calder said quickly. A new stock for a gun of quality was an expensive item.

'Then you'll have to leave me this one,' said Sir Peter.

'All right,' Calder said, laughing. 'I'll give it a coat of oil now and leave it with you, and collect it for finishing at the end of the season.'

'Fine.' Sir Peter handed over a cheque. 'I think this squares us up to date, including the cartridges. Are you coming up to the Hall for a dram?'

'Thank you but no,' Keith said. 'I'll need to be away shortly, so I'll get on with your stock. You just fetch your other gun while I make a start, and then you can have one with me.'

'All right.' Sir Peter hesitated. 'With all the kerfuffle yesterday, I never gave you a brace of birds. I'll bring them back with me.'

'No need for that,' Keith said. 'I collected a couple of runners after you'd gone.'

Sir Peter looked at him. 'You're a funny chap,' he said. 'I thought you'd probably gone after the runners, and I was – and am – quite prepared to give you another brace. And you've got the reputation of being the father and mother of poachers. Yet . . .'

'It may seem an impertinence,' Calder said stiffly, 'but I look on you as a friend – '

'Delighted, my dear fellow!'

' – and I don't poach off my friends, Sir Peter. The brace that I have will do fine, thank you.'

Sir Peter shook his head and turned away through the gate to the Hall garden. He looked pleased, but puzzled. He returned in a few minutes, carrying another gun but no pheasants, and climbed into the van.

A bottle and two glasses stood on the table. Keith was working at the cooker, putting a fine finish on the bare stock with a damp cloth, the gas flame, and the very finest of emery-paper.

'I thought you were just going to oil it,' Sir Peter said.

'I'm cleaning it first. No point starting to oil it over a rough surface. Help yourself, Sir Peter. Pour me a very small one, if you will, as I'll be driving.'

Sir Peter Hay watched, fascinated, as the skilled hands

put a new sheen on the surface of the wood. 'Sad business, yesterday,' he said at last.

'Very.'

'Odd sort of an accident, don't you think? I wondered if he'd taken a tumble and knocked himself out. He wasn't using safety-matches, because he gave me a light before we started and I remember, and if you fall on a box of the other sort, or lean on it heavily, you can set the whole box off. Did it myself, once, so I know. That could burn through his pocket and start a fire.'

'It could,' Keith said. 'I thought maybe he'd collapsed with a heart attack or something in the very act of lighting his pipe.'

'That could be it,' said Sir Peter. 'Or suppose he fell and his gun went off when it hit the ground. Could the muzzle-flash start a fire?'

Keith paused in thought for a moment 'I'd not like to say it was likely, nor impossible either.' He fetched his linseed oil, turpentine and a drying agent, and began to give the stock its first coat of oil.

'I sent Ronnie Fiddler up to McLure's place yesterday, to take the dog back and break the news if his wife hadn't already heard. She had, of course. Couldn't get away myself, but I'll pay a call tomorrow.'

'Upset was she?'

'Fiddler thought not. He said the dog was the more upset of the two. We had an awful job persuading it to leave the body. Well, I dare say we'll know more when the pathologist chappies have done their stuff.'

'No doubt.' Keith Calder held the stock up to the daylight. 'Nice piece of walnut.'

'Beautiful.'

'It'll go dull this time, of course. Just let my sister know when your pheasants are over and I'll pick it up again. You'll only be using the magnum after that?'

'True.'

'That's it, then. You can use it from tomorrow if you want. How's the deer situation?'

Sir Peter chortled. 'You mean when's Ronnie Fiddler going back up north? Not until December at the earliest.

The roe-deer on the hills here are getting out of hand, and the farmers are getting shirty. So he stays here until we can show them a good cull of does, and not even for the love-life of a friend will I say any different. It's a pity you two don't get along. Tell you what – I shouldn't do this, but come and join us on the Boxing Day shoot.'

'Thank you. I'd like that,' Calder said.

Sir Peter took his gun carefully in hand, avoiding touching the oily stock, and the two men climbed down onto the grass.

'Why, do you suppose,' Calder said slowly, 'was McNeill so determined to keep his Labrador away from McLure's Springer?'

'I didn't notice anything,' said Sir Peter. 'Season, perhaps.'

'They're both bitches.'

'Fleas, then.'

'Perhaps.'

Keith Calder spent an hour with a customer on Fala Moor, and by the time he slowed and stopped at the Forth bridge toll-gates darkness was almost complete. The lights of the bridge sprang away in a great arc across the river to Fife where the string of small towns sparkled along the coast.

The van had barely stopped before a uniformed constable appeared in its lights, signalling to Calder to pull out of the queue onto the bare apron at the side. Calder parked and switched off his engine, and the policeman came in through the nearside door.

'It is Mr Calder, isn't it?' he asked loudly.

Reluctantly, Calder killed the Berlioz tape. 'Yes.'

'Message from Newton Lauder. Inspector Munro wants to see you again, urgently.'

Calder sighed. 'What about?' he asked.

The constable was placid and impenetrable, armoured in ignorance. 'I wouldn't be knowing,' he said.

'I'm not taking this van all the way back, at fifteen to the gallon.'

'There's a car behind you to take you there. Leave the keys in the van. I'm to deal with it.'

26

Calder smiled. 'Why didn't you *say* before that it was the medical examiner's report on McLure.'

'I never said that!'

'Oh yes you did. Drive my van carefully.'

'You'll find it in the upper car-park when you get back.'

'There's a charge on that park,' Calder said. 'Leave it at the back of the motel, and the keys with the receptionist.' Calder spoke to Hebe, then climbed down and walked to the back of the van. A blue-and-white Rover was waiting, ticking-over. He dropped into the passenger's seat. 'You're to take me down to Newton Lauder?'

'That's right, sir,' said the driver.

'And back again?'

The driver hesitated, seeing his chance of dozing away half a night's duty slipping away. 'What makes you think you're coming back?' he said sourly, but he nodded all the same.

Keith Calder was whisked south again to Newton Lauder in a third of the time that it had taken for his heavily-loaded van to do the reciprocal journey that afternoon. Even so, the evening was well worn before they arrived at Newton Lauder's ugly, Victorian, police headquarters. The driver disappeared in search of the canteen, and Keith Calder was led upstairs.

Inspector Munro's room was typically institutional, the bare paint and varnished pine only slightly relieved by a few personal possessions almost as severe as the room itself. Group photographs including the inspector at a variety of ages were in evidence. Calder was only thankful that the inspector had refrained from hanging a selection of religious texts. The inspector, he decided, probably by now saw the room as homely and cheerful, but to its visitors it would always reek of gloom and Calvinism.

Sergeant Ritchie must already have been sent for tea. He entered on Calder's heels, bearing small paper cups of bitter machine brew. The waste-paper-basket was already half-full of cups, which suggested that the inspector had had a long day and many visitors.

'Sorry to fetch you back here, Mr Calder,' the inspector

said, 'but the sooner we got hold of you the less distance you'd have travelled.'

'Think nothing of it,' Calder said.

'There's your earlier statement ready to sign, and we have a few more questions for you.'

'I'm sure you do. But why are you still handling the case, instead of handing it over to your Criminal Investigation lads?'

The inspector was frowning at a sheet of notes that he had plucked from among the papers on his desk. 'They're badly under strength and have several other big cases on,' he said absently. 'Since this may be an accident, I'm carrying on.'

Calder leaned forward. 'What calibre of bullet was it?' he asked.

This time, the inspector did not miss the implication. He put down his notes and treated Calder to a glare. 'Who's been talking out of turn?' he demanded.

'Nobody,' said Calder. 'Why else would your colleagues be taking my van into Edinburgh, unless the ballistics were being done for you there and you wanted sample bullets out of my rifles?'

'Did they say they were going into Edinburgh with it?'

'No. But if they'd only wanted me to move it into the car-park, they'd have had me do that myself.'

'I see,' the inspector said slowly. 'I suppose you can infer what you like, I will just be getting on with it and taking a wee bittie further statement – '

'Why?' asked Calder.

'Why?'

'Yes. I have already given you an ample statement. Before I make another one, I want to know what the medical examination found. If I know what you're looking for I may even be able to help you.'

'I'm afraid your answers might be a little selective.'

'I'm not obliged to make a statement at all.'

'As a good citizen – '

'As just that, I'll give you a further statement when I know the cause of death.'

'This won't look good in the record.'

28

Calder laughed. 'Then put this in the record. First, I don't have to make a statement. Secondly, you haven't cautioned me. Thirdly, we can get this done much quicker if I know what you want. Fourthly, if I have anything to hide, then I already know whatever it is that you don't want to tell me. Fifthly – and note this down carefully, Sergeant – I believe that all men, guilty or innocent, lessen their chance of acquittal when they open their big mouths. By that, I mean that in the many cases in which an innocent man has been convicted of something – and you won't deny that such things happen, Inspector? – he wouldn't have been if he'd just kept silent. And – sixth and last – I may very well be called as an expert witness.'

'Why's that?' the inspector asked sharply.

'I was present, or at least nearby. And I'm qualified as an expert on gunshots and ballistics generally – remember what Lord Aves said in the High Court last year?'

Inspector Munro's face darkened. Lord Aves had complimented Keith Calder on his expertise and his lucidity, comparing him favourably with the expert witnesses put forward by the police.

'I don't quite see what you're getting at,' he said.

'I think you do,' said Calder. 'Unless you can give a definite assurance that no gunshot wounds were involved, I'm saying not another word until I know the basis of the p.m. report.'

The inspector leaned forward and pointed a bony finger into Calder's face. 'You're only guessing that he didn't die of a heart attack, and already you're trying to set yourself up for a fat fee.'

'At least I'm trying to keep my evidence intact.'

'You and Ron Fiddler,' the inspector said bitterly, 'no wonder you don't get along. You're the two awkwardest, scratchiest, *thrawnest* men I've ever known or even heard of. You must be like flint and steel.'

'Maybe. Now, are you going to tell me what this is about, or get the driver to take me back to my van?'

'You realise how awkward the police can be if you refuse to help them?'

Calder spoke very softly. 'I'm going to answer that remark, Inspector,' he said, 'and then I'm going to forget that you made it. But think twice before you threaten me again. I'm not refusing to help the police. I've already given a statement. I'm prepared to give another when I know how McLure died. I don't like crossing the police, but I don't like giving evidence blind either. Now, I may be the thrawnest man you ever met, but I'm probably also the most law-abiding. If you want to see the van's documents, my firearms certificates or dealer's licence, my dog licence, radio and television licences or my game licence, you're very welcome. I even have a permit to tape music off the radio.'

'And you're a notorious poacher.'

'Write that down, Sergeant, so that I can sue the inspector'.

'You were using the amateur wave-band for commercial messages.'

Keith Calder threw back his head and laughed at the grubby ceiling. 'You're getting desperate, Inspector,' he said at last. 'I'm properly licensed, and I have a commercial wavelength allocated to me, but whether it's any good or not depends on the weather, the time of day and the mountains. Sometimes I can't use it and I switch to the amateur band – it's a normal practice. It may be an offence, but only the Post Office can prosecute for it. If you think I've offended, Mr Thomson is the man to speak to.' Thomson was an old shooting friend.

The inspector leaned back in his chair. He gave a short laugh, and the sergeant grinned to himself. 'You're not easily pushed, are you,' said the inspector.

Calder half-smiled. 'I can be led but not driven,' he agreed.

'I'll tell you, but I'll ask you to keep it confidential for the next couple of days. We've other witnesses to see yet, and some folk can't help but remember whatever it is that they think will fit the facts.

'The pathologists dug a rifle-bullet out of him. Quite small. Point two four three calibre.'

Although he had justly boasted of a good memory, Keith Calder, when put to the test, was surprised at the irregularity of its performance. Those events of the previous day which he had noticed at the time were still clear in his mind, right down to who was wearing sunglasses and when, and what was playing on the various car radios as the guns arrived. But events to which he had paid no attention had faded already.

'You said that there seemed to be a feeling that two or three of the guests shouldn't have been talking to each other,' the inspector said at one point. 'Who were they?'

'I don't know. I was facing the van at the time, putting on my boots and cartridge belt, and I heard a man behind me say something like "We shouldn't really be here together, but as long as we don't chat I suppose it'll be all right". Words to that effect.'

'You've no idea whose voice?'

'Not for sure,' Calder said slowly. 'But it could have been McLure's.'

'Were the tones what you might call conspiratorial?'

'How do you mean?'

Inspector Munro cast up his eyes and made an uncomplimentary remark in Gaelic. 'I should have thought my meaning was clear to a witness of your expertise. Did he sound like a conspirator, as if he were saying "We shouldn't be seen together or someone may guess our secret"? Or was he just being careful and proper, saying "We shouldn't be talking together like this, as I'm interviewing you for a job tomorrow"?'

Calder, who understood Gaelic well and could even speak it with modest fluency, made mental note of another reason for disliking the inspector, but replied politely. 'Careful and proper, I think.'

'Can you think of any two guests, or small group, who didn't speak to each other after that?'

Calder looked into the dregs in his paper cup, and then threw it peevishly in the direction of the waste-basket. 'That's an impossible question,' he said. 'It's upside-down. I could probably make a list of who spoke to whom to my knowledge, other than the inescapable casual comments – you know what I mean? Things like "Your dog's got my bird" and "There's a gate over here" and "How the hell did I come to miss that one?". There were no obvious silences. And, of course, I don't know what conversations may or may not have happened outside my hearing.'

'We can come back to that later,' said the inspector.

Twenty exhausting minutes later, the subject was guns.

'Yes,' said Calder, 'of course I saw all the guns. In view of my trade, it'd be odd if I didn't. You've seen them too, of course. With one exception they were all double-barrelled, conventional guns of various quality. One sixteen-bore and one twenty-bore, the rest all twelve-bores. Two of those were over-and-unders, the rest side-by-sides. There were no single-barrelled repeaters. And the exception . . . William Hook was carrying a drilling.'

'Ah, yes. M'hm. That's the shotgun with an extra barrel, a rifle-barrel?'

'Correct. You saw one in my van last night. Hook's is a German one, sixteen-bore shotgun barrels. I don't know what bore the rifle-barrel is, but it was bigger than two-four-three, which is less than a quarter-inch diameter. His looked like nine-millimetre. But you'll have checked it yourselves.'

'What gun were you carrying?'

'A very nice Boss that I've had for years. I showed it to Hodges and Sir Peter Hay at lunchtime as an example of engraving.'

'I see . . . Nobody was carrying more than one gun?'

'Definitely not. Not a conventional rifle slung over the shoulder, anyway.'

Inspector Munro stretched, and fought back a yawn. It had been a long day, and it was far from over. 'But one of those knock-down guns that terrorists use? Could somebody have been carrying one of them?'

Keith Calder took his time and replied carefully. 'In theory perhaps. But there are three things against it. It wasn't a cold day so we weren't wrapped up – just tweeds or one of those slightly quilted shooting jackets. You could hide quite a lot in that sort of clothing standing still, but walking and climbing fences and shooting and lifting shot game . . . I very much doubt it. And those things take a little time to assemble and dismantle. Anybody seizing on the few moments that he might have while the rest of us were out of view would be taking one hell of a chance. And finally, at that kind of range the bullet would almost certainly have gone clean through him.'

'What about a pistol?'

Calder nodded. 'More probable. As I'm sure you've been told, there's no pistol made that would take a rifle cartridge like that, but any competent mechanic could take the mechanism and barrel of a rifle and fashion a pistol of sorts.'

'And that would be quicker to use and to hide again?'

'Obviously.'

'And more easily concealed?'

'Yes.'

'And of a reduced velocity?'

'If enough was cut off the barrel, yes.'

The inspector was silent for a moment, then nodded and moved on. 'What would you say were the possibilities of an adaptor-tube in a shotgun barrel?'

Calder scratched his head, and then he laughed. 'All right, Inspector, let's think around that one. Such things exist, of course, but usually for firing a small-bore shotgun cartridge out of a large-bore gun. In this case . . . the bullet had rifling-marks, of course – '

'How – ?'

' – because otherwise you wouldn't have asked about rifles and drillings. A rifle adaptor would tend to spin in the barrel from the counter-thrust of the rifling, which I should think would leave detectable traces – which could all have been polished away by now. It would have left him one barrel free to use while he waited for his opportunity, which would be adequate. But he would have had to get it out in the fairly short time that it took us to go down the wood to the bottom, and if it was loose enough to slip out easily I think it'd be noisy in use. Then he'd have to get rid of it somewhere in the wood. After all, he couldn't have known the body would be so badly burned that the bullet-wound wouldn't be spotted immediately.'

'That might have been the objective in starting a fire at all,' the inspector pointed out.

'Aye,' said Calder. 'Maybe. But not likely. Think how much easier it'd be just to blast him with your shotgun, and say "Sorry, I tripped and it went off by accident". You could never prove anything.'

Inspector Munro stretched and got up stiffly. He went to the window and looked down into the darkness. 'I know that well,' he said. 'But I must start off by thinking of every possible answer. That way the truth will not be missed.'

'Maybe.'

'Would you have known the difference by the sound of the shot, if someone had fired a rifle cartridge in the wood?'

Again, Calder took his time before answering. 'Probably but not necessarily. The sound of a shot changes with the gun, the cartridge, the distance, the angle it's fired at relative to the hearer, the humidity of the air, the surroundings and obstructions, and God knows what else. I *think* that all the shots I heard were from shotguns firing ordinary cartridges. But probably the guns standing down at the bottom would be better judges.'

The inspector turned away from the window and paced to and fro over the small area available to him. 'We'll ask them,' he said.

'I think you're barking up the wrong tree,' Calder said. 'But I think you think the same, yourselves.'

The inspector stared at him for a moment. 'Why?'

Calder smiled. 'Because if this was being treated as a probable murder, C.I.D. would be in charge, and you'd have at least a detective-constable sitting in. So you think the same as I think, that somebody on the hill nearby, say a mile away, let one off accidentally or fired at a deer and missed, and the bullet had to fetch up somewhere and McLure just happened to be in the way. That makes more sense to me. Where did the bullet hit him?'

'In the head.'

'At close range, a two-four-three would have gone right through. At least it does with a stag.'

The inspector paused in his striding. 'It was a keyhole wound,' he said.

'So the bullet went in at least slightly sideways! In fact, it may have been spinning end-for-end.'

34

'I've probably said too much for the moment, but at least you can see the problem.'

The inspector resumed his journey to nowhere, easing the muscles and joints that a long day spent sitting had stiffened.

'I see the problem all right,' Calder said. 'It could be a shot from a distant rifle, deflected in the last few yards by foliage, or even by ricochet. It could have been a ricochet all the way, except that somebody would probably have heard it whirring or whining as it arrived. It could be a ricochet, fired at close range. Or it could have been a near shot, travelling slowly and keyholing because it was fired out of a very short barrel. Is that about the size of it?'

'That's about it,' said the inspector.

'The rifling-marks on the bullet should tell you the maker of the rifle-barrel.'

'Except that anybody making an adaptor could incorporate a section from an old rifle-barrel.'

'That's true.'

'But it would take considerable technical skill, and the right tools and machinery?'

'True again.'

'So we set ourselves to wondering – '

' – whether there wasn't a time-served gunsmith nearby?'

'Just that,' said the inspector. 'Just that.'

'And you know that there was. And I'll tell you this for nothing. I could have taken an existing rifle-barrel and put a sleeve on it to make an adaptor that would go into a shotgun barrel. I can even think of a good way of locking it against the torque of the rifling. I could, but I didn't. And I'm damned if I can think of any way of ensuring that I could get it out again in a hurry. It would expand with the heat of the shot, remember.'

'So . . . You could but you didn't?'

'That is what I said.'

'Did you know the late Mr McLure?'

'I'd met him once. He was present when I spoke to the Lothians Gun Club on the assessment of shot patterns. Like several of those present, he asked one or two moderately intelligent questions; and he bought me a beer later. That was the only time I ever met him until yesterday afternoon. My life-style doesn't bring me much into contact with architects.' And, Calder decided, that was as far as reasonable answers to reasonable questions went, and if Inspector Munro wanted to push that line of questioning any further he'd get an earful that would send him home to his 'black house' with his tail between peat-stained legs.

The inspector, however, was away on another line. 'Would you say that the wood, near where the body was found, was thick enough for somebody to hide, and not be seen by the walking guns?'

'You've seen the place yourself.'

'Aye. That's right, Mr Calder. But I don't know how much attention it would get from the guns and their dogs.'

'All right. Yes, it was thick, Forestry Commission type coniferous planting both sides of that clearing. Easy enough to hide at the edge of the clearing. And, of course, if he'd shot the one man who was going to walk close to him, the others wouldn't spot him. But the dogs would.'

'McLure's dog?'

'That I wouldn't know. He had a nice Springer bitch, quite well-trained. They had a good relationship. But I don't think she'd have betrayed anybody – she's a quiet little bitch. She was very disturbed at his death, but we never heard her howling.

'But Hebe would certainly have told me if there had been a stranger in the wood.'

Inspector Munro nodded. There was no need to tell him how much a dog can tell its master. 'So, taking all in all, your own opinion would be that the bullet came from outside the wood?'

'I'm in no doubt of it at all.'

The inspector sat down at his desk. 'Now, Mr Calder, to come back to the matter of who might not be speaking to who. While you were talking I drew a little grid, with names down the side and names across the bottom. I'd like you to think back over the day, and each time you remember a conversation between two people, make a wee mark in the square that lines up with both their names. I'll do the same with the other witnesses, and we'll see if any interesting gaps develop.'

And so it went on. It was midnight before Keith Calder was returned to the Forth Bridge, where his van and an anxious Hebe were waiting for him, but at dawn he was stalking rabbits, quite illicitly, near Kinross.

CHAPTER 3

Two weeks later, and Keith Calder was driving north on the notorious A9 and into the mountains. The trees were almost bare now, a big wind overhead stripping the last foliage, and the roads were dangerous with wet leaves. A thin rain, managing to drive almost horizontally in the wind, kept the wipers going, and the van struggled hard to make its way northward.

But as he drove Keith hummed, in tune, more or less, with the ballet music of John Lanchberry coming by tape from the twin speakers. He had some reason to feel pleased with himself. A number of his ventures had gone well; not least that, that very morning, he had picked up a couple of hitchhiking neo-students near Dunkeld. By Pitlochry he had managed to provoke such a quarrel between them that the young man had been glad to be set down. Near Blair Castle he had pulled off the road and comforted the weeping girl on the pulled-out settee-berth, and had then restored her to her contrite beau whom they had found again at the roadside at Dalwhinnie. All in all, it had been a most satisfactory piece of poaching.

His destination that day was near Carrbridge, and in midafternoon he turned into a secondary road, and, after another mile, onto a track winding up a shallow glen. This came at last to a familiar place in a fold of the hills where what had once been a small farm was now turned into a modern home, with cedar boarding and double glazing and an oil tank in the treble garage where once the cows had been milked.

Jock Hendry came out in a hurry to meet him. While the two men greeted each other as real friends do, with few words but real meaning, Hebe gave a casual sniff of greeting to Sambo, her longstanding hunting partner and occasional husband, and then rushed by to roll at Jock's feet.

Keith's smile widened. 'That's a compliment she pays to nobody else.'

'A dog of sagacity,' Jock said, 'and also discernment. That's why I'm still waiting for my pick-of-the-litter.'

'Next time. It's her total addiction to the shooting field that does it. She just suffers from a delusion that you're a better shot than I am.'

'As I said, a dog of sagacity . . . Did you bring it?'

'Not this time, Jock. Circumstances were agin it. I'll tell you when we get inside.'

Over the tail-end of a good dinner cooked by Jock himself, Keith looked across at his old friend with affection. Jock Hendry was a small man, wiry, and dark to the point of having a permanent five o'clock shadow. His features were sharp, almost knife-like, and his face was brown except for his nose which was eternally red. Jock stemmed from the West Highlands, and his voice was like Inspector Munro's, soft and hissing. But Jock had emigrated early to Glasgow, to work first in the building trade, then becoming a contractor and finally making his fortune as a property developer, only to retire before fifty to live, mostly alone, among the mountains again. His many years in Scotland's industrial belt had infused his soft accent with the glottal stop of Glasgow, producing a strange hybrid that Keith thought he would recognise across a crowded room.

The talk had been of game – blackgame and capercaillie in the high plantations, grouse on the moor, pheasants down in such cover as the farmland below provided, but most of all the red deer. Jock leased miles of high moorland, and the management and stalking of the deer were his first passion.

'I see yon mannie McLure took a bullet at last,' Jock said suddenly.

'I was there.'

'I saw that. It was in the paper. What d'ye think happened?'

Keith helped himself to more coffee. The wind had dropped, and all was quiet except for the hiss of the open fire, and the dogs, well-fed, grunting and wheezing in sleep. 'They found a bullet in him,' Keith said, 'and we were carrying shotguns. The police were being very thorough, just in case, but I think they'll find it was just a stray shot from the hill. There's a lot of roe-deer thereabouts this year, and a lot of poaching of them going on. You know how it can be. A missed shot at a deer on the skyline, and it's got to come down somewhere.'

'I'd believe you,' Jock said, 'but that man McLure – somebody was going to shoot him some day.'

'You knew him, then?'

'I knew him, all right.'

'From when you were in building?'

'Knew him better than I liked him. The man was a crook. And not an honest sort of crook, if you take my meaning.'

'I take it,' said Keith, who was an honest sort of crook himself.

'If there's one thing I canno' stand it's a dishonest architect. He's in a special position of trust.'

'Surely that applies to any professional man? A doctor or lawyer?'

'Do you know one of those you can really trust? But an architect, now. There's an awful lot of money changes hands over a building contract.'

'Not through the architect's hands, surely?'

'Sometimes,' said Jock. 'Sometimes. That's how I first found out about him. We were doing a job for him. The payments were made by McLure himself, instead of him certifying to the client. It's an old dodge. Somebody consults him about a new building – a farmer, say, it's just the kind of thing a farmer'd fall for. McLure's asked for a probable cost. He looks at it and thinks, say, twenty thousand quid. But he says thirty thousand. And when the farmer's still dumbstruck, he drops hints that there's ways and means and he has friends, and says, very generously, that if the farmer gives him a cheque for twenty-six, or whatever, he'll see to the whole job for him. . . .

'But that was only the small fiddles, when he was a small man handling small contracts. On a big contract, every day the architect has to make decisions which affect the con-

40

tractor's pocket. And, mind you, those decisions are binding on his client. If he decides to sell those decisions – '

'McLure did that?'

'I'm afraid so. That and a thousand other ways of taking a cut. And then ploughing some of it back into wining and dining politicians and officials, to get more contracts and to sweeten them into looking the other way. Gifts and girls. And then maybe a little blackmail to follow up with. You know the kind of scene. It fair sickened me. I had to play that game a bittie, but only a wee bittie, and now that such things are being brought out into the light of day I'm glad. Glad that they're coming out, and glad that I stayed as clear as I could.'

'Was he in such a big way of business, then?'

Jock gave a short laugh. 'He liked to give the impression of a nice, middle-sized family firm. A lot of clients like it like that. They come to a converted manse where there were just the two partners and a half-dozen architects and some typists. What they didn't see, unless they needed to be impressed with his capability to handle the work, was half an office-block just down the street, crammed with draughtsmen and technicians and hacks, churning out the real work on a production-line basis. He was big enough, all right.

'I'll tell you something else. Once, I got into a dispute over the final account for a big contract I'd had. There was an arbitration clause in the contract, and McLure was appointed arbiter. As soon as I heard that, I settled, quickly. It lost me a good few thousand, but cheaper than going on.'

The ringing of the telephone ended their conversation. More than that, perhaps it was the moment when the peace and pleasure of Keith's existence ended, too.

'Your sister wants to speak to you,' Jock said.

'Elsie?'

'Keith? Is that you, Keith?'

'Yes, Elsie, it's me.'

'Keith, your fiancée – '

'Dammit, Elsie, I don't have a fiancée.'

'Well, you should have, Keith. At your time of life, you should be settling down with a wife and a family. It's what

Mother would have wanted. You can't always be racketing around chasing the girls and shooting things. You should have a gun-shop again. I don't know why you gave up the last one, unless it's just that you can't stick to a thing.'

Keith's voice went up an octave with exasperation. Elsie often had that effect on him. He could hear Jock strangling a chuckle in the background. 'You know perfectly well I was only the manager, and it was compulsorily purchased. And do you know how much this call's costing?'

'Aye, Keith, I know,' Elsie said patiently. 'It's over fifty miles, but it's the cheap rate time, so it costs just under two of those new sort of pence for a minute.'

'What did you want to *say*, for God's sake? If anything.'

'Now, Keith, there's no call to lose your patience, nor yet to use that sort of language. And if she isn't your fiancée, then she should be. She's by far the steadiest of all your girl-friends. And the nicest.'

'Are you talking about Molly? Molly Fiddler?'

'Of course I am, Keith. Are there so many – '

'Never mind that. Was she trying to reach me?'

'Aye, she was. She wants you to go back down, very urgently.'

'Did she say why?'

'Aye, she did. You mind yon fellow that was shot, the poor man?'

'Of course.'

'Her brother's been arrested for it.'

Keith Calder had a capacity for rapid thought that was useful in business, essential in shooting and invaluable at times in his other adventures. In the time that it took him to open his pocket diary, he had reached certain decisions.

'Elsie, phone Dingwall for me and apologise. Tell them that I'm delayed for a few days but I'll get in touch again.'

'All right, Keith.'

'Is Molly where I can call her back?'

'She was in a call-box. She's going to phone me again later.'

'Tell her I'll be there about this time tomorrow. And get onto Mr Edwards of Foster and Edwards in the morning and ask him if he'll stay open although it's Saturday and take fifty pheasants from me.'

'All right, Keith. I'll do that.'

'I think that's all, then.'

'Keith. The mannie that was shot. If Molly's brother shot him, is there any chance that he meant to shoot you?'

Keith swallowed. 'None at all,' he said. 'He's too good a shot to hit the wrong man.'

All the same, when he had hung up the phone he was more thoughtful than usual. The late Mr McLure had been not unlike him in appearance and dress.

Later, it occurred to him that he might have told Elsie that Molly's brother had no reason to try to shoot him. It would not have been true, but outside of business matters Keith Calder was not in the habit of letting such considerations influence him very much, if at all.

During the night, Keith drove southward in the van, pausing to visit the woods of a landowner who had once refused to pay for the re-blueing of a pair of gun-barrels on the grounds that the barrels had bulged a fortnight later, and who had been unimpressed when it had been pointed out that the muzzles had been plugged with mud at the time. Keith had been stuck with the bill for the blueing operation, but had taken many times that value off the estate since then. He took with him a bag of sulphur crystals. Just what he did with them is better not too widely known, but he returned to the van with his fifty pheasants and a few for the pot beside.

Keith's van was too slow and thirsty to be taken on a round trip of some three hundred miles when its facilities were not required.

Keith slept a few hours in the van on the forecourt of a garage where he was known, and in the morning he bargained for the hire of the proprietor's car, since the only hire-car was out. The proprietor was reluctant, but a brace of cock-pheasants helped to persuade him. Into the big Vauxhall he loaded Hebe, his remaining birds, some clothing and, more out of habit than anything else, a gun and some cartridges. He adjusted the seat and mirror to his liking, fiddled with the radio until he found some Bach, and set off.

In due course the obliging Mr Edwards gave him a fair price for the pheasants, ensuring that Keith's expenditure on the hire of the car would not be wholly a loss.

CHAPTER 4

The town of Newton Lauder is centred on one long main street, rather narrow but widening out at the Town Hall and the police headquarters into what is almost a square, from which several minor roads lead away to serve the villages around. At one time, most of the traffic between the north of England and Edinburgh had to descend into the valley and crowd through the town. Eventually, and at last, the main road was improved and diverted to by-pass the town, and Newton Lauder resumed the quiet that it had not known for two hundred years, to the satisfaction of almost everyone except the local hotelier and the garage proprietor.

Keith turned off before the Town Hall into one of the side-roads and again into a lane, and stopped outside the Fiddlers' cottage. It was already dark, with the beginning of a frost sparkling in his lights. On one side of him rose the shadows of a beech-wood and of the hills; on the other, the lights of Newton Lauder were two fields away. He could hear a pheasant chuckling in the wood. Overhead, the dark shapes of wood-pigeon were flocking in to roost.

With a silent prayer that Molly's big brother might not yet be exonerated or on bail, Keith rapped with his knuckles on the door. His prayer was superfluous, or perhaps it had been answered before it was made, for Molly came to the door alone. She was small, sturdily built for a girl and slightly inclined to plumpness, but with a delicate face on the borderline between mere prettiness and real beauty. It was a face created for smiles, with wide eyes and high cheekbones and a mouth always ready to lift and dimple, but now it was anxious and there were signs of tears. Her hair, which was as dark as her lover's, had been combed and left.

The cramped living-room of the cottage was dully lit by a single standard lamp by the chair beside the burning fire. The glass-fronted gun-cupboard was empty and Keith noticed that, although Molly had been sitting by the fire, there was no knitting, no reading matter, no sound, no sign of activity at all.

Her greeting was similarly muted. Usually she would run at him, beaming, and if space permitted he would catch and lift her and swing her round. Instead she shook his hand, something she had almost never done before.

She sat him down and went to make tea. His heart sank. It was as if he were a stranger, come to pay condolences after a death; and while he had no liking for her brother he could hardly bear to see Molly so troubled.

When she had sat down opposite him and poured his tea she said, 'I'm glad you came. I couldn't have borne it much longer.'

'It's that bad, is it?'

She nodded, and two tears spilled over. 'It seems to be as bad as it can be.' Her voice broke.

Keith jumped up and pulled her to her feet. He held her close, kissed her tears and then her lips. He sat down and pulled her into the deep chair with him, cradling her almost like a baby, and she wept on his shoulder with sobs that shook them both. When it was over she took his handkerchief, wiped her eyes and blew her nose and said, 'Better now.'

They pulled the table closer, and she spread the scones which she had brought. He was glad to see that she was suddenly hungry.

'Has he been charged yet?' he asked.

She swallowed her mouthful. 'They've charged him with a firearms offence, meantime.'

'Does he have a solicitor?'

'Yes. It's Mr Enterkin, in the town here. Sir Peter picked him. Sir Peter's been awfully good. He's paying the fees, too, although Ronnie could have got legal aid.'

'I don't know Enterkin,' Keith said, 'but I believe he's competent. Can't he get bail for your brother?'

'Mr Enterkin says that if he applies for bail just now he may force them to bring the bigger charge, and there'd be no going back. Keith, you didn't mind my sending for you, did you?'

'Of course not.'

'It's just that it's all about guns and things and I couldn't think of anyone else who might be able to help, and Mr Enterkin agreed. It's an awful guddle. Mr Enterkin can do the legal bits, but he needs somebody to help him. "Interpret the evidence", is what he said. He was expecting Ronnie to tell him what really happened, but Ronnie says he doesn't know a thing. And Ronnie isn't free to try and find out what did happen.'

Keith shifted her weight into a more comfortable position on his lap. 'Tell me,' he said.

She leaned her head on his shoulder again, taking a child-like comfort from close contact with another being. 'There's not a lot to tell. We'd heard about the death, of course, but everybody'd put it down as an accident. Then that skinny Highlander – '

'Munro?'

'Yes. He came round asking questions. I could hear them from the kitchen. Ronnie said that he was in the hills all day. He agreed that you could see the wood where it happened from the nearer slopes, but he'd been over the other side. There's a lot of roe-deer this year, and Sir Peter wanted the number of bucks reduced before they went out of season – next week, isn't it? – and then Ronnie was to start on the does.'

'How many bucks did he get?'

'He said five, and his records agreed with that, but only three went to the dealers as he'd sold two locally. He has Sir Peter's permission to do that,' she added quickly.

'Do many people buy whole carcasses like that?' Keith asked.

'Oh yes. Quite a few. Venison's expensive in the shops, but it's a big saving if you buy the whole beast and butcher it yourself and put it away in the freezer. Ronnie often brings one or two red deer carcasses back from up north, if people around here have asked him to.'

'And who would those be?'

'I've no idea. They never come to the cottage, they speak to Ronnie in the pub or leave a message at the Hall. Anyway, the police took Ronnie's rifles away, and then brought them back the next day saying that the bullet that killed Mr McLure hadn't been shot from either of them. Ronnie was angry because they didn't clean them again. And that seemed to be that. We heard that they'd been round every certificate-holder with that size of a rifle.

'Then they arrived again suddenly with a warrant to search the place. It was different men this time, from Edinburgh, and we heard later that there was a whole lot of them and they went to the houses of everybody known to use rifles, all inside of an hour or so. I suppose that was in case word went around and people moved things to safer hiding-places.

'Anyway, they found something – another rifle, I think, because they took Ronnie away and charged him with illegal possession of it. What's wrong?'

Keith forced his muscles to relax, before they betrayed him to her. Remembering the moment afterwards, he recalled the great weight that had settled in his stomach and how the colour seemed to have gone out of the firelight. 'Just that it sounds bad,' he said carefully. 'Go on.'

'That's about all I know. Ronnie swore that he'd never seen it before, but nobody seemed to believe him. And then I thought of you.'

Keith's mouth was dry. He just nodded and waited. She stumbled on.

'I mean, it's all very well having a solicitor to see that you get your rights under the law, and to try and pick holes in the other side's case and show that they haven't really proved what they say they've proved. But that isn't the same as finding out what really happened, and I'm sure Mr Enterkin wouldn't be good at anything like that. But you know all about guns and things, and if you were to look into the evidence and sort of advise him . . .'

Keith was breathing easily again, at last. 'I'm glad you thought of me,' he said. His mind was racing ahead. Between himself and Molly's brother was a deep antipathy, an antipathy that can only grow between two characters so similar that they know each other's faults and vices and how to strike home with insults. If Ronnie Fiddler had got himself into trouble unaided, Keith Calder would have gone his

48

way with no compunction. But Ronnie Fiddler might be innocent, at least in the matter of the rifle. Moreover, there could be danger to Keith himself if the law were left to grind slowly and small.

'Hop up,' he said. 'You're sitting on my bladder.'

On his way through the tiny hall he lifted the torch from the shelf. He switched on the lavatory light and off again as he pulled the door to, and he slipped very quietly out of the back door to a derelict wash-house where Ronnie Fiddler kept his gardening tools and sometimes hung the carcass of a deer. The ceiling was unlined, and a space ran back over the kitchen next door. Standing on a box, he probed with the torch, but there was nothing there but cobwebs and an old swallow's nest.

He reversed his tracks, pulling the chain in the lavatory, and was so preoccupied that he nearly took the torch into the room with him. There was no doubt about it at all.

'I'll see the solicitor in the morning,' he said. 'No, damn it, tomorrow's Sunday. I'll visit the place, ask a few people a few questions, and I'll see the solicitor and maybe your brother on Monday.'

She got up and faced him. 'Thank you.'

'And now I'd better be going.'

'Going?'

'Of course. I can't stay here. I'll go to the hotel.'

She moved against him and laid her forehead on his shoulder. 'But I don't want to be on my own. You've . . . stayed here before.'

'Not at a time like this. Look, Molly, your brother's in deep trouble right up to his stupid neck. You want me to look into it and see if I can help. He and I don't like each other much, but for your sake I'll do it. If I can find anything helpful, I'll be called to give evidence on his behalf. But, if it gets that length, the prosecution may want to destroy any part of my evidence that doesn't agree with their case. And if we've been openly cohabiting – and that's what they'll call it – they could make my evidence look very questionable. I can just hear Counsel's questions – "Are you asking us to believe, Mr Calder, that your – ah – relationship with the accused's sister had no influence on the evidence you've given today?" They'd suggest that you'd slept with me to persuade me to help out. You wouldn't want that, would you?'

'N-not if it hurt Ronnie. But I just can't take being alone, not knowing how it's all going to end. I've not been sleeping and the nights are so long.' The tears were very close again.

Keith felt his resolution wavering. Sometimes he felt that it wasn't that he really liked women, he just couldn't stand seeing them cry. 'I'd better go to the hotel all the same,' he said. 'You've got the dog for company. Reminds me, can you keep Hebe for me, or would Black Jake fight with her?'

'They'll be all right, Jake's as gentle as a lamb with bitches, it's other dogs he can't stand.' She blinked at him, her eyes almost luminous with tears. 'But, Keith, couldn't you book into the hotel and come back later?'

'Dangerous,' he said faintly.

'I can't bear it all alone, Keith.'

Keith pondered, but for only another moment. He needed a good night's sleep and it went against the grain with him to pay for a hotel room and then not to use it. On the other hand, Molly was far and away his favourite girl.

'All right,' he said.

CHAPTER 5

Keith Calder's life-style had accustomed him to getting by on minimal and irregular sleep, but the stresses of the previous few days and nights had taken their toll of him. His return to the hotel next morning was necessarily early, and he was glad to take a second sleep and a late breakfast. Bells were tolling and Sabbath-solemn parties straggling their way to kirk before he collected Hebe from the cottage and set off in the car.

Farmers are not always the best of church-goers, for the forces of nature observe no Sabbath. When Keith pulled up in the farm-yard, Janet Weatherby and her father were happily dismantling a tractor. Derek stood up and came across, but Janet contented herself with a cheerful wave and went on with her part of the work.

'Should have been a boy, that girl,' the farmer said.

'It's a bit late to think of that now, isn't it?'

'I'm afraid so. She's as much help now as a son would have been, but some day I suppose . . .'

'Yes.'

Convention demanded that talk be turned to polite enquiries after the harvest, the health of the beasts and the prices obtained, and it was some time before Keith could bring it around with the required deftness to the matter of McLure's death. He managed it at last by enquiring about damage by roe-deer.

'There's a lot of them about,' Weatherby said. 'It's a big year for them here. The weather's suited them and there's been plenty of feed, and the Forestry Commission have stopped shooting on the whole of Threeplow Moor. It's not just what they eat, it's the damage they start that lets the crows and pigeons in. I've seen around thirty at a time in my barley before it was cut.'

'You've mentioned it to Sir Peter, of course?' Keith said.

'Aye. I'm only the tenant. They're his deer. He was attending to it, but with Ronnie Fiddler in pokey . . .'

'A bad business.'

'It is that. I can't believe a thing like that of Ronnie. He's the most careful of lads with a gun, and as far as I know he'd never even set eyes on McLure.'

'That's what I'm up about,' Keith said. 'I've been asked by his . . . family to look into the evidence.'

The farmer gave him a knowing look but only said, 'I'm glad of that. I want to see him out and dealing with those deer.'

'So it's all right if I go up to the wood and take a look around?'

'Surely. Help yourself. But you'll find that the police have picked up every bit of garbage that's been dropped there for the past ten years. Take a gun with you if you like. I know you'll leave the syndicate's pheasants alone, but you might be able to knock off a carrion crow for us.'

'That'd be illegal on a Sunday.'

The farmer winked. 'Foxes are legal,' he said, 'and there's too many of them around.'

In the point of turning away, Keith thought of something else. 'Do you ever have a go at the deer yourself?'

'Now and again, with Sir Peter's agreement. I don't really have the time and patience to get near them.'

'You have a rifle, though, on certificate? Did you get the place searched by the police?'

The farmer smiled and nodded. 'They went through the place. Thoroughly. I didn't envy them the task. Janet and her mother have just about given up tidying after me. I asked them to keep their eyes open for a pair of snap-caps that I lost a few months ago, and I'm blessed if one of them didn't retrieve them to me like a spaniel.'

'About two years ago,' Keith said, 'I got you some thirty-eight pistol ammunition. I gathered that it was for something off-certificate. They didn't – '

Weatherby lowered his voice conspiratorially. 'Lots of places about a farm, you know. They didn't search the tractors – why should they? But I keep it in the tool-box

52

of a tractor. I sometimes get the chance of a pot-shot at a roe. Or a hare.'

'You'll get yourself in trouble one of these days.'

'Well, look who's talking!'

So Keith carried his gun and his game-bag up to the wood with him, and if he brought back a few wood-pigeon who could blame him? For a law that says that a national pest may be shot on Sunday in some parts of the country but not in others is a bad law. And Keith Calder had patience with no bad laws, and not many good ones either.

It was a calm day of thin mist, so that the hills stepped back in great jumps, each one lighter than the one before it. The leaves had fallen now, so that the trees in the valleys had turned from flame to smoke, as if a fire had burned out.

There were signs of many feet through the wood, and Keith was sorry that no miracle of prescience had guided him to study the site immediately after the event. It was now quite impossible to trace the movements of individuals and their dogs through the wood. If the murderer had passed that way on a pogo-stick the imprint might still have been discernible, but he had done nothing so distinctive.

From memory, Keith satisfied himself that his own route had passed well away from the clearing. He walked up the wood, against the direction that he had walked during the shoot, and checked that he must several times have been in view from the higher ground. Then he descended again to the burned clearing and again lifted up his eyes unto the hills. Again, his recollection was confirmed. Beyond the fence the ground rose fairly steeply to the first crest some two hundred yards away. Beyond that, the further hills were more than a mile distant.

He left the wood, vaulting the barbed wire, and walked up the slope, Hebe questing from side to side in front of him. Sheep, in their half-witted way, moved out of the path. The shoulder of the hill was bare grass, the heather only starting two fields higher. Keith walked along the line of the false crest to where a small outcrop of rock and some gorse broke the even flow of the cropped grass.

'That's what I thought,' he said to Hebe. 'This is the only

place a rifleman could take cover and not stand out like a turd on a shirt-front.'

Hebe grinned admiringly at this observation.

He lay down as a rifleman would, holding his shotgun. A branch of the gorse had been broken back to clear the view, so somebody had been here before him; but it was a logical place to lie in wait for deer passing down the flank of the wood. Looking down into the several clearings, Keith estimated that every memeber of the shooting party would have been in sight from this spot from time to time.

On the way back down to the wood, scent drew Hebe upwind and she put up a large covey of partridges. They erupted simultaneously in whirring flight. Keith resisted temptation, and enjoyed the sight of their rich colour.

Next, Keith started on the real objective of his visit – an inch-by-inch search of the area where McLure had died. First he took the charred circle in the clearing, and half an hour was spent in meticulous examination. But there was nothing to be learned. Any scrap of information not destroyed by the fire had been lifted by the police or trodden out of existence. He widened the search in an expanding spiral. Every scrap – wads, empty cartridges, even the carefully trodden-out cigarette-ends – had been lifted over the whole clearing and for some yards into the field and the wood.

The only fragments of human debris that Keith could find were some scraps of toilet-paper near the charred circle. Their revealing pink colour suggested that they had not gone unobserved but had been discounted as irrelevant. He was about to jump to the same conclusion when Hebe nosed one of the pieces, and her tail moved an inch either way. Keith lifted it and examined the staining.

'Aye, girl,' he said. 'Trust you not to miss that.'

It was his habit to carry a supply of small polythene bags in a pocket of the light shooting-coat which was his unvarying outdoor garb, and he stowed the frail pink scraps away in one of them.

When he was sure that he had missed nothing else, Keith relaxed. Wood-pigeon were following the line of the wood between their favourite roosting trees above and the stubbles below. He wedged himself for concealment between two conifers and began to drop them in ones and twos, making every cartridge count.

Later, he called in at Corner Farm to leave a few pigeon with Derek Weatherby. The farmer had disappeared but Janet was still working on the hydraulics of the tractor, the manual open on the ground beside her. She was a pretty girl, allowing for the oil-stains, and showed promise of becoming a spectacular woman. Keith, whose voice took on an involuntary mellow charm in the presence of any woman who attracted him, fought to keep the signs of downright lechery out of it.

'Is your dad in the house?' he asked.

She shook her head, and her fair pony-tail swung. 'He left me to it and went off in the car. He said that I seemed to know more about it than he did anyway,' she added complacently.

'You'll make someone a wonderful wife.'

'You for instance? I might consider it.'

'Well, I mightn't,' he said, laughing.

'Anyway, you're already bespoke.'

'No I am not! And this isn't what I came back to talk about,' he added. 'If I leave these pigeon on this window-sill, will you take them in to your mum when you've finished?'

She pulled gently on the torque-wrench. 'If the cat hasn't got them first,' she said.

'You remember the day Mr McLure was shot?'

'Of course.'

'When we walked down Oak Wood, you and your dad were outside it on my right. Did either of you come into the wood?'

She put down the wrench and rubbed her face, giving herself a Mexican-bandit moustache. Even so, she still looked all girl. 'I did once,' she said. 'Where that rocky hump is, in the middle of the wood, about a hundred yards or more before where he was burned.'

'What happened, exactly?'

'Well, you were slightly ahead, because I could see you, when somebody, it must've been Mr McNeill, put up a big cock-pheasant. It rocketed. Honestly, it seemed to go straight up, curving a bit over towards us. Whoever-it-was fired at it once and missed. I waited to see if he was going to use his other barrel, but he didn't, so I shot it.'

'Did you, by golly,' said Keith.

'Yes. And it came down thump, right on top of the rocky bit. Well, we didn't have Dinky with us. Dad said she was still in season, though it was finished the week before to my mind. So Dad said to wait until everyone was safely clear and then to go in and get it, and to be sure to come out of the wood before coming on to catch up, just in case. He's very sensible about safety things. So I waited and I went in and climbed the hump and got it.'

'Could you see anybody?'

'Yes. It's funny how much more you can see when you get up a bit. I could see down into the open bits, and I could see people's heads among the small fir-trees. You and Dad and Mr McLure were just a bit short of the place where it happened. Mr McNeill had just come out of a thick bit and seen that he was behind and he was hurrying to catch up and get back in line. And over the far side I could see Mr Payne a bit in front, and Hamish away out in the field chasing a runner with his dog.

'That was all I saw before I came down and hurried to catch up with Dad.'

'Have you told this to anyone else?'

'No. Dad gave them a short statement, and I was asked if that was how I remembered it, that was all. Why?'

'A couple of bits of what you told me just might be dangerous for somebody. I think you should either keep it absolutely between ourselves or go to the police and make a full statement so that it's all on record, and let it be known that you've done so.'

'How exciting! Which bits?'

'Never you mind just now. If you want to grow up to be a big girl just do as I say.'

She smiled wickedly and jumped to her feet. 'You're just trying to needle me,' she said. 'I'm a big girl now, aren't I?'

Keith was surprised to realise that she was as tall as he was. 'You're getting bigger every day,' he said.

She put her arms back so that her budding breasts pushed

out against her tartan shirt, and she moved against him and rubbed noses. 'I'll pass the age of consent in a few months,' she said.

Keith kept his hands firmly behind his back. After all, her mother might look out at any moment. 'Bully for you!' he said. 'May you never pass anything more painful!'

She sniggered, backed away and sat down to her work again. 'You've got quite a reputation as a ladies' man,' she said. 'I don't think you're so much.'

'You're not a lady,' he pointed out. And when she put her tongue out at him, he looked over her shoulder. 'You've put it together all wrong,' he said.

He chuckled all the way back to the car, and took the rest of his pigeons down to the Fiddlers' cottage where he scrounged his lunch. Janet's father, he thought in passing, would have to go on being 'careful about safety things'.

Sir Peter, like the good laird that he was, had set an example by attending the kirk with his lady, but unlike her had defeated the calculated discomfort of the pews and dozed through much of the service. At that point his deference to the Sabbath ceased, and Keith found him behind the hall, panting away as he dug manure into what had once been a small lawn. He seemed glad to straighten his back and lay aside the spade, and he dusted his hand on the seat of his kilt before he held it out to Keith.

'Don't tell the minister or he'll preach another sermon about me and I'll have to pretend I don't know who he's talking about. I'm going to put some more vegetables in.'

Keith raised his eyebrows. 'I thought you nobs had serfs and villeins to do that sort of thing for you.'

Sir Peter gave vent to his high-pitched laugh. 'I wish I did. But if I paid somebody to put my vegetables in they'd cost me more than buying them in the shops.'

'Don't your farmers provide?'

'Oh, I can get plenty of spuds and turnips, but my wife likes a little more variety than that. Truth to tell, she's the one that insists on all these little economies, and if I let on that we don't have to be quite so parsimonious I'd have to stop grumbling at her extravagances. Every time I spend a fiver she buys a new car or flies somewhere on a shopping spree. You know what wives are like.'

'As a matter of fact, I don't.'

'Or only other men's wives, I suppose,' said Sir Peter, with the tolerance that comes easily to one with no daughters and whose own wife would never have betrayed him with anyone of less than royal blood. 'Oh well, you'll know soon enough. I've no doubt of it. And a good thing too. Why should you be happy when the rest of us are married? Eh? Anyway, what can I have the pleasure of refusing to do for you today?'

'Ronnie Fiddler's sister – please do me the favour of not looking at me like that – she's asked me to look into the evidence and see if I can help.'

'Ah.' Sir Peter looked thoughtful. 'Better come inside. I could do with a cup of tea or something anyway.'

From the outside, the Hall looked like a film set awaiting the arrival of Sherlock Holmes; but the interior was worse, a gloomy Victorian image of how they thought their Scottish Baronial ancestors might once have lived. When Sir Peter shouted for tea, echoes came back like the souls of returning dead. He led the way into a study that reminded Keith of the worst kind of public library.

Sir Peter could hardly be unaware of the impression that the place created. 'I prayed this morning,' he said, 'that some day this dump would burn to the ground, preferably without too much loss of life, and that I could use the insurance-money to build my dream-house on the site.'

'Why don't you sell it, then?'

'What for, a lunatic asylum? The poor devils would only get worse in it. Anyway, I like living here. Wouldn't live anywhere else. It's just the house that I can't stand. And the Dawnapool place is even worse. My grandfather had a lot to answer for, but I suppose he's answering for it now.' He rambled on in similar vein until tea was brought in – not, as Keith had half expected, by a liveried flunkey but by an elderly woman in a flowered apron.

When she was gone Sir Peter said, 'Now, you know that I'm paying for the defence?'

'I didn't come to tap you for money.'

'Never said you did. All the same, if you need anything for expenses or loss of earnings you've only got to say so. But I'll assume that you have enough for present operating expenses and we'll discuss it again. I'm determined that Fiddler shall have every possible chance. He's a good man to me. What's more, I'm sure he didn't do it.'

'I know damned fine he didn't. Do you know if he knew McLure?'

'I can't think how he would. But – and this may come as a shock to you – the general theory is that he meant to shoot you. The police haven't said so, but I think they're prepared to use that if they're challenged as to motive. You were similarly dressed, as I recall.'

'That theory's a load of balls,' Keith said.

'I'm sure. Fiddler just wouldn't do that.'

'I wouldn't go so far as to say that,' Keith objected. 'In fact, I'm surprised he hasn't tried it. And when he gets out, I'll watch my back.' (Sir Peter looked shocked.) 'What I'm saying is that he didn't do it yet. For one thing, the only place he could have done it from is about two hundred yards from the spot. He wouldn't be using open sights at that distance, but through a telescopic sight – '

Sir Peter frowned. 'Two dark men, dressed similarly? I know he was bigger than you are, but there wouldn't be any standard of comparison in those circumstances.'

'No. But McLure was keeping his dog very close to him that day, and there's no way you could mistake a liver-and-white Springer for my black Labrador.'

'Good point,' Sir Peter said.

'But not proof in itself. Would you be satisfied with a "not proven" verdict?'

'No, I don't think I would.'

'No more would I. The best defence would be to find out what really happened. Impeachment.'

'Or that no crime had been committed. I mean, that the whole thing was a total mischance.'

'If it was true. But I'm afraid not. McLure was shot by somebody who set out to shoot McLure, and it wasn't Ronnie Fiddler, and I'm beginning to get some ideas about it.'

'I'm delighted to hear it,' Sir Peter said. 'Er – do you want to discuss those ideas of yours?'

'Not yet, if you don't mind, Sir Peter. I'm not ready.'

'Very well. If you won't let me be Dr Watson, then I shall await your pleasure in delighted mystification. And if I can help in any way – '

'You can,' Keith said. 'First, can you give me a list of private individuals who've bought deer carcasses off you, for several years past?'

'No, I'm afraid I can't. Ronnie Fiddler sold most of them and just turned the money over to me. I gave him a commission, and I'd just enter it in the estate books as "private sale of deer carcass". Sometimes he might mention that Joe Soap bought that one, but more often not, and I wouldn't remember it anyway. You'll have to ask Ronnie.'

'Right. Who drew up the guest list for the shoot?'

'What extraordinary questions you do ask,' Sir Peter said. 'You're sure you're not just piling on the mystery? Well, a fortnight before when we had our last grouse shoot, I asked the syndicate if anyone was interested in going after the pheasants on the First. Four of us were, and the others agreed to it. Then one dropped out, so that left Andrew Payne, Derek Weatherby and myself. With Derek's daughter and my wife and Hamish Thomson, the keeper, that was still only six of us, which isn't really enough. I knew that you're your own boss, so I got onto your sister to pass the invitation along. I asked Payne and Weatherby who they'd suggest to make up numbers, and between them they suggested Captain Hodges, Oxter and Bill Hook, plus a couple of others who couldn't accept. I think it was Hook, in turn, who mentioned McNeill's name to me.'

'And McLure?'

'I don't think anybody even suggested him. His name got mentioned, I forget how and why, as being a good shot; and since I'd met him at some do or other in Edinburgh and his firm had done work about the estate from time to time I thought I might as well give him a ring.'

'You can't remember who mentioned McLure's name?'

'Not at the moment, but it'll come to me eventually if I don't think about it.'

'Forget it for the moment, then,' Keith said. 'Think about this instead. I know something which would help the defence. It would probably get Ronnie off the hook altogether, but not necessarily. And it would certainly get me into dire trouble, probably lose me my livelihood, so I'm not keen to produce it unless it's absolutely necessary. I'm going to tell his solicitor about it in the morning, in absolute confidence unless it becomes necessary in order to prevent him being convicted. But I think I should also make a written statement, just in case I walk under a bus. Will you witness my signature and then hold onto it for me?'

'Yes, of course.' Sir Peter fidgeted for a minute. 'A bit tough on Fiddler, though, isn't it? I mean, you could get him out of the clink now, but he has to stay inside because of some peccadillo of yours.'

'Believe me,' Keith said, 'I'm not taking this line without having given it a lot of thought. Yes, it's hard on Ronnie and it's hard on you. But in the long run I'll get us both out of trouble or I'll take my medicine. It'd be quixotic of me to give up now, and, anyway, even if I was believed it might not be enough, and then there'd be nobody on the outside investigating.'

Sir Peter sighed. 'I may be a fool,' he said, 'but I trust you. All right, go ahead, we'll do it your way. But I think you might tell me a little more.'

'I'm sorry, Sir Peter.'

'Oh, very well. But on condition that once this is all over – '

'I'll buy you a dinner and tell you the whole story, in Technicolor,' Keith said.

'You're on.'

On his way out, Keith noticed an enormous paraffin heater supplementing the ancient and inadequate central heating and adding its smells to those of wax polish and mould. 'Kick that over,' he thought, 'and the poor old stick can build his dream-house.' But he walked on past.

CHAPTER 6

By nine-thirty the following morning Keith was in the solicitor's cramped and crowded office in an old stone building off the square, quite prepared to wait but determined to be the first appointment. To his surprise, Mr Enterkin was already there and saw him immediately.

Enterkin was a portly man, bald as an egg. His was not the muscled stockiness of Derek Weatherby nor the flabby fat of Jonathan Oxter, Keith noticed, but a rounded bounciness as if he had been compounded from rubber balls of various sizes. It was his habit to blame his weight on his metabolism and to complain that he only had to get the smell of a chip-bag to put on a pound, but Keith was later to find that the solicitor was, in fact, a lover of good food and inclined to indulge an appetite that Keith considered frankly phenomenal. Apart from this little piece of self-deception, though, Keith found that he had a quick and enquiring mind. His manner was brisk and his eyes sharp.

'I'll be glad to have your help, Mr Calder,' he said. 'These criminal cases always pose a problem. When bail isn't allowed, you find yourself with a client who isn't available to go out and hunt up the necessary evidence. That, I suppose, is why defences are so often defensive, if you follow my meaning – relying on shooting holes in the prosecution's case and disputing their proof, instead of proving by positive evidence that it couldn't have happened. I like to attack the facts when I can. But the police aren't too keen to help with facts that run counter to their own case. Private detectives are too expensive for most purses. And, of course, lawyers aren't detectives, can't spare the time, aren't good at it and don't get paid for it, but we sometimes have to do it all the same. However, Sir Peter seems to have a high opinion of you, so I'm hoping you'll provide some good ammunition for counsel's brief.'

'It's going to go that far, is it?'

'No doubt of it, I'm afraid. I've been asked to go over at ten and be present when they charge him with murder.'

Keith slammed his hands down on his knees. 'Damn, damn, damn,' he said.

The sharp eyes twinkled. 'In the circumstances, a very moderate outburst.'

'Can you get me in to see him?'

'Easily. But I gather that there's some hostility between the two of you? In the circumstances, would it not be better if I were to act as an intermediary?'

'Mr Enterkin,' said Keith, 'I've got a personal interest in the success of Ronnie Fiddler's defence, and I'd rather have a few words with him than try and use you as a post office.'

'And what's your "personal interest"? The sister, perchance?'

'No,' said Keith shortly. 'The fact is that I've got information which is vital to the case but harmful to me. By the bye, I'm making a holograph statement of it, which I'll leave with someone, to be produced if I drop dead. That'll protect Ronnie's interest. But because it would put me in serious trouble I'm not prepared to release it unless and until it's necessary to get Ronnie off in the High Court, and I'll only tell you now between ourselves, orally and unrecorded, without witnesses and on your promise to treat it as absolutely confidential short of the same circumstances.'

'Why not leave the written statement with me?'

'I'm not your client – Ronnie is, and you might feel the call of duty to be stronger than any other. You follow me?'

Mr Enterkin smiled. 'I am insulted and intrigued at the same time,' he said. 'You appreciate that your silence, and mine, may be the cause of Mr Fiddler spending several months unnecessarily in the clink?'

Keith nodded emphatically. 'That's why I think you might weaken, and why unless I get your promise I'll tell you damn-all until he's on trial and not going to get off any other way.'

The solicitor looked at his watch, and then sighed. 'All right,' he said, 'you have my word.'

They both sank deeper into their chairs. A new relationship had been formed.

'You know,' said Keith, 'that an uncertified rifle was found behind Ronnie's home?'

'Yes. It's now been confirmed that the bullet that killed McLure was fired from it.'

'I was afraid of that,' Keith said. 'They would hardly be charging him otherwise. They're going to spring on you that the number on the mechanism matches that of a rifle that Ronnie Fiddler reported having lost a year ago.'

Enterkin pursed his fat lips. 'That's not good,' he said.

'It doesn't get much better. Now I'll tell you the full story. About a year ago, Ronnie took out a visiting stalker, a Belgian, on the estate up north. The man's own rifle developed a fault, so Ronnie lent him this one. The Belgian took a tumble down a steep scree, almost a cliff in parts, and broke both his ankles. Ronnie carried him over his shoulder for several miles to the Land Rover and drove him to hospital. That long carry injured Ronnie's back, and he was longer in his bed than the Belgian was. He never found his rifle, wasn't even sure of the exact place. The grateful Belgian presented him with a new rifle, the insurance company paid up on top, and Ronnie came out of it quite nicely, thank you. Mind, he deserved it.'

'He did indeed,' said Enterkin.

'Rather later, a very good friend of mine got into trouble. He leases quite a skelp of ground up north – I'm not saying where – and goes in for deer management. He was working closely with his neighbours, and they were doing a lot of good and the deer were coming along well. You know what you can achieve with selective culling and attention to habitat and winter feeding?'

The solicitor nodded.

'Unfortunately, the area came to the attention of one of the big Glasgow poaching gangs. They paid two visits with a lorry, spotlights, rifles and a couple of Bren guns.'

The solicitor tutted and shook his head in disgust. He was not unacquainted with minor poaching matters, but had only read in the newspapers of the big business methods that are sometimes applied in other areas.

'When they made the second visit my friend got wind of it, and there was something of a battle. He was lucky not to be killed. But he shot up their lorry so that they had to leave empty-handed, and they were caught on the road a few miles away.'

'I can't say I'm sorry to hear it.'

'But there was a man in the lorry when my friend shot it up, and he took a bullet through the hip. My friend was charged on about a dozen counts, and had to plead guilty to several of them. Because he'd been fired on first, the court took a lenient view and he was admonished.'

'That seems like a satisfactory ending to the tale,' the lawyer commented.

'If it had been the ending it would've been. But the chief constable refused to renew his firearms certificate, and he was forced to get rid of his rifles. As you probably know, chief constables have a wide discretion.'

Enterkin nodded. 'Undesirably wide, some think,' he said.

'That's right! And some of them interpret it even wider. Well, that left my friend good and stuck. As you probably know, we've just had a couple of very good breeding seasons. There was danger of the deer outgrowing the available feed and destroying their habitat. Some very second-rate beasts were coming onto the ground and surviving to breed.'

'And,' said Enterkin, 'he was deprived of both his stalking and his venison.'

'Locally he got a lot of sympathy. A rifle was loaned to him from time to time, and he was able to get his neighbours, plus occasional visiting friends, to do some culling for him. But it was all very tiresome, and he decided to buy one off certificate.'

'A somewhat dangerous proceeding.'

'Not very,' said Keith. 'The rifle that he was able to borrow from time to time belonged to the local Bobby – that's how feelings were running up there.

'Anyway, he came to me. Now, it often happens that I'm offered goods to purchase which are slightly warm. Not stolen, you understand. I wouldn't buy stolen goods, but there are occasions . . . Even licensed collectors often collect items which have never been on certificate, and getting them legitimised can be difficult.'

'I understand.'

'A rifle was brought to me. It had come down from a height onto its butt, and the stock was shattered and the telescopic sight would have made a good tyre-lever, but the barrel and action were perfect. I thought that it might be the one that Ronnie had lost, so I checked the number discreetly and it was.

'Well, by that time Ronnie had a new rifle and the insurance had been paid. If the rifle had been handed back, Ronnie would have had to return the money, which he'd already spent, the insurance company would have had to cough up for a new stock and telescopic sight, which on top of their administrative costs would have mopped up just about all that they recovered from Ronnie, who would have ended up with an extra rifle which he didn't need but might have been able to sell for a bit less than the insurance money that he had in the first place.'

'And who you didn't like much anyway.'

'We were getting on all right at that time – it was a week or two later that we fell out over his sister. He started coming the heavy brother, and I wouldn't have it.'

'So you agreed to repair it for your friend?'

'Not so much a repair as a rebuild. A new detachable skeleton stock and grips, and a new and better telescopic sight, and the whole lot folding in half. The arrangement was that my friend would get the rifle now, and as soon as he could get his certificate back he'd return it to me and I would either legitimise it or get rid of it.

'Unfortunately, it was in my van when McLure got called to the hereafter. It seemed quite possible that there'd be a search, so I hid it immediately. There was, in fact, a rather casual search at the time. But the death was rather unusual, and it seemed quite on the cards that evidence of foul play would be found at the post mortem. A much more thorough search of the van would then be likely. The one place that seemed safe was the derelict wash-house behind Ronnie's cottage. I certainly hadn't expected that they'd find a rifle bullet in McLure.'

Enterkin's eyes, usually mildly twinkling, were sharp and stern. 'It didn't occur to you that if the rifle was found the numbers would be particularly damning to Fiddler, suggesting that he had never lost the weapon at all? Or – '

'I never thought of that,' Keith said. 'Truly, it never occurred to me at all. I never thought they'd find a rifle bullet in him.'

'Accepting that for the moment, for lack of reason to the contrary, why didn't you file off the numbers?'

'The numbers are in several places, and they're too deeply punched in for it to be practicable. You've really got to cut the whole bit out or they can be developed again by acid etching techniques.'

The solicitor pursed his plump lips in a way that made them look like something novel in the way of human anatomy. This was his habit when deep in thought, to the amusement of his friends and clients. 'It fits together,' he said at last. 'But if the rifle was taken from your van – '

'You'd better leave that to me,' Keith interrupted. 'All I've got at the moment is a theory and a few scraps of evidence. But you just believe that I can get your client off the hook at my own expense and that if necessary I will.'

'I'm not sure that I can rest on that assurance,' said Enterkin. 'The police might very well suggest that Fiddler took that rifle out of your van.'

'He didn't and he couldn't, and I can prove it. Just leave that in my hands. Aren't you in danger of being late for your appointment?'

The solicitor glanced at his watch and bounced to his feet with no apparent effort.

As they crossed the quiet street, Keith asked, 'How important is motive in a criminal case?'

'The prosecution don't have to prove motive; but juries don't like motiveless crime, and tend to expect a higher degree of proof.'

'Ah. What's the status of the case now, as far as the police are concerned?'

'As far as they're concerned, it's been a murder case

since the bullet was found. They set up a murder room in the gymnasium at the back of their headquarters, although I suppose they'll be dismantling it soon.'

'Who's in charge of the investigation?'

'Because of a manpower problem, a number of men were drafted in from Edinburgh. Munro's been given the temporary rank of detective chief inspector and has local charge, but he's responsible to a superintendent in Edinburgh. A clumsy arrangement which seems to please nobody.'

'I see.' Keith sounded unhappy. The arrangement did not please him either. He had a number of friends on the force, but Munro was not one of them.

'I'll go on in,' said Enterkin. 'Give me about twenty minutes to half an hour, and I'll have left word to have you brought to us.'

So Keith Calder did a little shopping while Molly's brother, in the presence of his solicitor, was formally charged with the murder of Ronald James McLure, in that on the first day of October he did shoot at the said McLure, whereof he died.

Keith was taken to the door of a small interview room, guarded on the outside by a constable. Inside, Ronnie Fiddler and Mr Enterkin were seated at a small table. Keith thought that Fiddler would have made three of his sister, and been preferable that way. Fiddler was a large, square man with a large, red face and a jaw like the bucket of a blue-stubbled bulldozer. His dark hair, which had a curl that Molly had often envied, had been wetted and slicked down carelessly to either side.

'Molly'd no right to go to you for help,' was his greeting.

Keith took the chair opposite Fiddler. 'She had every right,' he said calmly. 'She came to me as a friend.'

'You're no friend of mine. Just as long as that's understood.'

'I'm a friend of hers, and she can come to me for help any times she likes, even if that involves helping you. It's time that was understood, too.'

'We do need help,' Enterkin said, emphasising the first

68

word, 'and Mr Calder has just the experience to be able to give it.'

'Help I need,' Fiddler said. 'His help I need like a second arse-hole.'

Keith shrugged and got up. 'A third, you mean,' he said. 'Well, just as long as we know where we stand, I'll get back to earning a living.'

The solicitor knew that Keith was bluffing, but played up to him. 'Sit down, Mr Calder,' he said with a warning frown. 'My client has an exaggerated sense of independence. But you're not just helping him, you're helping the defence as a whole.'

Keith hesitated, and panic flickered somewhere at the back of Fiddler's blue eyes. Then Keith sat down.

'Well . . . just don't let me catch him making it an excuse to hang around my sister.'

'I don't make excuses.'

'Just as long as that's understood.' Fiddler avoided saying what was to be understood, and Keith let it go.

They spent an hour going over and over Ronnie Fiddler's account of how he had spent the day of McLure's death, but it was all wasted breath. He had, he insisted, spent the day in the hills. He had met nobody, seen nobody. He could describe his route in detail, and the wild-life that he had seen and watched. He could take them through each stalk and shot in a detail that compelled belief, except that the detail could as easily have come from the day before or the day after. There was no flaw in his account, but also there was no corroboration.

'You took your empty cartridge cases home with you?' Keith asked.

'Yes. I always do.'

'Will the estate records not bear you out?' Enterkin asked.

Fiddler shrugged and looked dour. 'Not really,' he said. 'They're in my writing, the deer records; and the venison-dealer doesn't come every day.'

There was nothing there at all, Keith thought. There was no point in tracking over the route, nothing would date any traces that Fiddler had left behind him. It is as easy to drop yesterday's newspaper as today's.

'You're absolutely sure that you didn't come down close to Corner Farm all day?'

'Absolutely, definitely, positively certain sure.'

There was a brief silence.

'There's a small patch of cover on the crest above Oak Wood,' Keith said. 'Do you ever lie up there to wait for the roe-deer?'

'I have done, in some weathers.'

'But not that day?'

'I've already *said* – '

The solicitor intervened. 'Have patience with our questions, Mr Fiddler. We must make absolutely sure. We must gather every fragment of evidence. And we must be sure that the prosecution don't have any surprises for us.'

'All right, all right, all right.'

Fiddler watched fascinated as the solicitor pursed his lips in thought. 'You know that the police theory is that you shot Mr McLure in mistake for Mr Calder?'

'Aye. It's damned nonsense. I've no need to shoot him. The toe of my boot's good enough for the likes of him.'

'You and whose army?' Keith asked, amused.

The solicitor smacked the table, and all his bulges bounced. 'Stop this childishness at once,' he said, and the two men jumped in their chairs. It was like being snarled at by a pet rabbit. 'May I remind you, Mr Calder,' he went on, 'that you're here to help and not to hinder, and you, Mr Fiddler, that any hostility between yourself and Mr Calder will only strengthen the police case. So, both of you, keep the heid and don't be provocative.'

There was a silence, as if neither man could think of anything unprovocative to say. Ronnie Fiddler was the first to break it. 'It's important to my case?' he asked.

'Very.'

'All right, then. For that reason and that reason only. Just as long as that's understood.'

Keith broke another silence. 'There's a better reason why that theory won't wash. If a rifle was used it was at two

70

hundred yards, near as dammit. At that range, on a slowly-moving target, would you use open sights?'

'No way,' Fiddler said.

'Well, through a telescopic sight, you couldn't possibly mistake McLure for me. Except maybe from the back, but you'd have seen him side-on. And even if you did, he was keeping his dog very close to him that day, and there's no way you could mistake a liver-and-white Springer for a black Lab.'

'That's true,' Ronnie Fiddler said, and for the first time his voice sounded almost friendly.

The solicitor pursed his lips again before he spoke. 'That's not an argument likely to convince a court on its own, but it's a useful point and useful points all add up together.'

There was one question that Keith was hesitant to introduce, but that would have been conspicuous by its absence. Now was a better moment than most. 'The rifle that was found at your cottage – is that the one that you lost last year?'

'Aye. I'm damned if I know where it's been or how it got there. But they showed me the rifle, and the number in my old certificate. It's the same one, right enough. The stock's been changed, of course, and a new sight fitted. At first I thought you'd done it – it seemed the kind of caper that you might get up to. But the workmanship's better than you could ever do. The police were admiring it.'

Keith would have loved to reply, but instead was forced to keep his face a blank. Ronnie Fiddler was watching him with secret eyes, and Keith was surprised to find that Molly's brother could be so subtle. 'Some day I'll tell him,' he thought.

'Were there any fingerprints on it, do you know?' asked the solicitor.

Ronnie Fiddler shrugged. 'Aye. One of his and one of mine, they told me. But they were old ones, I saw them – you know how a permanent fingerprint can get etched in rust where you've left an acid print on bare metal? It was under the magazine-slide. I've never had it out since I had that wee fault with it and we stripped it down together.

That's when we must have left them, and I told the police so.'

'And they accepted that?'

Fiddler shrugged. 'They seemed to,' he said. 'The rest had been polished clean, and the box it was in was a rough plywood one, too rough to take any prints, somebody said.'

As he and Enterkin were about to leave, Keith felt a stab of compunction for the prisoner-on-remand. 'Is there anything you want?' he asked.

'All I want is for you to stay away from my sister.'

Keith ignored the dig. Nobody gets all that he wants. 'There's nothing that you'd like sent in to you?'

'Molly's quite capable of seeing to what I need.'

'Right. One more thing. Would you make a list of everybody you can think of who've bought deer carcasses off the estate – here or up north – for at least the last couple of years? I think that's all,' he added to Enterkin. 'Could you get me a look at the evidence?'

'I think so. We can but try.'

As he left the room, Keith thought he heard Ronnie mutter 'Thanks', but he could not be sure so he made no reply.

Inspector Munro was in the murder room, but a message fetched him out to meet them.

Mr Enterkin, without wasting any words, was explicit. 'Mr Calder has been retained by the defence, to look into the evidence and to advise on all matters especially those pertaining to guns. We'd like him to see the evidence.'

Munro hesitated, then nodded curtly. He led them into the murder room which lay at the end of devious passages. The large room was cluttered at one end with screens and furniture and spattered with photographs and diagrams. but there were signs that, now that a charge had been made, it was about to revert to its usual function. The furnished part of the room held only a middle-aged constable sifting papers, but two men were bringing the vaulting equipment out of store.

The acting detective chief inspector took the rifle and its

box from a locked cupboard, and opened the box. 'Have you ever seen this before?' he asked.

Keith looked at it, as if with curiosity. 'If, as I'm told, this is the barrel and action from the one that Ronnie Fiddler lost last year, then I've certainly seen that much of it before. I mended it for him before he lost it. Of course, it's been altered a lot since then.'

'So you wouldn't be surprised if we found your finger-prints on it?'

'I wouldn't be surprised if you found them inside the action. I'd be surprised as hell if you found them anywhere else.'

'What can you tell me about it?'

'From memory, it was a standard barrel and action in good condition. From what I see now, it's been shortened. It seems to have a Bokson scope instead of the original Bushnell. The walnut stock has been discarded completely, and a new skeleton stock made up with rubber hand-grips and shoulder-pad. It seems to be designed to fold. And the metalwork has all been browned.'

'Why would anybody use brown instead of blue?'

'I'm only guessing, but a good browning job is easier for an amateur to do. Blueing needs more equipment. Of course, brown is less conspicuous when stalking.'

'You'd rate this as the work of a skilled amateur?'

'Either an amateur, or done on the cheap. The workman-ship's a bit rough.' This was true. Keith had grudged doing a polished job which, eventually, was likely to be consigned to the depths of some loch.

'Could Fiddler have done it?'

'Not him,' Keith said fervently. 'He's a butcher with metalwork.'

'Do you ever do browning instead of blueing?'

'Often on antique guns, especially Damascus barrels. By the way, whoever stripped the gun for fingerprinting put it back with the sight turned through ninety degrees.'

Munro allowed no expression to cross his bony features. 'Did you make – or re-make – this gun for Ronnie Fiddler?' he asked abruptly.

'Certainly not,' Keith said truthfully, but he flicked a glance at the solicitor, who stepped into the breach.

'I must advise Mr Calder,' Enterkin said, 'not to answer any further questions along those lines. They're only designed to fish for material to discredit a possible defence witness.'

'In that case – ' Munro made a gesture implying that the interview was at an end.

'I'd like to see the fatal bullet, and the comparison photographs,' Keith said quickly.

'That seems a reasonable request,' said Enterkin.

With evident reluctance, Munro opened the cupboard. Keith glanced at the bullet, and then studied the photographs with care. These each comprised two strips, upper and lower, each showing, greatly enlarged, the surface of a bullet in a strong side-light so that the tiniest blemish was thrown in high relief. The photographs had been adjusted to bring similarities in the pattern into register with each other – rather like matching wallpaper, Keith thought. There was no doubt that the bullets had been fired from the same rifle.

'Can you tell me which strips were the fatal bullet?' Keith asked.

'I have not the faintest idea,' said Munro.

'Can we have one print to take away?' Enterkin asked.

'Very well.'

'Now,' Keith said. 'I'd like to see the material that your men picked up in the wood.'

'It has been examined most thoroughly. There is nothing of any significance in it.'

'I would still like to see it.'

'But I've already told you – '

'Come away, Mr Calder,' Enterkin said gently. 'I'll look forward to hearing counsel explaining to the judge that the defence have been denied access to the evidence.'

Two spots of high colour appeared on Munro's prominent cheek-bones. 'Who says that it's evidence?' he asked.

'Who are you to say that it isn't?' asked Enterkin. 'For all we know, your searchers lifted a great deal of evidence that supports a defence theory.'

74

'So the defence have a theory?'

'I didn't say so.'

There was a pregnant pause, and then Munro sighed with all the martyred patience of a mother tolerating her children. He turned to another cupboard and produced a cardboard carton which he emptied onto a table and spread out. Then he stood back, folding his arms. 'You see?' he said. 'Rubbish.'

Keith, keeping his hands carefully in his pockets, looked at the varied collection carefully. The only objects of any size were two fertiliser bags. There were plastic shotgun cartridge-cases, and the brass ends of paper cartridges, a child's gym-shoe, cigarette ends, a cigar-butt and some matches, empty cigarette packets and sweet-papers, several pieces of binder-twine, the ferrule of a shooting-stick, a handkerchief, a lens from a pair of sun-glasses, a pen-knife so rusted that it was barely identifiable, a number of various types of cartridge wads, and other human debris.

When he was satisfied, and long after Munro had started to fidget, Keith asked to see McLure's personal effects. These occupied another carton, but were separately enclosed in polythene bags. Very little remained to be examined. McLure's wristwatch, gun and knife, together with a few coins, had survived although greatly damaged; the rest was cinders and barely recognisable.

Enterkin peered at the polythene bag that contained a recognisable cartridge-belt. 'I'm surprised to see this more or less in one piece,' he said. 'Wouldn't the cartridges go off in a fire.'

'They'd explode, but not violently,' Keith said. 'They need to be confined in a gun before they'll go bang. Obviously, they helped the blaze along.'

'Have you seen enough?' asked Munro.

'Yes.'

'I hope you have learned something.' There was the trace of a sneer in his voice.

'I have, thank you,' said Keith. 'I have indeed. Good day to you, Acting Chief Detective Inspector.'

'Good day,' echoed Mr Enterkin.

They walked back across the square together, the energetic gunsmith shortening his pace for the fat solicitor. They maintained a ruminative silence until they were back and seated in the latter's office.

'Thank you for getting me off the hook,' Keith said. 'He was all set to press me hard.'

Enterkin grunted. 'Maybe I shouldn't have. I did it on the spur of the moment, and because I never could stand that man Munro. But it might have been to my client's advantage to let you put your foot in it.'

'And it might not. I might have been out of the way and unable to look at the evidence for you.'

'We could have got bail. Anyway, take away the rifle and my client has nothing to answer.'

'I wouldn't be so sure of that,' Keith said. 'You could see the line that Munro wanted to take – that I'd converted the gun for Ronnie Fiddler. That wouldn't have stopped him using it on me later.'

'Maybe. You were lucky with the fingerprints.'

'I'm surprised they found any at all, but with Ronnie fussing about and interfering I suppose I was careless. I always finish off each part with a good rub in a lightly greased cloth, and part of the reason is that it's so easy to leave acid fingerprints behind, and they're a sign of a bad workman.'

'Have you written out that statement yet?'

'I'll do it this afternoon. And would you, for your part, give me a letter – To Whom It May Concern – stating that I'm enquiring on behalf of the defence? Give me a few photo-copies as well, just in case I don't always get it back.'

'Yes, that I can do,' said Enterkin. 'Can you call for them tomorrow?'

'In the morning, yes. I'd like to see Ronnie Fiddler with you again tomorrow morning, if I can, and then I'll be for off.'

Keith lunched with Molly again, and then retired to his hotel bedroom where, in his neat italic script, he wrote out a full account of the rifle's history and added some notes about his theories and discoveries to date. These he took up to the

Hall, and Sir Peter and his housekeeper solemnly witnessed his signature before the papers were sealed in an envelope and safely locked away. Sir Peter was almost incoherent with curiosity; but he was also inclined to be a chatterbox with anyone whom he regarded as trustworthy, a category which included most of the human race, and Keith did not want the contents of his statement bandied around.

His last call of the day was on Hamish Thomson. Hamish, who doubled as the syndicate's half-time gamekeeper and as a general farm-worker to Derek Weatherby, lived alone in a cottage on a remote edge of Corner Farm, and there Keith found him overhauling a set of Fenn traps on a bench outside the door. A row of repainted pigeon decoys was ranged along the low garden wall.

Keith's description of Hamish, given to Inspector Munro as 'the big chap with all the hair', was, if anything, an understatement. Keith, who was no midget, felt dwarfed beside Hamish's broad six-foot-five, while the rarely-cut curly brown hair and ginger-tinted beard left little but Hamish's nose and his friendly eyes on view, peeping out of the undergrowth like wild creatures.

Keith picked up one of the traps, and set to cleaning it as they talked. Keith told him of a fox's earth, for which Hamish was duly grateful, and they discussed the past nesting season before Keith got down to business.

'Hamish, do you know what a bullet sounds like, when it goes by overhead?'

'I was in Ireland wi' the Borderers,' Hamish said simply. 'And I've done my share of butt-marking.'

'If McLure was shot from the hill, there's only one place it could have been from. Most likely the bullet would have passed not far over your head. Did you hear anything like that?'

Hamish shook his shaggy head. 'A bullet at full speed plinks like somebody leaned on the lid of a biscuit-tin. Bird-shot just hisses. I'd've noticed.'

'What about a bullet that's been deflected by passing through something?'

'Ah. That's different. That may whine if it's been deformed, or it may whistle or it may make a plunking sort of sound.

But if it's spinning it'll whirr, and I might've mistaken that for the swoosh of shot. You hear that often enough, keepering, wi' some o' these dangerous boogers around.'

'Thanks, Hamish.' Keith put down the trap and picked up another. 'Did you notice anybody firing singles when he might have used both barrels?'

'Only McNeill, but he was complaining of one barrel misfiring. He took one out of his gun an' showed it me, an' right enough there was a fair wee dent in the cap. He loads his own, an' I doubt he's doing it wrong. But for the others, I wouldn't ha' noticed. Often, a mannie'll miss wi' the one barrel, an' wait for the bird to fa' down out o' the sky.'

'True,' said Keith.

As he took the hired car back down to Molly's cottage, Keith thought that Hamish had never commented on being asked such questions. But then, he thought, no doubt the fact that he was working for the defence was all over the place by then. Newton Lauder was always a hotbed of gossip.

CHAPTER 7

The Tuesday morning, for Keith, was a morning of shocks almost from the very moment of awakening in Molly's bed. He awoke to find Molly in her quilted dressing-gown bending over him, and his first thought was that she looked better, younger and more wholesome than most girls her age did in the mornings.

'Oh, Keith,' she said, 'how awful!'

He yawned. 'What is?'

'Did you not hear the knocking?'

'No. What's awful?'

'There was a policeman at the door. He wanted to know if you were all right.'

'Why wouldn't I be?' Suddenly the urge to yawn left him completely.

'That's what I asked, and he told me. There was a fire in the hotel kitchen almost under your room. It was only a wee one, but there was a lot of smoke and the alarm was set off and the firemen came. All the guests came out – except you!'

'Holy damn!'

'And they thought they'd better make sure you hadn't been overcome by smoke or something, so they opened your room with the master-key. And you weren't there. So, just to check up, they wanted to know if you were all right. And they came here. Well, I couldn't have them list you as a missing person, or whatever they do, so I had to say that you were all right. But, Keith, whatever made them think to come here?'

The human female is capable of amazing feats of self-deception, not least concerning the continued secrecy of her secret loves.

If Keith had thought to mention that rude awakening to

Mr Enterkin, the solicitor would no doubt have seen the danger-signs and advised precautions. But Keith, accustomed over the years to thinking in terms of angry husbands and brothers rather than of tactics on a more legalistic plane, thought it better to keep silent and hope for the best.

The two men met by appointment outside the police building. The lawyer handed over the letter of authority complete with extra copies and they went inside. After a wait of a few minutes a constable escorted them to the same interview room, where another officer was guarding the door. Ronnie Fiddler was seated inside, glowering from his hard chair.

As the door closed, Fiddler erupted. Before Keith had time for more than an impression that he was being charged by a snorting, rampaging bull, he was grabbed by the coat and slammed against the wall. Fiddler's furious face was inches from his own and scarlet with fury.

'How dared you?' he demanded. 'Me in here, and you sleep in my bed!'

Keith was too startled to guard his tongue. 'I didn't sleep in your bed,' he said before he could think. The frenzy of Fiddler's reaction brought home to him that he had said the wrong thing. There were only two beds in the cottage.

With a muted growl, Fiddler shifted his grip to Keith's throat, lifted him clear off the floor and thumped him to the wall again. Keith found himself in very real danger. He might have freed himself, but only at the expense of serious injury to the other man. He could only drag at the squeezing hands in the hope of minimising the killing pressure and at the same time try for a leverage with his knee. His pulse boomed in his ears and the world turned grey.

Enterkin tried for a few seconds to force himself between the two men, then, giving in to the inevitable, he shouted for help. The two constables bored into the room. They were both past their first youth, but they were highly practised in handling recalcitrant prisoners. In a matter of seconds, Fiddler was hauled off and Keith could breathe again.

'Go over to my office and wait for me there,' Enterkin said urgently.

The officers dropped Fiddler into a chair and held him

down with practised ease, despite his still furious struggles. 'We'll need a statement,' one of them said.

'Nothing to say,' Keith croaked. Ronnie Fiddler's threats and curses followed him along the echoing corridor.

Keith waited in the solicitor's office, among the bound volumes of session cases and the pink-garlanded dockets. He waited a long time. Soon, he drew out a volume of Irons and Melville. He became absorbed. His reading had always been catholic, a characteristic which may have saved him from becoming an extraverted and hedonistic boor.

When the solicitor returned, he was clearly upset. He slumped into his solid old leather swivel-chair and puffed for a minute before he spoke. 'What a mess,' he said at last. 'Tell me what brought that on.'

With some embarrassment, Keith explained about the early morning fire and the visit of the police to the Fiddlers' cottage.

'Why for the love of God didn't you tell me all this?' the solicitor burst out, so vehemently that his cheeks bounced about on every second word.

'I didn't think it was going to matter. Damn it, I couldn't know that it was going to get back to Ronnie.'

'Didn't you even *think*? You're supposed to be a consultant to the defence, and you aren't even capable of coherent thought? Sir Peter spoke highly of you, which makes me wonder about *his* intelligence.' He paused, and rubbed his face. 'I must keep calm and try to get this over to you without getting angry, even if I burst a blood-vessel in the attempt. What would you do if you were on the prosecution's side and you had a chance to drive a wedge between the defendant and his principal witness? Wouldn't you do it? Of course you would. But what's more, their case is based on the supposition that he hated you. That made your helping the defence doubly damaging to the prosecution. In their shoes, wouldn't you have leaked the information to him?'

Keith preferred to treat the question as rhetorical. He stared silently at his knees.

'That isn't even the worst of it,' Enterkin went on. 'He

was in such a state of rage that I couldn't shut him up. Even after he was cautioned he went on ranting about what he was going to do to you. I couldn't get through to him at all. He seemed to take a special pride in the fact that he'd bested you in a fight. I gather that there have been some – ah – fisticuffs between you before?'

'Some,' Keith said unhappily. 'He didn't say that, did he?'

'He was very explicit about it. It seems that he'd always come off worst in the past. So he was boasting that he had you helpless, and that if they hadn't pulled him off you he'd have screwed your head clean off and done something with it which I won't repeat. You and I know, of course, that he would certainly have stopped short of killing you; but just imagine his words being read out in court, in a flat and unemotional voice. It lends a lot of credence to the rest of their case.'

'But can they use it if I don't press charges?'

'You don't have to press charges. An indictable offence was committed in front of two officers and subsequently admitted by the accused after he had been cautioned. If they bring this to trial before the murder charge and get a conviction . . .'

'All right,' Keith said. 'All right. I blew it. I admit it and I'm sorry. What can I do to minimise the damage?'

Enterkin pursed his lips and blew out his cheeks. He seemed to relax, and the high colour faded in his face. 'Let's deal with one other thing first,' he said. 'When you got back to the hotel, had there really been a fire?'

'There was a smell of smoke – I haven't seen the kitchen. You don't really think it was a fake do you?'

'Probably not. But it would be easy enough to knock on the lassie's door and say that there had been a fire, wouldn't it? But if you smelled smoke it was probably a real fire and just bad luck that it happened at this particular time.'

'And that I was too stupid to mention it,' Keith said.

'That, too. And if you'd allowed me to produce the evidence about the rifle sooner, we could probably have got him out and the damage wouldn't have been done,' the solicitor said grimly.

'It would have been done to me,' Keith pointed out.

82

'True but irrelevant. But you asked me to trust you, and you blew it. So now I think you'd better spill the beans.'

Keith fidgeted under the solicitor's beady gaze, and then capitulated. 'All right,' he said. 'I didn't want to say anything before I had to, in case the line I was working on got about and somebody covered his tracks. The fact that I'm making enquiries at all is bound to be known, but – '

'I understand,' said Enterkin. 'Your theories shall not be bruited abroad.' His annoyance seemed to have spent itself.

'McLure was killed by a bullet fired from a shotgun,' Keith said abruptly.

The solicitor sat back and protruded his mouth until it looked like an elephant's trunk in embryo, and his eyes rolled up to study the ceiling. For fully ten seconds he looked, Keith thought, like something from outer space trying hard to assume human form. Then he relaxed. 'Ah,' he said profoundly. 'Go on.'

Keith said, 'I'll try to take you through it in sequence. I knew with absolute certainty that the rifle was secure in my van when McLure died. There seems to be no possible reason to doubt the time of death – we'd all seen him a few minutes before.'

'And his dentist identified him by his teeth,' said Enterkin. 'Quite so. But how secure is your van?'

'It's an ex-bank-van, and it's secure. A gunsmith's premises have to be. The workshop half has a very special lock on the door, a grille over the only window, and the door's lined with steel. On top of that, the rifle was in a secret hidey-hole which nobody knows about but me.'

'That seems to settle that. So the bullet was not fired from the rifle.'

'Not at that time. But the nature of the wound – what's called a "keyhole" wound – suggested that the bullet was either deflected from its proper course or fired inefficiently. There's only one place I could imagine a rifle being used from, and there's nothing between to deflect it. I've heard of a freak case in which a bird flew between a stalker and a deer and got killed, and the stag had a keyhole wound, but that really was a freak. And I couldn't see any sign of a dead bird near the line between the two points.'

'I think you've gone far enough along that line,' said Enterkin, 'although, of course, if the bird had been a pheasant the keeper might have picked it up.'

'If his dog had brought it to him, he'd've thought it had retrieved somebody else's bird,' Keith said. 'But there's other evidence. Hamish, the keeper, was out on that side, and if the bullet had been spinning he'd have heard it, almost certainly.

'So I thought about the possibility of explaining the rifling-marks by the bullet being fired out of a shotgun after it had been fired and retrieved once already. You follow me?'

'Your logic is better than your syntax, but I follow you,' said Enterkin. Under the stimulus of reasoning and the comfort of facts he was returning to his more usual, sprightly self.

'I leave the polished grammar to you,' Keith said. 'I'll just make do with the facts. I must fire some test shots soon, but I've no doubt it's practicable and will bear out some other bits of supporting evidence. For a start, you'd have to wrap the bullet up pretty tightly in something. Soft lavatory-paper would be very suitable, and who'd think anything of a few bits of it lying around in a wood? But I know, from shooting muzzle-loaders, that if you use paper for wadding it often comes out burning – for instance, you just don't use it shooting rats in a barn or you'll set the whole place up. Doesn't that make a credible explanation for the fire?'

'Yes,' said Enterkin slowly, 'I believe it does.'

Keith took the polythene bag out of his pocket and laid it on top of a pile of papers on the desk. 'Found near the burned patch in the wood. Look at the powder-staining, in little lines over half of it, as if it had gone up a dirty barrel. We're lucky it didn't all burn. It's scorched, but sometimes you'll find bits that have blown themselves out from the blast and the speed they were travelling.'

The solicitor stared at the scrap of paper. 'Maybe,' he said. The twinkle was back in his eyes. 'Maybe. I never thought I'd be glad to see a tiny piece of dirty lavatory paper, but this is the first physical clue that we've obtained that points away from the unfortunate Fiddler. Have you any more little goodies like that?'

'Yes, but it's in the hands of the police. What do you know about shotgun cartridges?'

The solicitor shrugged vastly. 'Only that they go bang when you hit one end,' he said.

'You need some form of wad between the propellant powder and the shot. It keeps them separate, forms a gas-seal, and cushions the shot from being deformed by the enormous pressure up its tail. Rifle cartridges manage without, because the bullet's a gas-tight fit, more or less. One type of wad used in some factory cartridges and by nearly all home-loaders is made of plastic. It's a bit like a three-legged challenge-cup on a base. The base is like a saucer and forms the gas-seal. The three legs collapse, and so cushion the shock. And the cup contains the shot and protects it from abrasion against the barrel wall. You still follow me?'

'I'm probably ahead of you, but then I'm jumping to conclusions. Tell me.'

'It seemed to me that that kind of wad would be just the thing to use, if I were loading a rifle bullet into a shotgun cartridge-case. In particular, it would prevent the gases popping the bullet out of its wrapping before it got up speed and so negating the whole thing. What I'd do is to re-prime the case, put in the powder, put in a plastic wad, and then wrap the bullet in just enough paper to bring it up to the diameter of the barrel, or a little less over the short length that would be inside the shot-cup.

'Now, wads of that type often fly pretty straight, and I was afraid that it might have fetched up in the fire. But if it missed McLure it could have gone right past the fire. I couldn't find it, so I looked among the rubbish that the police picked up.'

'And?'

'There were a dozen of that type. All but one had the deep imprint of the shot in the plastic cup that happens from the pressure on the shot as it's hurled up the barrel. You often find them lying around. If whoever-it-was had picked up a used one and used it again we'd've been at another dead end. But he didn't. There's one in the box that has no shot-marks at all, although it shows signs of having been discharged from a gun.'

'There's no other way that it could have arrived there? No alternative explanation?'

'None that I can think of.'

'Then I'll get a court order at once.' Enterkin scribbled a note in his diary.

'Without letting the cat out of the bag? I'd hate to have that wad vanish.'

'And so would I. I'll get the whole lot listed, photographed, sealed and impounded.'

'That's fine,' said Keith. 'Next thing, it would help if you could get that list from Ronnie. The obvious place for somebody to obtain one of his bullets is by finding it in a carcass.'

Mr Enterkin's jollity dimmed again for a moment. 'If he ever cools down again, I'll ask him.'

'Ask him if he ever lent the rifle.'

'Of course.' Enterkin made another note. 'Any other evidence?'

'One thing. Let's see that photograph, the comparison one of the two bullets.' They pored over it together. 'I thought so,' Keith said. 'It would help if we knew which was the fatal bullet and which was the test one, but it doesn't really matter. Take a good look. These big markings are the rifling, the others are tiny blemishes caused by imperfections in the surface of the rifle-barrel. Some of them may wear away a bit over a long period of use, and you can reduce them by "lapping", which I haven't done and I'm sure nobody else has. Of course, new scratches can be added, usually by grit between the bullet and the barrel.

'Now look. Most of the lines run right through from one half of the photograph to the other, so there's no doubt it's the same gun. But each half, and that means each bullet, has a few small lines which don't appear on the other half. Now, between the firing of the murder bullet and the firing of the test bullet you might expect some extra blemishes if the rifle had been fired a lot; but how could it also lose a few lines?'

'You tell me.'

'Because I cut a few inches off the barrel length. The worst scratches are often near the muzzle, because grit can so easily be introduced there, blown by the wind.'

Enterkin pulled his face again. 'You're arguing,' he said at last, 'that, because certain scratches have *not* been reproduced on the test bullet that were on the fatal one, the fatal bullet must have been fired before the barrel was shortened?'

'That's it exactly.'

'Could you stand up to cross-examination on that one?'

'Up to a point, yes. But I'd have to admit that there were other explanations, possible but less likely.'

'Nevertheless,' said Enterkin, 'it would be contributory. Is there anything else?'

'Nothing physical. The fact that a shotgun was used suggests that we look very hard at Andrew Payne, who was walking just outside the wood but quite close to McLure, and David McNeill who was next to him on the other side.'

'That seems logical.'

'I want to go away and go through the same motions. Fire test bullets through a shotgun until I've got it right, and then see what traces I've left. Then I may know what else to look for. Nobody can do anything without leaving traces behind. Then I want to think about what I'd've done myself to cover up those traces, and look for traces of *that*. And I want to see if I can find connections between McLure and anybody else on that shoot.'

The solicitor sighed. 'I won't say that I'm sorry that I blew up at you, because you deserved it. But I will say that you're pulling your weight now. Come and have some lunch. Or are you expected somewhere?'

'No,' said Keith. 'I'm not expected. I'd like to.'

The various published guides to good eating tend to pass lightly over Newton Lauder, pausing only to murmur a brief benediction over The Willow Tree, a restaurant that had been created by an immigrant Frenchman out of the former coach-house behind a local inn. It was to here that Mr Enterkin led Keith Calder, and in its atmosphere the solicitor seemed to fit, reminding Keith of the photographs in natural history books of animals in their native habitat. Keith himself, however, was accustomed to taking his pleasures where more concern was given to value-for-money, and was not at ease.

They took a sherry apiece at the bar. At the table, Mr Enterkin's duckling was preceded by *paté* and accompanied by a red wine. Keith, whose living depended on his driving-licence, took a beer with his omelette. He could drink with the next man, but not before driving.

'Could you find us another expert witness who would take the same view of the evidence as yourself?' Mr Enterkin asked suddenly.

'I suppose so,' Keith said, surprised. 'Why?'

'If you go in the box as a witness, you may be faced with a stiff cross-examination.'

'It's happened before.'

'Suppose you're asked point-blank whether you converted that rifle. It would be a fairly obvious question for the other side to ask, and I think it would be allowable.'

Keith thought that over. 'You're right. I'd better not give evidence for the defence. Thanks.'

Enterkin waved a fat fist, dripping orange sauce onto the cloth. 'Don't thank me. You're not my client, I remind you again, and if I have to choose between your interests and those of Mr Fiddler, you lose.'

'I trust you all the same,' Keith said.

'Unwise. Just as long as that's understood. Damn it,' added the solicitor, 'I'm even beginning to talk like my client. But I'm envisaging you being asked that question on oath. You can lie, which would be perjury to add to your other sins. Or you can tell the truth, to your own detriment and that of my client. Or you could refuse to answer on the grounds that your answer might incriminate you, which would just about damn the validity and impartiality of your other evidence.'

'All right. I'll find you another expert who takes the same view as I do. Anything else I can do?'

'Yes.' Enterkin held his glass up to a gleam of thin sunshine that found its way through the windows. 'You can help by staying away from the attractive Miss Fiddler.'

'I can't do that,' said Keith. 'She needs somebody around. She begged me to stay. I warned her of the danger, but she said she couldn't bear to be alone.'

'Doesn't she have any other friends? Girl-friends?'

'I don't think so. None that she'd trust to stick by her in bad times. I *can't* leave her to stick it out on her own.'

'Then,' said Enterkin simply, 'marry the girl.'

Keith's mouth fell open. 'It's a conspiracy,' he said. He pointed a finger at the solicitor. 'Sir Peter told you to say that!'

'He certainly did not! And – ' a quick grin flitted across the roly-poly features ' – I may say that my client certainly didn't.'

'I believe you.' Keith shook his head. 'You married folk – '

'I am a bachelor,' Enterkin said. 'I nearly said "A bachelor gay am I," but that word has developed certain unfortunate connotations. I deeply sympathise, and I should no doubt react similarly in your predicament. I enjoy being a bachelor and intend to stay one.'

Keith was less interested in Mr Enterkin's status than in his own. 'I'm only thirty-four,' he said plaintively.

Enterkin laughed, and choked on his wine. He mopped his face. It was not a small face and he took his time, still chortling. 'I'm fifty-three,' he said at last, 'and I still consider myself far too young to marry. I have a very comfortable arrangement with a nice lady not too far away, and I see no need to clutter up my life with the daily trappings of feminine company. So you see that, as an adviser, I could hardly be less biased.'

Keith was not impressed. He had comfortable arrangements with more ladies than he could comfortably remember. 'But,' he said. 'But . . . but . . .'

'Do shut up a moment, my dear boy. You sound like an outboard motor. As I said, I sympathise; but consider your position. If you're not called by the defence, you certainly will be by the prosecution. Now, they can't cross-examine you, and would certainly avoid the matter of the rifle. But it would be very much to their interest to bring out every reason that Fiddler might have for putting a bullet through you. And in the process, I'm afraid the young lady's reputation would suffer. Not to put too fine a point on it, she'd come out looking like a tart.'

'I know all that,' Keith said. 'I told her much the same myself. But I don't see what difference marrying would make.'

'You make it sound like a rare perversion,' said Enterkin ruminatively. 'And who's to say you're wrong? But don't be obtuse. It would make all the difference in the world. There could be nothing so disarming as the reply, "Sir, you are speaking of the lady who shortly thereafter did me the honour of becoming my wife". In your own less polished words, of course. It would go a long way towards showing the sincerity of you both and thus shaking the credibility of any theory based on the supposition that you were the intended target. It would be all very well painting you as the seducer of Fiddler's baby sister; your image as having been his prospective brother-in-law at the time would be far less credible as a prospective murderee.'

'But I wasn't his prospective brother-in-law at the time.'

'Very difficult to convince a jury of that, *post facto*,' said Enterkin.

'And it's not as if I'm a desirable brother-in-law.'

'Bless you, *you* know that and *I* know that, but the jury won't know it and I doubt if anyone will convince your fiancée of it either. And it should stop my fool of a client from making a bigger fool of himself than he has already.'

'More likely to make him worse.'

'You do yourself less than justice. You may not be anybody's ideal of a brother-in-law, but as a brother-in-law you'll be considerably more acceptable than as a successful seducer of young maidens. You used to be on good terms with him, didn't you?'

'We tolerated each other, in an aggressive sort of way.'

'Let's say that you had a mutual respect based on antipathy,' said Enterkin, twinkling. 'And it was only when his sister grew up and you became attracted to each other that hostilities commenced?'

'Yes.'

'There you are, then.'

'You ask him whether he wants me for a brother-in-law,' Keith said desperately. 'You just ask him.'

'We don't always get what we want in this world,' said the solicitor. 'Sometimes we only get what's good for us.'

'He won't want to lose his sister.'

'He'll have to some day. Perhaps he'll look on it as gaining a brother instead.'

Keith sighed. 'It's a terrible big step to take.'

'It is. But I know you'll take it. You have a high regard for the young lady, and more sense of duty than you would care to acknowledge.'

'There's no tearing hurry, is there? It's not a thing to rush into.'

'The sooner the better, all the same.'

'I'm not going to say that I'll do it, mind. But I'll go this far – will you help me with the mechanics of getting a licence and so on?'

'Of course. That's what solicitors are for. Regard the prospect with equanimity, my boy. You might even find that marriage, like other institutions, is really quite tolerable when you get into it. In time, you may even come to enjoy it.' He raised his glass. 'Bless you, my children.'

'You're a cynical bastard,' said Keith. 'I suppose it wouldn't do if *you* married her?'

'I'm afraid not. It wouldn't have the same impact at all.'

'Did anyone ever tell you the story about God saying to the devil "You'll hear from my solicitor"?'

Mr Enterkin positively beamed. 'And the devil said, "Where would you find a solicitor?" Frequently, my boy. Usually when I've just told them that they haven't got grounds for divorce.'

CHAPTER 8

Keith homed back to the cottage with conflicting feelings, an unusual state for a usually single-minded man. Molly was not yet back from receiving lunch and reassurance from the Hays at the Hall, and the cottage seemed dead. Keith let himself in and, as much as anything to overcome the emptiness, washed out his laundry and left it for a final soak. He spent a few minutes admiring the wildlife photographs on the walls.

When he looked out again, Molly and the dogs were coming up the lane. The bitch saw him first and, true to her training, stayed at heel although she tensed in every muscle. When she saw him produce the whistle, her tail began to go, and at the first peep she bolted to him, whining with pleasure and relief. The girl contained her dignity until she was only a yard or two away, when she threw herself at him in her old way, and he swung her around and set her on her feet again, and they kissed and then looked at each other. She was still troubled, Keith could see, but she was out of the terrible depression. They went inside, hand-in-hand. Hebe walked sedately behind them with Black Jake, but her tail was thrashing like a branch in a gale.

'I'll have to be away shortly,' Keith said. He started wringing out his laundry into the sink.

She said 'Let me do that,' and took over the task.

'I'll be as quick as I can,' he said. He lounged back, leaning against the cooker. 'I've got to get round my customers up north. If I hurry, that'll take maybe a fortnight. I'll try to bring some work back to keep me going. Then I can still be earning a living while I make the rest of my enquiries down here. Can you get along all right that long?'

'I'll manage. Sir Peter said that if anyone could sort it all out it'd be you.'

'If you can't stand it on your own, I'm sure the Hays would have you up at the Hall.'

'Don't be silly.' He couldn't see her face.

'It's a pity you're not on the phone. Call Elsie every night. No, better than that, be in the phone-box at nine every night and I'll call you unless something makes it impossible. Don't wait after ten past. Would that help?'

She nodded, without speaking.

Her hands, he saw, were nervously tangling away at his laundry, and suddenly he found the right thing to say. 'Hey, hey, don't get my knickers in a twist!'

She stopped and turned. There were tears on her face, but first a smile and then a laugh came bubbling up. She put up her arms, pulled his face down and kissed the tip of his nose. 'Oh Keith,' she said, 'you are an ass.' Water from a pair of his pants was running down his back, but it seemed a small price to pay. Their bodies shook together as they laughed at the silly little joke. He could feel that, this time, she was really herself again.

'Stay for a meal while I get this lot dried,' she said. 'I've made a pigeon pie.'

He was tempted. The common wood-pigeon is not the easiest bird to prepare, tending towards toughness and an earthiness of taste, but in one of Molly's pies, with a little wine, and herbs, and nutmeg and bacon, and the very lightest of pastry, it was delicious. But, if he stayed, he would lose a day.

'I'd better go,' he said. 'I'll bag this lot and dry it when I get back to the van.'

'Take the pie with you, then.'

'Put it in the freezer and we'll have it together when I get back.' He lifted her by the waist and sat her on the work-top, so that their faces were level. 'Molly, can I ask you a hypothetical question?'

'Yes, of course.'

'You know what hypothetical means?'

'It's an iffy sort of question that doesn't mean more than it says.'

'Right.' He swallowed. 'You must have thought about us

getting married some time. How do you really feel about it?'

She considered the question seriously and unemotionally, as if it had always been tacitly there between them. 'There'll never be anyone else means as much to me,' she said simply. 'But I wouldn't want a husband who's always away after the other girls, like some I can think of.'

'I don't make promises lightly,' he said, 'like some of the others. When I make them I mean to keep them. That's why I'm in no great hurry to make a promise that I won't lightly break.'

'That's all I'd ask,' she said.

'You wouldn't try to change me into a stay-home-and-mind-the-baby sort of husband?'

She thought again, with her head on one side, and he almost decided to change his mind and stay the night. 'That's what any girl would want,' she said. 'But with you . . . I wouldn't want to change you. I'd just hope that you'd change yourself a bittie, because it was what would make me happy.'

Keith Calder drove the hired car northward through a dark afternoon and an occasional shower. Hebe lay very still on the passenger's floor. When her master looked and acted thus, she knew that it was a good time to be inconspicuous.

Keith, for his part, wondered if his mood resulted from his parting with Molly. Thinking back, each parting in recent months seemed to have been more of a wrench than the one before. But he dismissed the idea as fanciful, no more than the mind's attempt to come to terms with his probable fate. After all, he had more than the average man's experience of partings.

After some thought, he decided that his malaise must come from being separated from his beloved tapes. He hated driving in silence, but the radio gave him the choice between a talk which bored him, pop music which he despised, and a composition by Musgrave, a composer for whom he had conceived such a consuming hatred that, had he ever met the lady, he would have been quite unable to express it without risking arrest.

A few miles on and his practised eye spotted a movement

to the left of the road, almost at the periphery of his vision. He pulled in to the side. With binoculars, he confirmed a large hare. His shotgun and a point-two-two rifle were lying, bagged, along the back seat. At slightly over a hundred yards he shot the hare through the head, and sent Hebe away. Guided by the silent whistle she homed in, found its scent and picked it up. On two blasts she lay down, inconspicuous in the rough grass, while some traffic went by. Then, at a series of quick pips, she came home with a rush.

Keith emptied the hare's bladder out of the window and dropped it on the floor at the back of the car. Hebe knew better than to touch it again. He drove off, feeling happier, without having left the car at all.

Instead of slipping round Edinburgh by the so-called Ring Road, Keith plunged into the confused traffic of the city centre, crossing the Royal Mile and Princes Street by way of the Bridges. He found a vacant parking-meter just off George Street. His destination was the firm of Henderson, McLure and Groag, and he found them, as Jock Hendry had suggested, masquerading as a small family concern in one of a terrace of large, Georgian houses. The pulse of activity suggested a much larger firm.

Keith sent in a copy of Mr Enterkin's letter, and admired the perspective drawing hanging on the walls for a few minutes before being invited into a clean, bright room and offered a seat in a chrome-and-leather chair.

Eric Groag was a thin man with protrusions – ears, nose and Adam's apple – so that Keith thought that he looked like a clothes-pole painted pink. He had long, wavy hair surrounding a bald pate.

'Glad to help in any way I can,' he said. His voice was high but mellow like an oboe. 'I gathered that you were among those present, as they say, when my partner joined the majority?'

Keith was not there to give information, but to receive it. 'I was on the same party. But as the letter says – may I have it back, by the way? – I've been asked by the defence to look into the evidence, and I wanted to start by knowing a little about McLure, to put everything else into context. And this seemed to be a good place to start.'

Groag blinked. 'I thought he was supposed to have been shot in mistake for somebody else . . . but that, I suppose, is the very supposition that you want to upset?'

'Probably,' said Keith. 'It certainly seems to be the only possible motive that can be laid on the man they've arrested. But it might be helpful if we could show that McLure had enemies.'

'Yes, I take your point.' Groag seemed to have not the least reluctance to discuss his late partner. 'He could certainly make himself disliked. He was a tough, thrusting sort of man, arrogant, selfish, utterly self-confident. The type most likely to make enemies, I suppose.'

'Could he have made enemies in the way of business?'

'Not the least doubt of it. Not that I know of any that he did make, but his part in the firm was two-fold. He was the bringer-in of business; and also our man on contract law, which meant mainly settling disputes with contractors. With clients too, sometimes. Easy subjects to get hot under the collar about. There are few things quite as emotive as money, and I suppose he'd cut quite a few throats in the way of business.'

'And in the way of pleasure?'

'Do you know, I haven't the faintest idea? We were business partners, but I don't remember ever meeting him in a wholly social context or talking anything but business. We were opposite characters, which made us complement each other in business but gave us nothing whatever in common outside of it.'

'You're more the architectural designer, then?' Keith hazarded.

'Good God no.' Groag sounded quite shocked. 'Designers are ten a penny, and very rarely do they work their way up the ladder. Every newly-fledged student can design. Nine out of ten that make it to the top do so because they can *manage*. I'm the firm's manager, administrator, personnel man and general bottle-washer. But I'm not the type to go out into the large and cruel world and drag commissions in by the scruff of the neck.'

'So McLure will be a loss to the firm?'

'Not really,' said Groag. 'He was very good at bringing

in the work, but his expense-account was gigantic and he refused to account for most of it. Given that sort of budget I should think anybody could bring in business, but I had to turn the work out at a hell of a rate to balance the books. Anyway, one of our associates is just another such social butterfly with the knack of grovelling properly before the controllers of the purse-strings, so I dare say we'll continue to get our share.'

'And financially?'

'The same and more so. As I've said, he was an expensive man to have around. But he was well insured. And, on the other hand, he was talking about going abroad and wanted to be bought out. I gathered that he saw wider horizons and a less suppressive state elsewhere. Anyway, buying him out would have been an enormous burden, financially, whereas the partnership insurance takes care of the whole matter very nicely. Just as well, isn't it, that I don't shoot and that I was addressing a conference at the R.I.B.A. at the time?'

'Very lucky,' Keith agreed, forcing a smile. 'And your associate – the "social butterfly" – was he there too? He seems to have had something to gain.'

Groag laughed. 'Jeffreys? Like me, he's the indoor type, more likely to fake a suicide with sleeping tablets or push him downstairs.'

'So it only remains to clear up after him.'

'Tidy him away? I'm afraid that's it exactly. It sounds very callous, but I dare say somebody will miss him. He left everything in pretty good order, thank God, except that he was about to start hearing a fairly lengthy arbitration, and he was doing without a legal clerk, so I've got to unscramble the situation and work out who it goes back to for a fresh nomination.' He flicked the papers in front of him.

Reading upside down, Keith could decipher the heading on one of the papers. It read 'A. Payne & Co v. Lothian Flooring.'

'Is that Andrew Payne, who was on the shoot?' Keith asked.

For the first time, Groag seemed concerned. 'Here,' he said. 'These are supposed to be confidential,' and he swept the papers into a drawer.

'I'm sorry,' Keith said. 'It just happened to catch my eye.'

'Well, do me a favour and forget that you saw anything. And now, if there's nothing else I can do for you . . .'

'Can you give me any more clues to his character?'

Groag shrugged. 'I thought I'd about said it all. He was selfish and pleasure-loving, liked good suits, lunches, wines, women. He was unemotional and pitiless. He had occasional streaks of sentimentality which could be mistaken for the heart that he didn't have. He could turn charm on, quite deliberately, like a spotlight, for the sake of a client or a woman. Or a dog, for the matter of that. I never could decide whether he enjoyed his pleasures, or felt he owed them to himself, or that he pursued them to keep himself from relapsing into some inner hell. I never knew, and frankly I never cared as long as he pulled his weight.'

'Can you point me in the direction of any of his friends?'

'I don't think he had any. Not friends as you and I would understand the word. Hundreds of acquaintances, of course.'

'Girl-friends?'

'Undoubtedly. But I wouldn't have the faintest idea where to look. If I were you,' Groag added, 'I'd go and see his wife.'

On his way out of Edinburgh by the Queensferry Road, Keith detoured to find a large house, built around the turn of the century, standing alone in an ample garden and screened by its own trees. In that part of Edinburgh it spelled money. Dark had crept in while he was questioning Groag, but the light of the street-lamps, filtered through the trees, was enough to show that the garden was maintained to a higher standard than most people's clothes. Keith stooped and ran his finger over the grass, but it was real.

He sent in a copy of Enterkin's letter by way of a maid in cap and apron. The carpets were noticeably shaggier than the lawn. The signs of affluence were all present – signs that, Keith well knew, did not necessarily mean that money was there, only that it had been there before it was spent on the signs of affluence. He wondered whether the partnership insurance had been all that stood between the widow and Social Security.

Mrs Elena McLure, when she received him in an immaculate drawing-room, was exactly as he had expected. She was beautiful, a platinum blonde, either genuine or very recently refreshed. The slim elegance of her was typical, in Keith's experience, of the woman of a prosperous philanderer – a woman for show rather than for comfort. She was in black, but Keith felt that if black had not suited her blonde beauty then she would have gone to the grave with her late husband rather than wear it. From the boundless warehouse of his experience, Keith was sure that he could make a very accurate guess at the style and colour of her underwear as well. The thought was interesting, and if her cared-for slenderness had not suggested an uncomfortably bony body he would have been tempted to protract the interview and find out. He would meet no great opposition to doing so. Although her manner was condescending, she was sending minute signals to him whether she knew it or not.

McLure's dog, the young springer spaniel bitch, was on the rug before the log fire. She looked up listlessly as Keith came in, but her head went down between her paws.

Mrs McLure returned the letter, and motioned him to a chair opposite her. 'I don't know why you should be looking into my husband's death,' she said. 'I thought that was the job of the police. They have all the facilities.' Her voice was meant to sound English, but it sounded upper-class Edinburgh.

'The police have the facilities,' Keith said, 'but they're not very interested in using them to prove facts that don't suit their case.'

'But they've already arrested somebody,' she said, as if that closed the matter.

'They have. But surely he's entitled to have somebody look for facts that may help him prove himself innocent?'

'I suppose so,' she said. 'And that's you?'

'That's me.'

'Are you some sort of a "private eye"?'

'I'm acting as one. I'm a gunsmith by trade.'

'Oh? You must look at his guns for me before you go.' She sounded bored, as if that departure might not be far distant, but Keith noticed that her posture was always a mirror-image of his own. 'I don't know how I can help you.'

'No more do I,' said Keith. 'If I knew, I wouldn't have to bother people and ask questions. Does the name David McNeill convey anything to you? One of your husband's friends, perhaps?'

She shrugged. 'If he's the man I'm thinking of, my husband brought him to a cocktail party here several years ago. Tall, with a beaky nose and not enough chin?'

'That's the man,' Keith said. 'I believe he's in the building business.'

'I wouldn't know,' she said. 'But my husband didn't usually cultivate anybody who wasn't in building.'

'Remember anything about him, or anything your husband said?'

'Ron said he was a bully, but that he collapsed if you stood up to him.'

Keith nodded. That had been his own impression of McNeill. 'What about Andrew Payne?' he asked.

'What does he look like?' she asked after a moment's thought.

'Tallish, wrinkled, bald, always beautifully dressed.'

She nodded. 'We met him at some reception or other. One of those pompous professional affairs with people wearing chains of office. He seemed rather sweet. I was going to ask him to dinner but Ron vetoed him. He said that if I'd shaken hands with Mr Payne I'd better count my fingers. And he said that Payne was one of those people you could turn your back on or not, it didn't matter, he'd just as soon stab you in the front.' Mrs McLure seemed to enjoy recounting her late husband's more slanderous comments.

'Derek Weatherby?'

'Doesn't ring any bells.'

'Janet Weatherby?'

'I don't know the name.' She raised her eyebrows.

'She's only about sixteen anyway,' Keith said with a smile. 'What about Hamish Thomson?'

'That's the man that brought her back.' She pointed her toe at the springer bitch. 'He needn't have bothered.'

'Sir Peter Hay?'

'Invited him out that day. It was the first time I'd ever

heard of him. Then he came to pay a duty call. Nice old boy, but thick as a plank.'

'Ron Fiddler?'

'Isn't that the man they've arrested?'

'Yes. Had you ever heard of him?'

'I couldn't forget a name like that. No, never.'

Keith took her through the names of the shooting-party. Apart from William Hook, who had been to dinner the year before and whom she had disliked intensely, she said that she had never met any of them and as far as she was aware her husband had met them for the first time at the shoot. Keith had an acute ear for the truth in a woman's voice, and recognised it in hers.

'How would you describe your husband?' he asked.

'Did you ever meet him?'

'Yes. But he had his social face on.'

She laughed. 'You've met him all right,' she said. 'That sounds just like him. A social face, a business face, an enemy's face, the face of a husband or a lover or a friend. A multi-faced man. He could put them on and take them off to suit himself. Like a hat.'

'And behind all the faces?'

She sighed deeply. On a bustier woman it might have been interesting, but it did nothing for Keith. 'I never saw behind the faces. When I thought I was seeing behind, each time there was just another face but not a real person. The only characteristic that came through that wasn't assumed was . . . inconsideration. He didn't give a damn for anyone else's wishes unless it suited some damn purpose of his own. He was a good provider, though – I'll say that for him. Would you like a drink?'

'Something very small.'

'Help yourself, and make me a Martini.'

Keith did as he was bid. The glasses were Edinburgh crystal. The stock of drinks would have been worth the price of a thousand cartridges. 'Did you fancy going abroad?' he asked as he poured.

'Not a lot, no,' she said. 'He had a sudden opportunity – overall consultant to a new capital city, with a chance to build an enormous new practice of his own. Money and power galore. So he was busting to go immediately. I didn't really want to go out there – one of these new African states, all sweat and sandflies probably – away from my friends and civilisation. But we agreed that he'd go out first, and I'd fly out and join him for a bit, and if I thought I could tolerate it I'd come back and see to the house and so on. I was quite willing to give it a fair try.' Keith recognised that the last statement was either a lie or a self-deception.

'I'm afraid the problem seems to have been solved the hard way.'

'It does, doesn't it,' she said. 'Well, it may seem a hard thing to say, but perhaps better now than after we'd up-rooted ourselves.'

The callousness of the remark would have been shocking except that Keith had already decided that, of all the hard women that he had known, she came within the top three or four.

He was saved from any need to reply when the dog wheezed in her sleep. 'That was his dog, of course,' Mrs McLure said. 'Would you like to take her?'

'She's quite valuable,' Keith said. 'She works well. You should sell her quickly – it's a good time of year.'

'There's no pedigree with her. Nobody wants an unpedigreed and unregistered bitch. Anyway, she's been down in the dumps since he died. Nobody's interested in a lackadaisical gundog.'

'Why doesn't she have a pedigree?' Keith asked.

'I've no idea. Perhaps she was the result of an accidental mating.' And Keith was quite sure that this was a lie.

'Did he have any particular men-friends?'

'Not intimates. Just men who were in a position to be useful to him, at any given time.'

'Girl-friends?'

He could see the struggle between the woman-of-the-world taking pride in her permissiveness and the woman who could not bear to admit that any man might prefer any other woman. 'If he had any, he'd hardly discuss them with me,' she said at last; and even that obvious statement failed to ring true.

'Did he have his own secretary?' Keith asked.

'At the office, yes.' She smiled sardonically. 'I chose her.'

Keith decided that he would visit the secretary when next he was in Edinburgh. A secretary would be more likely to know about a boss's amours, which might provide some motive; and she might also know about any affairs in which Mrs McLure was indulging. He, himself, could not imagine any man killing in order to obtain the slim and chilly widow for himself, but there might be such a man.

'Did you know any of his shooting cronies?' he asked.

'He brought one or two of them back for drinks occasionally. Boring people, and never the same one twice. I wouldn't even remember their names.' Keith judged this to be true.

'Will you marry again?' he asked loudly.

He had hoped to detect some flicker of expression that might give him a clue to whether there were any loves in her life, but her immediate reaction was to apply the question personally. 'Is that an offer?' she asked.

'I might do worse,' he said laughing.

'You might not do at all,' she said. But she crossed her legs, and she must have known that those low chairs did not allow legs to be crossed in short skirts unrevealingly.

'I doubt if I could afford to keep you in the style you've become accustomed to.'

'You have a point there,' she said. But before he left he bought one of her husband's guns and some loose gear, and when she saw the thickness of his wallet she brightened, and there was warmth in her invitation to return if he had any more questions.

Before leaving Edinburgh Keith found a phone-box and compared diaries with his sister. He went for a snack in a small café, and returned in time for his call to Molly.

She answered on the second ring, and they chatted for a few minutes. She seemed to have adjusted to the strain, and Keith was happy to listen to her voice.

'Do one thing for me,' he said. 'See Mr Enterkin in the morning. Tell him that McLure was hearing an arbitration, A. Payne and Company against Lothian Flooring. Got

103

that? It may be the A. Payne who was on the shoot. Ask him to find out all he can about it.'

Keith drove north through the night with the radio playing. As he crossed the high arch of the Forth Road Bridge he was listening to Kabalevsky's piano concerto *Youth*, and then he became interested in a talk on astro-physics which kept his mind occupied for much of the length of the M90. But the talk gave way in due course to the Brahms variations on a theme by Paganini. At the second repetition of the tedious chords he shut it off.

In the near-silence, and under the hypnotic influence of the advancing lights, his mind turned to a train of thought which he had been avoiding.

Why, he wondered, had the police been so shy about investigating the question of who had converted the rifle? The fact that Mr Enterkin had warned him, in Munro's presence, against answering any questions should not have prevented those questions being asked.

Acting Detective Chief Inspector Munro, Keith thought, was likely to follow a line of reasoning which ran:

I have a body with a bullet.

I have the rifle that fired that bullet.

The rifle belonged to the accused, was reported lost, but turned up again still in his possession.

In the interim, it had been converted from a conventional deer rifle into a folding and silenced rifle suitable for poaching and other naughtinesses.

The accused is a stalker by profession and has no need to poach, but he might be a spare-time poacher for money or for the sake of the challenge.

The conversion was carried out by a skilled metalworker. Who?

The most probable culprit is Keith Calder.

Calder may have been the intended victim, but when the rifle was lost they were still on speaking terms.

Why did Enterkin advise him not to say whether or not he did the work? If Calder admitted converting the rifle, the defence could make some advantage out of the admission.

Do I care who did the work? Yes, I do. Very much.

Firstly, the knowledge might help to prove the case against Fiddler.

Secondly, offences have been committed. The insurance company was defrauded, and the Firearms Act smashed to smithereens.

Thirdly, I do not like registered gunsmiths who convert honest rifles into unregistered, silenced, folding weapons. Such people should not hold dealers' licences.

The gun looks like new so the work may have been recent, in which case traces may be left in the culprit's workshop.

But if the work is recent, it was done after they quarrelled.

·Damn.

Either way I still want to know.

So I think we'll just take another wee look in Mr Calder's van and see if we can't match any traces.

At this stage in his thinking, Keith began to get seriously worried. He was not afraid that traces might be found, for he was exceptionally careful when engaged in matters of doubtful legality. He had disposed of all off-cuts, and had swept the van out thoroughly and several times. But why, oh why, had Munro not been after him or the van before now?

In Perth, Keith stopped for a cup of coffee, and he and Hebe stretched their legs and relieved themselves. Then it was north again and the last stretch. Keith tried the radio again. Stravinsky was sampled and left to pulse in the ether unheard.

It was almost the first time in Keith's life that he had felt other than completely self-contained and self-reliant. It would be nice, he thought, to be able to share this worry with someone close. The life of a loner was losing its charm.

Was the prosecution reserving a challenge, to throw in his face during cross-examination of the defence's expert witness? If so, the substitution of a different expert would

105

be a disappointment to them. Keith occupied himself for a minute in considering possible nominations for the alternative expert, but his nagging mind came homing back, like a tongue to a sore tooth.

Next, Keith tried putting himself in the place of Munro who, in his turn, was putting himself in the place of Enterkin. What would Munro think Enterkin thought were the most desirable shades of truth to the defence. Keith thought about it until he almost ran into the back of a lorry.

It was a relief to arrive at the van and to find two patient constables waiting beside it in their panda car. With great politeness they presented a warrant, and for the third time the van was searched. This time, the police knew what they were looking for, and samples were taken of materials. They also vacuumed every corner of the van. Then they thanked him politely, accepted a cup of coffee apiece and drove off.

Keith went to his bunk and slept easily.

CHAPTER 9

Another grey, misty day, and Keith set off north again in the van, cheered by the laughing melodies of Weber.

His usual tour of customers in the north and west was a leisurely and sociable affair, business being well diluted with the pleasures of shooting, drinking and chatting with old friends, and dalliance with his 'comfortable arrangements'. This round would usually extend to two months – or even more, depending on the weather, the availability of game for the bag and the comfort of the arrangements.

On this trip, however, Keith intended to complete his circuit in a quarter of the time, by concentrating mainly on business, or at the least by confining his pleasures to the hours when business was not available. He made a few shooting forays, mainly wildfowling trips on the firths, but while these were both fruitful and (to a case-hardened hunter prepared to rise long before winter's dawn and brave the mud-banks and a wind with the breath of the arctic) enjoyable they were primarily aimed at making contact, on their own ground, with the most industrious gossips in the shooting fraternity. These contacts were mostly unproductive, discounting a vast volume of scurrilous allegations quite unrelated to his enquiries, and only on one occasion was he given food for thought.

On the shore of the Cromarty Firth, within sight of the giant aluminium complex, Keith was ready to go back to the van for a late breakfast. Three geese were already in the bag, and Hebe was away after another which was hard hit but had gone on away over the sands, first planing and then running. Keith was not displeased with his outing, although the omniscient chatterbox he had hoped to meet had not made an appearance. While he waited, Keith fell into conversation with another fowler, a man he had not met before,

and who was on holiday from a small town in the Strathclyde region – 'to get away from the wife', as he put it.

This man went by the name of Hardy, and lived up to
it too, Keith thought, since his upper half was clad only in
a khaki shirt and that with the sleeves rolled up. He rose
to the bait as soon as Keith mentioned that he had been
present at a shooting fatality.

'Down by the Borders?'

'That's right.' Keith managed to sound surprised.

'I saw it in the papers,' said Hardy. 'Funny, somebody
else I know was on that shoot. Bill Hook.'

'Muscular sort of chap? Big wheel with one of the district
councils?'

'That's him all right. He lives quite near me. My wife's
friends with his.'

Keith had made this kind of second-hand contact on previous occasions, and it had never produced anything more
useful than a little shading-in of the background; but at
least he had learned how to keep people talking. 'Seemed
a nice, reliable sort of chap,' he said.

Hardy snorted. He had a long chin and a short upper lip,
so that his mouth seemed to be climbing up his face as he
talked. 'I can't stand him. Or her. Matter of fact, I can't
thole any one of the three of them.'

'You saw that there'd been an arrest?' Keith asked.

Hardy nodded. 'It'll be manslaughter, I suppose?'

Keith shook his head. 'They've charged him with deliber-
ate murder. I think it's a load of nonsense, myself. Matter
of fact, being a gunsmith to trade, I've been consulted by
the defence . . .'

At this point the subject became mislaid, as Hardy wanted a free consultation as to the cost of having his gun
tightened and fitted to him, and having a number of dents
removed. As Hebe chose this moment to return, mud-
stained and exhausted but happy, with the now dead goose
in her jaws, Keith suggested an adjournment to the van.

Over a breakfast of bacon and eggs and toast and coffee
– the kind of breakfast, in fact, that spells heaven after a
morning's fowling – Hardy agreed to help if he could.

'I don't think I can be much use to you,' he said. 'But

108

I'll tell you this, for some months Hook's been a worried man.'

'What about?'

'Well, he wouldn't tell me, would he? But a friend of mine who's a surveyor says that he was playing patsy with McLure for years, and the fraud squad people who're chasing down corruption are looking at him pretty hard. I think he might have been glad to see McLure where he couldn't let any cats out of bags. What do you think?'

'If he did it, I can't see how,' Keith said.

Breakfast over, Keith tightened the action of Hardy's gun and removed the dents for him, and was careful to get paid for the work before producing another gun in visibly sounder condition and a much better fit. After the customary period of haggling, Keith accepted a cheque for a substantial cash adjustment.

Hardy went on his way, a happy man, and Keith gloated alone over his new acquisition. It was a Dickson Round Action, and after a little more cosmetic work would be almost the most valuable gun in the van.

In a late afternoon, and in a deserted quarry near the shores of Loch Lochy on the Caledonian Canal, Keith was tired, sick of the smoke from the nitro-powder, and half deafened. This last effect annoyed him most. He was still subject to moods of divine discontent coupled with a sense of insecurity. He had searched out from his collection of tapes those that cheered and comforted him most – Schumann's *Carnival*, the Lanchberry ballet music and tape after tape of Haydn and Mozart and of Beethoven in his jollier moods – but the music that was lilting from the van's speakers was marred by a singing in his ears and a loss of sound in the higher frequencies.

Keith had spent the whole day testing his theories, and now was surveying what he had learned. Hebe, who had spent the day shut in the van in an agony of frustration at being excluded from any activity that involved shooting, was now on the loose. Keith and the van were on the higher level of bare rock, but a few yards away the level dropped in a twelve-foot step. Here, in the lower part of the quarry, grasses, brambles and blackthorn had become established, and Hebe was hunting happily in the jungle, her tail going like a windscreen wiper.

That morning, Keith had started by setting up an open drum, which he had brought for the purpose, and filling it with water. He brought out a point-two-four-three rifle, and fired a box-load of cartridges down into the water. He bared an arm and recovered the bullets.

Keith then brought out the table-top from the van and set it on the drum, brought out his loading tools and materials and a shotgun, and started work. He spent most of the day loading rifle-bullets into shotgun cartridge-cases and firing them at a succession of paper targets in front of an earth bank, recording his results with meticulous care in a large note-book that he had bought for the purpose.

By late afternoon, when the shadows of the hills were creeping towards the quarry and the evening chill was back in the air, Keith had satisfied himself of a number of things. He had proved to his own satisfaction, for instance, that there was no way that a spent rifle-bullet could be fired again through another and larger rifle without affecting the original rifling-marks. He had successfully fired bullets through a shotgun, and had found that the loading method that he had described to Mr Enterkin was the best that he could discover, reliable enough to hit a six-inch target at thirty yards with reduced but still adequate velocity, although more than half would have produced 'keyhole' wounds. He had even tried firing one of his bullets from a smooth-bore pistol – a reproduction flintlock – but the shorter barrel-length made it impractical.

So far, he had only proved to himself what he was already sure of, and satisfied himself that another gunsmith would come to the same conclusions. Now he set out to study the ground, inch by inch as he had in the wood, to see what traces he had left. The man who killed McLure must have followed much the same processes.

The ground was littered with plastic wads, and he gathered them up carefully. Half-a-dozen of these showed the typical imprint of shot-pellets, but these were wads which Keith

110

had re-used. Mentally, Keith filed away the knowledge that the murderer was either less than thorough or had had to prepare his materials in a hurry. The debris of his wrapping materials he studied carefully. Some of the lavatory-paper had burned, some had not. He had also experimented with newspaper, but he found sufficient scraps left to identify the edition and date.

One other trace remained – the churned-up and dug-over bank of earth could hardly be camouflaged until nature did the job. And if the murderer had used a box of sand or sawdust, he might expect to find some spillage.

As Keith gathered up his chattels and stowed them in the van, he ruminated. In his mind, he turned over a variety of ways by which a bullet might be introduced into a human being, from using it as the tip of an arrow to stabbing the victim with a spike within a tube and pressing the bullet down the tube after the death; but not one could he make cover all the facts. He decided to take Hebe for a walk of contemplation, and then, if he could find no convincing alternative, go ahead bald-headed on the single theory.

As he turned away from the van, he almost bumped into the man who had come up behind him.

'Mr Calder?' The voice was flat and without any accent that Keith could detect, which probably meant a slight and neutral Scottish accent.

'I'm Calder,' Keith said briefly. He looked the man over and wondered why he distrusted him. The face was ordinary, or at least any departure from the norm was too small to be noticed. And yet a wealth of information can be conveyed by a shift of dimension in a facial muscle, even in the focus of an eye. Something told Keith that this man would never be anything but an enemy. 'Who are you?' he asked.

'Who I am doesn't matter. I'm only an intermediary.'

'Go ahead. Intermediate.'

'Funny! You're asking a lot of questions and making somebody nervous. You don't know anything, but you might set somebody else wondering.'

'Now who, I wonder,' Keith said, 'would pay you to be nervous for him?'

'You're not getting the idea. That's just the sort of question not to ask, or it could be bad.'

'Who for?'

'Who do you think? It could be bad for you, or the girl, or it could be even worse for her brother.'

'Somebody prefers things the way they are?'

'Now you're getting warmer. But if things are left as they are and nobody rocks the boat, then there's five thousand for Fiddler and another thousand for yourself. He stands trial, and if he gets off that's okay, and if he goes down he takes his medicine like a little man. Got it?'

'I've got it,' Keith said. 'So somebody thinks I'm getting that close?'

The intermediary made an impatient, shrugging movement. 'I wouldn't know, and frankly I don't care. I'm only here to make the offer because whoever-it-is could hardly discuss the thing with you without telling you just what he doesn't want you to know. I don't even know who it is myself, there's somebody else between me and him, so don't think of doing anything silly. Well, what about the offer. Does it grab you?'

'If it grabs Ronnie Fiddler,' Keith said, 'then it's all right with me.'

'I need an answer now.'

'You don't get one.'

'If you don't say yes now, then the answer's no and the offer closes.'

'Then it's no.'

The intermediary, Keith found, was also a poker-player. His expression had never altered, but now he nodded over Keith's shoulder, and Keith found himself gripped in a bear-hug from behind.

'Let me know when you change your mind,' the intermediary said. He danced forward, neatly avoiding a kick. Keith took a punch in the belly that forced the wind out of him. For the first few blows Keith thought that he could bear the pain, that the intermediary was a novice at hurting; and then the pain began to grip him until he yelled aloud, as much with rage as with the pain itself, and he knew that the man was a professional and that if it went on for long he himself would be destroyed, reduced to a timid shell. But he knew, too, that nothing would make him betray his task, even though he was being offered a way out of his own dilemma. Keith roared defiance and tried again to kick.

A black demon from the pit came up over the rim of the rock, eyes blazing, lips asnarl showing terrible fangs, rumbling like a volcano. Hebe was coming with blood in her eye.

Keith had no wish to see Hebe hurt or, worse, put down for savagery, so he took instant advantage of the distraction. He was reputed to be among the best pub-fighters in southern Scotland outside of Glasgow, and he used his hard-bought skill. He gripped behind him and twisted, and stamped with one of his heavy boots on the instep of the man behind. As his arms came free, he drove back with an elbow.

The intermediary had tried to kick Hebe away, and she had him by the leg. He was trying to balance on that foot and kick with the other when Keith came up beside him, chopped him across the stomach and, as his chin came down, brought up a fist in a haymaker under the angle of his jaw that slammed him up and back to land with a crack of his head on the bare rock.

At a word from Keith, Hebe lay down, chewing on a strip of tweed.

The man who had grabbed Keith from behind was bent double but feeling in his pockets. Keith grabbed him by the lapels, leaned back, pulled and swung. In half a turn he had built up the energy that he needed, and he let go. The man back-pedalled frantically across the rock, one hand caught fast in his pocket and the other arm flailing, and disappeared over the edge.

Keith drew breath, nursing his hand which felt broken. His mouth was dry, his legs shook and his face and ribs still pained him, but he had not lost his capability for rapid thought. How best could he unscramble a foul situation?

Logic suggested that he should pursue two aims – gathering information, and forestalling further hostilities.

Hebe was not trained as a guard-dog, but at least she would give audible warning of any change in the situation. Keith stood her over the unconscious man, who was breathing but lay as limp as a wet towel, only a rim of white showing at his eyes.

Keith took a shotgun and a few cartridges out of the van and locked up carefully. Then he went to the edge of the rock step, and cautiously looked over.

The second assailant looked back at him, with understandable apprehension. He had landed on his back in a thorn-bush. It was the grandparent of all blackthorn bushes, large and thick, amply branched and over-provided with the inch-long spikes that serve the blackthorn instead of thorns. The man had hit it centrally and descended into its midst, and the bush had closed lovingly around him. He would have been no more helpless, and much more comfortable, encased in concrete. He was an unpleasant-looking man, thin and vicious, with greasy hair and a scar that puckered one side of his face.

When he saw the gun in Keith's hands, the man tried to cringe even deeper among the thorns. 'You're not going to – ?'

'I don't have to, do I?'

'Get me out of here, then.' The voice was deepest Glasgow, so deep that it would have been unintelligible to a Londoner.

'I'm coming down in a minute,' Keith said. 'And then we can take up the question of what you ever did for me that I should help you.'

Keith turned back from the edge and took his wounds over to the oil-drum. He soothed his swelling face with a soaked handkerchief, and dunked his hand for a minute until he began to feel that it might not be broken after all.

The intermediary was still limp. Keith emptied his pockets, wallet and keys and all, but found no weapons. He put the items into his own pockets. As an afterthought, he drew the knife that lived in a sheath taped across the back of his belt, cut the man's shoelaces and threw his shoes into the bushes fifty yards apart. Finally, he slit the man's clothes from collar to trouser-cuffs, right to the skin, without scratching his flesh. Skinning rabbits, he thought, was good practice for that sort of thing. The return of consciousness would not be followed by any sudden activity.

He left Hebe on guard again, and, satisfied that his rear was reasonably secure, went down to the lower level of the quarry.

The other man had struggled, and had sunk deeper into his bed of thorns. Blood from a hundred cuts was dripping slowly into the drift of dead leaves below the tree. He stared back at Keith with the sullen defiance of a trapped wildcat.

Keith shifted the gun, cradled it in his left arm. With his right hand he drew the knife again. He had forged it himself, years before, and it was always with him. Suddenly he slashed with the knife and the man flinched. A branch of thorn fell across the man's face. Keith sliced again and again, severing the branches that prevented him reaching the man, but careful not to touch any that held him trapped. When he was within reach of the man, he stopped cutting.

'You're not going to get me out, then?' The Glasgow twang conveyed no sense of surprise.

'Like I said, now would be a good time to remind me of anything you ever did for me. . . . No? Then tell me who sent you and I'll think about it, and if you ask me nicely I may get you out of here.'

The man shook his head as much as he could between the thorns. 'No way!' he said firmly, but there was a quiver in his voice.

'I've been coming here for years,' Keith said, 'and I've never seen another soul.'

'C'mon now, Jimmy! You don't know what they'd do to me.'

'You don't know what I'll do to you. Turn out your pockets. If you've got a gun bring it out butt first or I'll blow you in half.'

'I've no gun,' the man said. He struggled to reach his pockets with one hand or to extricate the other, but by now his entanglement was so complete that every movement was checked and aborted.

'Don't bother,' Keith said. He slit the man's pockets, one by one.

'Hey!'

'If you don't like it, do something about it,' Keith said absently. A razor fell to the ground, followed by some small change, a handkerchief, a cosh, a car-key, some bank-notes and other papers, a comb and a vicious-looking knuckle-duster. Keith stowed them away in his poacher's pockets, all but the handkerchief. 'Who sent you?' he asked again.

The man clamped his lips and said nothing. Although the light was going, Keith could see sweat on his face.

'Too bad,' Keith said. He slid the knife into the neck of the man's shirt and, as he had with the other, slit his clothes all the way down. He finished again by removing the man's shoes. 'You're going to stay away from me in the future, aren't you?' he added.

In many words, and in an atrocious accent, the man made it clear that he would never forget Keith, He began to go into great and unnecessary detail as to just what would happen to Keith when next they met, but in the full flood of his peroration his voice suddenly dried up.

'No, that wasn't very clever, was it?' Keith said. 'Now what, I wonder, would you do if you were in my place?' He laid the point of his knife in the man's navel and twiddled it gently. 'There are two things I can do. I can scare you away from me for life, or I can kill you. I'll let you choose.'

'I won't go near you again,' the man said quickly.

'I know you won't. And you've got a very few seconds to make up your mind why, or I'll choose for you.' He rotated the knife-point suggestively.

The man's eyes were popping. 'Just a *minute*, Jimmy! Don't kill me!'

'All right,' Keith said reasonably. 'That gives me two more choices, and I'll let you choose again. I can maim you, so that you just physically couldn't annoy me again, like blinding you maybe, or taking off your fingers with a bolt-cutter. Or I can do something so abominable to you that you'd rather die than come within a mile of me again. Which would you prefer ... ?'

The year before, Keith and Hebe had been roundly de-

116

feated in a field trial by a man whose control of his chocolate Labrador had been little short of telepathic. Keith had followed him into a nearby hotel, determined to pick his brains, and had never regretted the cost of the many drinks he had bought him. The victor had been a psychologist, who had applied his studies of motivation very effectively to the matter of dog-training. Keith had picked up many tips, and had made profitable use of them, but one casual comment thrown out by the psychologist in his cups had never before seemed to have a practical application. *'There's no quicker way of breaking a man down,'* the psychologist had said, *'than forcing him to choose between a series of options, none of which are acceptable to him.'*

This, Keith found, was true. Giving full rein to his imagination, he led the man through a series of shocking alternatives, forcing a choice from him at each stage and lending reality to each suggestion with a touch of the knife-point. Keith himself would never have believed such a bluff, but the man, because he was capable of the execution if not the invention of such atrocities, could believe every word, and Keith watched him disintegrate. It was a process that would normally have aroused his compunction. In five minutes, the man was reduced to a snivelling wreck, and when he was finally offered a choice between losing his tongue or his scrotum he broke down altogether. Had it been his, he would have given away the secret of everlasting life. Unfortunately, his actual knowledge was of much less value, and beyond the fact that the man's name was Alex Paisley, the knowledge that Keith managed to extract from him was patchy. Paisley referred to the intermediary as Johnny, although he had also heard him addressed or referred to as Seamus, Hughie, Scratcher and The Gingerbread Man. Paisley's employment had been on an irregular and piecework basis, and he had no more than a vague idea that Johnny lived in the Springburn area of Glasgow and was reputed to be independent from any of the known gangs.

One other fragment Paisley produced under a little extra pressure. Johnny had referred to their client as 'a pillar of the bloody Kirk'.

Keith went up to the van again, to check on things while

he thought it all over. Johnny the Intermediary had not moved. Keith stood over him and opened and closed his gun, and got no reaction. Hebe had quite lost interest in him, although her training was too strong to let her wander off and she still glanced his way from time to time.

The sun had escaped from the clouds at last, but was now touching the hills. It blazed in the berries and the dead leaves at the quarry's rim, but left a pool of blackness below.

Keith fetched his tow-rope from the van. As he moved around, Paisley's nasal voice followed him from below, explaining ever more sincerely that *no way* would he ever disturb so fine a gentleman again. Keith turned the van, attached the tow-rope to the back bumper and dropped the other end over the edge. He went down again. Paisley's face was a pale blob in the dusk, but the panic on it shone out like the moon.

'What exactly were you sent to do?' Keith asked.

'Fix you, or put the frighteners on you or the girl,' Paisley said.

At the mention of Molly, Keith felt his heart trip over its beat. It had not occurred to him before that pressure on her would be as effective as if it had been applied to himself, or that his offensive against the two messengers might put her in deadly danger as soon as word got back.

'I haven't got time to open you up like a banana this trip,' he said. 'Just remember that I've hardly started on you. If I ever see you again, or you go near the girl, if I even hear that you've said an unkind word, I'll come after you and start where I left off, and next time I shan't stop until you're in bits. Do you believe me?'

'I believe you,' Paisley said.

'You'd better. All right, you can go.'

'But, mister, you can't leave me here to starve. You got to get me out!'

Without answering, Keith took two turns of the rope's end around Paisley's ankle and added two half-hitches.

'Hey, now!'

'Something wrong?'

'You pull me out like that an' you'll leave half my hide behind and all my clothes! Can you not cut the branches?'

'No time,' said Keith, 'and I can't be bothered. It's your choice. Do you want to stay there until you rot, or don't you?'

It was too dark now to see the tears on Paisley's face, but Keith knew they were there from the quiver in his voice. 'I want out, but – '

'If you're getting what you want, don't complain about details.'

Followed by shrill, whining protests, Keith left him and went up to the van for the last time. He called Hebe away from the prone figure of the intermediary and took her into the van with him, and then he hardened his heart and drove the van forward a few yards. He could feel the resistance, and hear the noise as Paisley told the world what was happening to him.

When he jumped down, one of Paisley's feet was showing at the lip of the rock. He glanced to his right. The figure of Johnny the Intermediary was gone.

It would be useless to pursue the man in the gathering dusk. Hebe had never been taught to follow a human trail. Keith had no way of being sure that there were no weapons handy to the man. Rapid action was to be preferred.

Keith drew his knife and slashed the rope. A thump and a squawk confirmed that the wretched Paisley was free.

Back in the van, Keith put on his lights and accelerated to the mouth of the quarry. Here, just out of sight from where the van had been parked, a Cortina stood beside a huddle of giant boulders. Keith adjusted the wheel a fraction and nudged the rear of the Cortina with the van's front bumper. The Cortina shot forward. It seemed to make for a gap between two boulders. The gap was a foot too narrow, but the car ended up half-inside anyway. Nobody was going to drive that car again that night. Keith hauled the van out onto the road and turned for Spean Bridge.

After twenty impatient minutes, Keith came to a place which he knew from past experience was the least bad for miles around for radio reception. He pulled into a familiar lay-by. He was early for his contact with his sister but he was lucky. Elsie answered almost immediately.

'Keith? Is that you, Keith?'

'Elsie, this is urgent. Get on the phone to the police at Newton Lauder. Tell them that I have good reason to believe that there may be an attack on Molly Fiddler. Ask them to give her protection until I get there. I've more than two hundred miles to cover, so I may not be there until around midnight. Have you got that? Over.'

'I've got it, Keith. Over.'

'Then phone Sir Peter, and tell him about it. And, just in case, call the phone-box at nine, and if Molly answers tell her to get somewhere safe, like the police station, and stay there 'til I come. Got it? Over.'

'I'll do all that, Keith. Don't worry. Over.'

Thank God, Elsie was in one of her less garrulous moods. Keith felt that he would have exploded otherwise. 'Good girl,' he said. 'When you've called the police and Sir Peter, phone ahead and see if you can find anywhere still open where they can hire me a faster car. If it's much of a detour off my road it wouldn't be worth it. I'll be going – ' he paused for a second and reviewed the map in his mind ' – by Glen Coe, Glen Dochart, Lochearnhead, Stirling and down the bittie of motorway, straight on down to Carluke and across the wee road by Peebles. Use the map and the yellow pages. All right? Over.'

'All right, Keith. I'll try. I hope she's all right. Over, Keith.'

'So do I. I'll leave my receiver open. Keep me posted.'

The van had never been built for speed, but early in his ownership Keith, bored with its performance on main roads for which it was not designed, had fitted an overdrive made simply out of an extra gearbox back-to-front. On downhill stretches, or on flat roads with the least help from the wind, the van now had a respectable turn of speed, and even uphill gradients could now be started on the run. Keith began to use his two gear-levers as if he were stirring porridge, nursing the heavy van over the road as fast as it could be induced to go.

As he drove, his mind picked again over the equation that he had first solved almost intuitively. 'Put the frighteners on you . . . *or on the girl*.' Again, he tried to put himself

120

in the other's place. Quite apart from the need to complete the job and earn his fee, Johnny the Intermediary might well be out for revenge. What was more, in those circles to fail was to lose value in the market-place.

What Keith could not know was whether the intermediary had been part of a larger organisation. Paisley had thought not, but Paisley had known almost nothing about the man. But even if he were a lone wolf, he still might be able to use the telephone to call on some other of Paisley's type. When he got to a phone...

What would the two men do? Paisley was probably too hurt and demoralised to be back in the field for days or weeks. But Johnny the Intermediary was a different proposition. Assuming that he could overcome his concussion – and during their brief chat Keith had learned that whatever he lacked it was not will-power – and assuming also that he would or could not use the phone to whistle up reinforcements, he would first have to overcome a clothing problem. He might have luggage in the car, possibly in the boot, which with a little luck might be jammed. If Johnny the Intermediary was unlucky, then he had a problem, but Keith felt that, in the same situation, he could have bundled and tied his riven clothes somehow. Thereafter, no money, no transport. What would he do? Keith put himself in his place, endowed with ruthlessness. He would steal a car. Probably he would simulate the victim of a hit-and-run accident, take the first car to stop, take its owner's money, and go. But it would all take time. Keith had a start.

But how much of a start did he need? Mentally, Keith did the run in the van, and again in a good car with a bad concussion. Allowing for the traffic conditions, he guessed the difference to be an hour and a half. Did he have that long? Keith cursed himself for a fool. He should have put the local police onto Johnny the Intermediary. He picked up the microphone from the passenger's seat, but he was among the hills and the radio was dead.

At Glencoe, he stopped for petrol and filled right up.

He was at Ardchyle before Elsie's voice came through to him along the length of Loch Tay, to tell him of a car for hire at Crianlarich, ten miles and more behind him. Even so, mathematically it might have been worth the return journey; but it was against his instincts to drive the wrong way. He turned south and drove on. She spoke to him again an hour later. He could get a car in Stirling. But that would mean a detour into Stirling's crowded streets while he could be bowling down the motorway; and, besides, by Stirling he would have made more than two-thirds of the distance. He looped down onto the motorway and wrung more speed out of the van, ignoring as best he could the bruises on his face and body and his swelling hand.

Soon, he was sure that he had picked the wrong route. A humid day was being followed by black frosts, and ice was forming. Because of the van's limited speed, Keith had chosen to miss some miles of motorway in order to avoid the traffic of Edinburgh's ring road. As long as he was on the main road south he made as good time, but when he turned across country he was on roads that did not carry enough traffic to de-ice them, and he had to contain his speed or risk the van waltzing on a sudden icy patch. A fast car following him would probably opt for the Edinburgh route, and find that a thousand warm tyres had kept it clear. But that route was prone to fog . . . Keith pressed on, hoping against hope. Logic told him that, having invoked the police, there was no need for him to hurry; but instinct, primitive and raw, drove him on.

At last, long after midnight, Keith swung the van through the square and turned down the lane. The tension within him was almost unbearable, yet he did not know what to expect and could have believed anything from a pitched battle or its aftermath to a bored Bobby pacing up and down outside the cottage.

What he found was a large car, parked half-facing him with its lights blazing on the cottage whose door was open. A wisp of steam was pulsing from the car's exhaust.

Leaving his engine running and his own lights adding to the blaze, Keith piled out of the van so violently that he nearly took the door with him.

The scene had appeared deserted, but behind the hedge among the rose-bushes he found one of the middle-aged constables who had pulled Ronnie Fiddler off him in the

122

police station, looking dazedly around him and nursing a growing lump on the side of his head.

And as Keith reached the door, Johnny the Intermediary came out, blinking in the bright lights. When he saw Keith, he checked and gave a swallow. 'She's all right,' he said huskily, but Keith never took the words in until later.

Considering that the fight was between a case of concussion and another of multiple contusions, it was fast and furious. Keith relieved his opponent of a truncheon with a jerk that snapped the intermediary's teeth together audibly, dropped it underfoot, and used his one good fist, his head, elbows and knees, and, when Johnny the Intermediary was down, his boot. Along the way he collected some more bruises, but he was unaware of them until later. When he was quite sure that there would be no more aggression from that quarter, he ran inside.

Keith dashed from room to room, but there was no sign of Molly. He thundered up the stairs, taking the narrow flight three at a time, and at the top he nearly bowled her over. In an orgasm of relief, he grabbed her up and she clung to him.

'I hid in the attic,' she said at last. 'I was waiting for you, so I looked out when I saw the lights of the car. I saw him hit poor Mr Murchy, so I got up into the attic and dropped the hatch and stood on it.'

'He never thought of looking up there?'

She shuddered. 'I don't think he had time.'

'You shouldn't've come down until I called.'

'You didn't call,' she pointed out. 'But I heard you swearing when you were fighting him. Are you all right?'

'Just a minute,' Keith said. 'You put the kettle on. I'll be right back.'

He felt very tired. All his bruises ached, and his head was like a throbbing tooth. He went down the stairs like a very old man and out into the glare and the frosty night.

The policeman was on the mend. He had recovered his truncheon and was leaning groggily against the door-post.

'How're you doing?' Keith asked.

The constable smiled lop-sidedly. 'All the better for seeing you do him up,' he said. 'But don't quote me.'

Johnny the Intermediary had dragged himself as far as the car and was sprawled in the driver's seat, trying to reach the door to pull it shut. He was not a pretty sight. Several teeth were missing, and the blood on his face looked black. He glared at Keith as he came to the gate. 'I *told* you she was all right,' he shouted peevishly.

'I'm sorry,' Keith said. Even as he said it, it sounded stupid.

Johnny the Intermediary looked up towards the moon. 'Now he says he's sorry!' The sibilants whistled in his broken teeth. He trod on the accelerator and the car shot away, the door slamming as it went. Keith started to run, but he was too late.

Methodical as ever, Keith stopped the van's engine. It was very quiet, all of a sudden.

CHAPTER 10

Mr Enterkin was at his most avuncular. 'Don't bolt your food,' he said. 'There's plenty of time. It's only just across the road, and Sir Peter's meeting us here first. The special licence is in my pocket and the ring, I hope, is in yours. So there's nothing to worry about and no hurry. Nothing to do but to enjoy the occasion. Not,' he added severely, 'that I approve of the bride lunching with the groom before the ceremony.' He tried to frown at Molly but without any real success. She was looking too happy to be frowned at with conviction.

The three of them were lunching at The Willow Tree. Enterkin was revelling in the meal, Molly was enjoying it and Keith was nibbling. 'I'm not letting her out of my sight again until this is all over,' Keith said.

Molly's sigh held a nice balance between a new happiness and an older trouble. 'What a pity Ronnie couldn't be here,' she said.

It would have been the wrong time to contradict. 'How's he taking the news?' Keith asked.

'Mollified a little,' Enterkin said. He blinked. 'No pun intended. He's not exactly jumping with joy, but he seems to have stopped fulminating for the moment.' Ronnie Fiddler, in fact, had been specific about the disasters which he prophesied his sister's marriage would bring down on her head, but Mr Enterkin had too much sense of the occasion to mention them.

'Couldn't you get them to let him out for his own sister's wedding?' Molly asked.

'I didn't try.' Mr Enterkin filled his mouth with chocolate gâteau, and they waited patiently. 'We couldn't risk the possibility that he might lose his head again, and on such an occasion. Think of the possible effect if that came out at the trial.'

'Think of the possible effect on me,' Keith said. 'They mightn't have been able to pull him off me in time again.'

'A minor consideration,' said Enterkin.

'Can we get married again?' Molly asked. 'Properly, I mean, in church. When Ronnie gets out, of course.'

Keith touched her hand. 'Of course we can,' he said fondly.

Enterkin cleared his throat. 'Let's get back to the matter of seeing that that happy event isn't too far off. I'd like to know whether you think the police accepted your story, and whether you found out any subsequent history from them.'

'Why wouldn't they accept my story? It's true.'

'So, I'm led to believe, is that of the unfortunate Mr Fiddler.'

'I see what you mean. Well, they *seemed* to accept it. They didn't ask any trick questions or anything. After all, they'd had a constable clobbered, and I'm told Paisley was found wandering, tearful, penitent and starkers on the Lochy Bridge road, and confirmed as much as he knew which was no more than I got out of him. They found the wrecked car; and the other car, the one that the other man got here in, was reported stolen from near Corriegour and turned up abandoned at Bonnyrigg. Oh yes, and a house was broken into near Corriegour and clothing stolen, including a black overcoat, which is what I think he was wearing when he came out of the cottage, although I must admit I wasn't paying much attention to sartorial details.' Keith paused for breath. 'And then Sir Peter phoned as soon as he got my message, which wasn't until this morning, and he turned up at the police station where he seems to pull a lot of weight, wanting to know all about it.'

'They must have believed you,' Enterkin said. 'Otherwise your favourite policeman wouldn't have told you so much about what the police have learned.'

'It wasn't Munro that I saw, he's off duty,' Keith said. 'I saw the duty inspector, and he didn't seem to mind passing on the news as it came in.'

'Did they not get that man with all the names?' Molly asked.

'Let's just call him Johnny. No, they'd not got near him, the last I heard, and they probably never will.'

'I think it's a shame,' Molly said hotly. 'He beat you up –'

'No, he didn't. I beat him up. Twice.'

'Well, he hit you first. And he hurt poor Mr Murchy, and tried to make you stop helping Ronnie, and Ronnie's still in jail and they can't do a thing.'

'They'll try, all right,' Keith said. 'If there's one thing they don't like it's witnesses being got at, even defence witnesses. Right?'

'Quite true,' said Enterkin. 'But a man like that, a lone wolf not connected to any gang, who picks up his help in pubs when he needs it and probably has no permanent address – sounds a bit like you, come to think of it . . .'

'I suppose it does, a bit.'

'Not any more,' said Molly.

'Anyway, he'll have gone to ground by now. And if he lies low I don't see the police catching him, not without a stroke of luck. Even if they do get him, I don't see him saying a word. His livelihood depends on a reputation for absolute confidentiality.'

The waiter brought coffee. Mr Enterkin started on a cheese whose bouquet made Molly's eyes water.

'Do you think that man's prepared to have another go at us?' Molly asked.

'He's had two good thumpings,' Keith said. 'On the other hand, he mustn't fail if he wants to go on making a living that way. Not that it matters – if it isn't him, his client may just as easily go looking for someone else. That's why I don't want you out of my sight.'

Mr Enterkin nursed his brandy in both hands, and peered at Keith over the top. 'He'll be more careful next time, and better prepared. I don't want you two to take any chances. Why don't you brief another gunsmith and then go for a quiet honeymoon, somewhere secret, until I call you back?'

Keith gave him a secret frown. 'It's tempting,' he said, 'but I have some more work to do first. I'll be better prepared too, and a little less open about where I am.'

'How *did* they know where to find you?'

Keith laughed. 'My van's well kenned, and of course

several folk who have appointments with me could make a good guess at where to look for me. But it's simpler than that. Somebody phoned Elsie saying that he wanted to get in touch with me urgently, and she told them where to look for me. She won't do that again,' he added grimly. 'How's Ronnie's case going?'

'Trial's been called for the end of January, which doesn't give us very long. Sir Peter's stumping up for a good Q.C., and I'm seeing him on Monday to start detailed briefing. I may have some questions for you to work on after that.'

'Right,' Keith said. 'I'll see Joe Quaich in the next day or two. He's a very good gunsmith with a reputation to match. What's more, although he's getting on a bit now, he has a lively mind. He'll grasp all the implications. Also, he makes a good witness. He's unflappable.'

'That's the kind we want,' Enterkin said, 'if we must let it get as far as court. But I'm sure you'll not forget the desirability of clearing up the whole affair before it gets that far.'

'Why's that?' Molly asked.

'You surely don't want your brother to stay in jail longer than necessary,' Keith said smoothly.

'Not to mention the legal costs to Sir Peter,' Enterkin added.

'I've not finished up all my own business yet,' Keith said. 'But while I do, I'll be trying to find out who on that shoot might be called a "pillar of the church", and I'll be looking for places where our man might have carried out the same sort of tests I did, and I'll be listening to gossip generally. Can you think of any other line I can follow?'

'Not at the moment, but I may be in touch after I've seen counsel.'

'Speaking of counsel reminds me,' Keith said. 'Did you find out anything about that arbitration?'

'Ah!' Enterkin sniffed his brandy. 'You may have struck oil there. You were right. A. Payne and Company *is* your Andrew Payne, and he seems to be up to his neck in litigation which he can't afford to lose.'

'I thought litigation meant going to court,' Molly said. 'Surely arbitration isn't that?'

'No, but it's an enforceable legal process. I had the very devil of a job finding out about this one, because arbitration is essentially confidential unless the parties agree otherwise. In the end I was driven to bribery – you'll keep this under your hats, both of you. A niece of mine shares a flat with a girl who types for Henderson, McLure and Groag. For a consideration, she took copies of the papers in that office, and they put me onto some other sources.

'According to the Minute of Submission, Mr Payne leases a factory in which certain building components are fabricated, using a lot of synthetic resins, whatever they may be. The floor was in poor condition, so advice was sought from specialist flooring contractors, and Lothian Flooring got the job. I haven't been able to find out who's behind them, by the way – not yet. Just why the thing all went wrong is the subject of the dispute. Payne and his independent experts say that the job was to the wrong specifications and wrongly carried out, and that the nature of the agreement was that they would be given a satisfactory floor, which they weren't; but Lothian Flooring and all *their* independent experts say that the floor failed because of the nature of the chemicals used in the factory, and that nobody told them that certain processes would be going on in there; to which Payne replies that they certainly were told all about his processes, in support of which he produces the carbon copy of a letter which the other side deny ever receiving, and reading between the lines the letter does seem to be somewhat questionable. Meantime, of course, poor Payne has lost a lot of money, lost a lot of customers, and lost his patience. The contract is embodied in an exchange of letters so vague that you can read almost anything into them. It's all very sad, but if people would only use a solicitor at that stage they wouldn't need a barrister later.'

'If they'd had solicitors,' Keith said, 'nobody would ever have got around to doing anything at all.'

'And they'd both have been very much better off,' Enterkin pointed out. 'Anyway, the one thing that was clearly expressed was that the contract was subject to an arbitration clause, and McLure was duly appointed. I suppose, in a vague way, it could furnish a possible motive, if Payne thought that McLure was going to award against him.'

'What's the time?' Keith asked. 'My watch stopped, after all the jolting it got.'

'Plenty of time,' Enterkin said. 'Plenty of time.' He signalled the waiter again.

'Am I right,' Keith asked, 'in thinking that once an arbiter's been appointed it's very difficult to get rid of him again?'

'Hullo! You've been doing your homework.'

'While I was waiting in your office, after that time that Ronnie had a go at me, I dipped into a book on it.'

'Irons and Melville? Dated, but still largely valid.'

'I think that's why I pricked up my ears when arbitration was mentioned in McLure's office.'

'Well, you're quite right. The law is unclear and the authorities contradict each other on certain points, but generally speaking once he's appointed an arbiter can't even resign, and even in the case of gross misconduct the processes for having him removed would be time-consuming.'

'Suppose that the arbiter suddenly went abroad, for keeps?'

Molly watched, fascinated, as Enterkin made his thoughtful face. 'That would certainly hang things up. Probably for years,' he said at last. 'Leaving Payne, of course, whistling for his recompense. In fact, the death of the arbiter would certainly be the quickest solution to the problem. Not, mind you, a solution that one would suggest to a client, but – '

'A motive for murder?'

'Probably a very good one. If Payne knew that McLure was going abroad.'

Molly was consulting her own small watch. 'Are you sure we aren't late, or has my watch gone fast?' she asked.

Enterkin put his wrist up to his ear. 'My God,' he said, 'my watch has stopped too. We're going to be late. Get your coats. Waiter, the bill!'

Keith got up and pulled back Molly's chair, a new departure in courtesy for him. 'Who have you been fighting with?' he asked.

'Nobody,' Enterkin said grimly. 'But I'll have a go at that

waiter if he doesn't bring the bill within the next ten seconds.'

Keith and Molly were duly married by the registrar, and then attended a reception for a dozen or so close friends at the Hall, graciously given for them by Sir Peter and his lady. Lady Hay, at least, was gracious; Sir Peter was his usual affable self.

The couple then departed on a working honeymoon, in Keith's van.

It was perhaps fortunate for the whole future of their marriage that Keith embarked on it in a mood that was far from his usual independence and self-reliance. It was not surprising that a day spent standing in an ice-cold quarry, followed by two savage fights separated only by a long drive in a heavy vehicle in a hurry, should have induced in his taxed muscles a stiffness that persisted for more than a week. Keith chose to interpret his symptoms as the onset of rheumatism, or possibly arthritis, and nothing that Molly could say would shift him from that view. This reminder of his own mortality, and more particularly of the decrepit old age which now seemed to be looming over him, turned his thoughts to the advantages of having a strong young wife to minister to his declining years. Thus Molly was delighted to find that, in addition to Keith's usual passion, there was a new tenderness and a sense of needing, and whenever the stiffness returned she would rub him down with liniment, an attention without which no honeymoon is quite complete.

A remarkable harmony developed in the van, where the crowded conditions might have provoked friction. Molly had deemed it necessary to bring along Black Jake, Ronnie's half-bred Labrador, but the two dogs had settled down together surprisingly well. If Molly was looking forward to coaxing Keith into a more spacious and less nomadic life she was sensible enough not to say so. And although Keith found his solitary world suddenly invaded and his life-style influenced forever, the availability of a second pair of hands to share his chores and help him get through twice as much in a day was an adequate compensation.

As befitted a farmer's daughter, a stalker's sister and a gunsmith's bride, Molly was quite familiar with guns and a passable shot. She was willing, if pressed, to carry a gun and perform useful tasks such as blanking-off the end of a covert when required, but she had none of the enthusiasm of the true hunter. Instead, she produced another talent which Keith found of great value. He had known that she was addicted to the taking of nature photographs – he could hardly have failed, with the cottage so liberally hung with her flower and bird pictures. But he had not realised how competent and knowledgeable she was, nor how well equipped. This last had been paid for by the sale of the skins of foxes that Keith and her brother had been in the habit of bringing her, neither man realising the price that a fox's pelt fetched.

Keith himself was a dedicated scribbler, and part of his income was derived from many articles on technical and sporting subjects in a variety of magazines devoted to field sports. His problem had always been to illustrate his articles. It is never satisfactory to carry a gun and a camera, nor to work a dog and photograph its action as well. Moreover, Keith had no real feeling for photography. Molly, on the other hand, could compose and catch a picture on the instant, or stop a bird on the wing or tumbling dead in the air; and her photographs of gundogs at work were of the very best, somehow bringing out the pride and pleasure that good dogs take in their work.

Soon Molly was to become a familiar sight, trotting beside Keith in the shooting-field or along the foreshore, never with less than two cameras bouncing on her pretty bosom and always grinning like a pup because she was so happy. Of her brother's ultimate fate she had no fear. After all, Keith was looking after the matter so it was bound to be all right . . .

One of the first calls that they made together was on Joe Quaich, the gunsmith, at a shop on the outskirts of Musselburgh. They spoke in the van, away from the many ears in the shop where Joe's partner sold cartridges and fishing-tackle. So as not to spoil the value of his testimony Keith told him as little as possible, asking only that Joe experiment until he had satisfied himself as to the best method of firing a rifle-bullet from a shotgun, and then take note of what clues might be left behind.

Joe Quaich, a sharp and bristling little man, brisk of movement and voice, nodded his grey head. 'Give me a week,' he said. 'Then come back. I'll have a draft report ready for you, but when I know what you're really after I'll make out a full precognition.'

'That suits us fine.'

'I'd be a fool,' Joe said slowly, 'if I didn't guess that this stems from that shooting down Newton Lauder way, the one you were present at. I was reading about it. You're for the defence?'

'That's right.'

'Sir Peter Hay's stalker?'

'Yes.'

'And this'll be his sister?'

'How did you know that,' Molly asked, wide-eyed.

He chuckled. 'Bless you, good news travels fast around here. And this man getting himself married, that's good news to a husband or two, I'm guessing, but there's a few lassies that'll not be so pleased.' He looked at his watch. 'Can you wait and take a dram with me?'

'You'll take one with us,' Keith said firmly. He got out one of his special bottles from under the bunk-seat, and poured a large tot for the older man, a lesser one with water for himself, and the merest whisper for Molly.

Joe Quaich raised his glass, wished them long life and happiness, and drank. His eyebrows flicked up. 'Now where would you get the like of that? It never belongs in that bottle!'

Keith laughed. 'The exciseman at one of the distilleries was determined that what he wanted was a Purdey.'

'Not that Purdey that you got from me?' Joe rolled up his eyes. 'But it was clapped-out!'

'I worked and worked on it, and put on a new stock to fit him. He got just what he wanted out of it, but I wouldn't take money. So he's paying it off in instalments – may it take him another ten years!'

'He always had an eye for a bargain,' Joe said to Molly.

'The locks were so rusted I was sure it could never be fired again.'

'Ah,' said Keith, 'but you could still read the name on it. Joe, do you know any of the men that were on that shoot?'

Joe stopped chuckling and became very serious. 'Not well enough to worry about,' he said.

'I wasn't thinking of that. But are any of them among your customers?'

Joe was lost in thought for a second. 'I know Andrew Payne,' he said. 'He bought a gun from me last year, and he gets his cartridges here. And materials for reloading.'

'Does he have his own shoot, as well as his gun in the syndicate?'

'Not that I know of. He seems to use a lot of large shot, BBs and the like, so he'll be doing most of his shooting on the foreshore.'

'Does he pay cash on the nail?'

Joe laughed. 'It's a very special customer that gets credit from my partner.'

'And Andrew Payne isn't in that bracket?'

Joe shrugged. 'I've no reason to believe otherwise. I've heard rumours, mind, that Payne was having a bad time financially; but you hear that about them all, one time or another. I'd not believe it at all, except that he's one of those men that goes about looking worried.'

'That's right,' said Keith, 'he does. All the time. Even while he's enjoying himself. I'd forgotten that.'

'You've only met him once or twice,' Molly said. 'Maybe he's not always like that. You may have met him when he had something to be worried about.' Keith looked at her sharply.

'I never saw him look any other way,' said Joe. 'A pleasant chap, softly spoken and always very well dressed. But I wouldn't want to have him around, or he'd have me looking worried too.'

'What about David McNeill?' Keith asked.

'Councillor McNeill is that? Tall man with a thin face and a big, hooked nose? Dark hair, greying?'

'That's the man.'

'He's been into the shop a few times. A free spender, but

I could do without his custom. Nothing wrong with his money, but he's an arrogant man. He looks down yon great beak of his, as if he's doing you the grandest favour in the world just by being there and it's your privilege to give him the best service at the best possible price. And then a nod's as good as thank-you to him.'

'Does he reload?'

Joe scratched his head. 'I don't think so. I seem to remember him buying a box of primers once, but then, some people use them to make blank cartridges for dog-training. Mostly he buys cartridges, number sixes.'

'If he does dog-training it doesn't show,' Keith said.

Joe grinned. 'If it doesn't show he's all the more need to be doing it,' he said. 'Now, that one does have his own bit of shooting, at the back of Lanark somewhere.'

They discussed personalities for twenty minutes, but Keith learned nothing new. It was only at the last moment that he thought to ask about McLure.

'McLure,' Joe said thoughtfully. 'I never met him, that I know. Faces come and go in the shop, and unless they pay by cheque or want a receipt you never hear their names. But I did hear something about the man. Ask me in about three weeks' time and I'll tell you. I'm not one to make trouble for a widow.'

And with a word of farewell he jumped down and trotted back into the shop.

Keith and Molly stared at each other. 'What the hell would three weeks have to do with it?' Keith asked, and Molly could only shake her head.

Prompted by Keith, Molly phoned the office of Henderson and Groag – the name of the deceased partner had already been dropped – and asked if she might speak with Mr McLure's secretary. Miss Scobie, she was told, had left the firm and was now living at a Dunfermline address. Dunfermline was almost on their planned route, so the two presented themselves the following morning at a small house overlooking a golf course.

Miss Scobie was a tiny woman with pointed features and unnaturally bright yellow curls. Keith guessed her age at forty, Molly at fifty-five. She had a clear, educated voice almost free of accent, and a shy smile that transformed an otherwise plain face.

'Come in, my dears,' she said. 'It's too cold for talking on the doorstep. Cold enough for snow, d'you think?'

She led them into a stuffy, cluttered room where an open fire blazed. There were Christmas cards already among the ornaments on the mantelpiece, and Keith blinked at this reminder of the passage of time.

Miss Scobie read Mr Enterkin's letter with quick, bright eyes and handed it back. She proved willing enough to talk, but first expressed a reluctance to say anything that might upset the course of true justice. 'You see,' she said, 'the police have a difficult enough job to do, and Mr McLure was a good employer to me, and I wouldn't want to do anything to make their job harder or to help the man that killed poor Mr McLure to get away with it.'

'We wouldn't want that either,' Keith said.

Molly leaned forward. 'Miss Scobie, if I thought that my brother did this awful thing, then I wouldn't ask my husband to help him. But surely he's entitled to have us find out the truth, so that he can prove that he didn't!'

So far from confusing Miss Scobie, this seemed to allay her doubts. 'What do you want to know?' she asked.

'What was he like to work for?' Molly asked.

Miss Scobie licked her thin lips. 'He was demanding, inconsiderate, selfish and utterly charming,' she said at last. She sighed. 'He drove me quite ruthlessly without a word of thanks, and then suddenly, perhaps one Christmas in three, he'd remember and give me an enormous present and a word of thanks and I didn't mind any more. The office paid my salary, but Mr McLure, he'd have me doing a thousand things that were nothing to do with the office, and if I didn't have time to do his typing – and usually I didn't – it just went to the typing pool. I did his personal letters and paid his bills for him, looked after his Christmas shopping, posted his parcels, ran errands, passed messages, booked hotels and made travelling arrangements . . . oh, everything!'

'It doesn't sound as if Mrs McLure had to do much for him,' Keith said, 'except maybe darn his socks.'

Miss Scobie gave a ladylike snort. 'I don't see her mending socks! I wouldn't have put it past him to bring them to me, but I suspect that he just threw them away when they got holes in them.'

'Did you help him with his business entertaining?'

'Yes, of course. After all, it was for the office, wasn't it? He only asked me to come as his hostess once or twice, for respectable clients,' she said regretfully. 'Mrs McLure usually did that sort of thing. But I made all the arrangements, and sometimes I had to arrange for . . . other sorts of entertainment.'

There was an empty little silence.

'We did understand,' Keith said slowly, 'that Mr McLure sometimes entertained his male clients with . . . young . . .'

'Tarts,' said Miss Scobie briskly. 'Of course he did. All part of getting in the business. He usually left the arranging to me.'

Molly turned slightly pink. 'You didn't mind?'

'Bless you, no. Mind, I wouldn't have anything to do with his affairs with proper ladies, and he knew it. I mean, I didn't mind choosing a present or booking a table, but I wouldn't take messages about assignations, or arrange hotel rooms. It wouldn't have been right. But with those sort of girls, well, men are like that, aren't they?'

'Are they?' asked Molly. 'All of them?'

'All of them,' said Miss Scobie firmly. 'I got to know some of them quite well, the girls I mean. They used to send me Christmas cards. I got quite used to keeping a little card-index on them – under lock and key, of course – and picking out the right young woman to call if Mr McLure wanted to entertain a client, a councillor or someone like that, and paying the bill afterwards.'

'You mean they sent in a bill?' Keith asked incredulously. He edged back, away from the heat of the fire.

'They put in a chit to me, and I paid them,' said Miss Scobie. 'How else? It's just good business practice.'

'And then you accounted to the firm?'

'Not in detail, no. Mr McLure never wanted that sort

137

of detail to go to the firm. He had me keep detailed accounts of his entertaining, and put a claim monthly for reimbursement. He wouldn't have me give any details, ever, but he was strictly honest about it, never made a penny extra although he could very easily have done.' Miss Scobie seemed quite unaware of the effect of her disclosures which, surprising as they were, were doubly devastating in association with herself.

'Who – ?'

Miss Scobie shook her head. She was almost arch. 'Now, you mustn't ask for names. These things are highly confidential, you understand. It wouldn't do to tell tales. I was in a position of trust.'

This shading of ethics was a little too subtle for Keith. 'But if one of them's a murderer – '

'Why should there be any connection?'

'Doesn't it occur to you,' Keith said, 'that if McLure was giving those sorts of bribes, he was in a position to put pressure on people?'

'He never said anything about bribes,' Miss Scobie said indignantly. 'I'm sure he wouldn't have done such a thing. He referred to "sweeteners". But I never had anything to do with that, just the entertaining.'

'But you know,' Keith said, 'that McLure went a long way over the borderline between legitimate entertainment and corruption.'

As soon as he said the word, a shutter came down blotting out all expression from Miss Scobie's face. It was only as the expression vanished that Keith recognised it for what it had been – a curiously innocent delight in vicarious naughtiness. But the shift of interest from naughtiness to downright corruption was beyond the scope of Miss Scobie's mental elasticity.

Molly stepped in quickly. 'We do understand about the entertaining,' she said. 'And I'm sure that you wouldn't have lent yourself to anything that you felt to be dishonest. Everybody gives "sweeteners" of some kind or another, even if it's only a bottle at Christmas . . .'

'That's right,' said Miss Scobie.

'But Mr McLure couldn't do a lot of that sort of entertaining without finding out a lot about some people's nastier habits. I suppose you too . . . ?'

Miss Scobie brightened. 'You'd hardly believe it,' she said.

'But,' said Molly, 'somebody killed poor Mr McLure, and we're looking for every possible reason that anybody might have had. And one possible reason might have been that he knew something discreditable about somebody, and even if he wasn't exactly holding it over that person's head there might be circumstances that made that person think that Mr McLure might be going to let the cat out of the bag. What do you think?' She took a pencil out of Keith's top pocket and started writing.

'I suppose it could have been something like that,' Miss Scobie said slowly.

'If that was it, then you might be in danger too. When you left the firm, what happened to your card-index?'

'I lodged it at the bank, to protect myself. So, you see, it wouldn't do anybody any good . . .'

'But they wouldn't know that,' Keith said.

Molly looked up from her scribbling and gave him a warning shake of the head. 'Miss Scobie,' she said, 'here's a list of the men who were on the shoot when Mr McLure was killed. I've put where they live, so that there's no muddle over people with the same names. Would you look at the names and tell me whether any of them ever had any special sort of entertainment from Mr McLure?'

Miss Scobie ran her eye down Molly's clear, rather childish writing. 'Oh yes,' she said. 'More than one.'

'But you don't want to tell us which?'

Miss Scobie was enjoying this piquant new guessing-game. 'You can't expect me to give away the secrets of perfectly respectable businessmen who may have had nothing whatever to do with Mr McLure's death. If you had a particular suspect, now . . .'

Keith looked hard at Miss Scobie and called on his years of experience in interpreting the finer shades of female expression. She was suggesting a trade of information. He decided after a moment that she was merely curious on her own behalf. He took the paper, ringed two names and handed it back.

'Those two?' Miss Scobie sounded surprised, and disappointed. 'No, neither of them.'

'And as far as you know neither of them received any kind of "sweetener"?'

She shook her head. 'No. I think they've both phoned up and asked to speak to him at one time or another. I wouldn't know what about – perhaps just to ask him shooting or something.'

'I see. Without betraying any confidences, can you tell me anything about the arbitration that he was hearing?'

'Confidences or not, Mr Calder, I can't tell you anything about that. There was going to be a lot of typing to it, and it wasn't part of his normal business, so McLure got one of the pool typists put onto it. I remember seeing the Minute of Submission when it came in, but after that I never even heard of it again. But I had an idea – and I was only guessing – that it was worrying him just a little bit.'

'Why did you guess that?' Molly asked.

'Only that he seemed worried at a time when everything else was going well. A secretary gets to know a boss's moods, better than his wife does sometimes.'

'Could it have been woman-trouble that was bothering him?' asked Keith.

Miss Scobie shook her head. 'No. He never let them bother him. If there was any bothering to be done, he did it.'

Keith and Molly raised eyebrows at each other. 'I know you're too discreet to name names,' said Molly, and the irony in her voice went over Miss Scobie's head and under Keith's nose, 'but would you take a last look at the names and addresses on the list and tell us whether you think that any of Mr McLure's lady-friends might be connected in any way to any of those gentlemen?'

'Cherchez la femme?' Miss Scobie looked down at the list. 'I didn't think that angry husbands or brothers did that sort of thing any more.'

'Nor did I,' said Keith, 'but the police seem to have old-fashioned ideas.'

Miss Scobie sighed. 'I can't help you,' she said. 'I didn't

keep cards on them, and the nearest I ever had to an address was the occasional call-back phone-number. And some of these are such common names around Edinburgh. McNeill . . . Thomson . . . Hay . . . No, I can't help you.'

'You've helped a lot,' Keith said.

After the hot room, the cold outside cut like a whip. 'You nearly blew it,' Molly said as they walked back to the van, 'talking about corruption like that. The old biddy was thoroughly enjoying acting as Madame to McLure's circus, but she's shut her mind to the rest of it. She only wanted to remember the fun things. I should think that that was as near as she ever got to sex.'

'Incredible hypocrisy.'

'Not really. These things do go on, and I suppose that behind any big businessman who wheels and deals and all that there's got to be a secretary who does most of the dirty work and convinces herself that it's all right,' Molly said tolerantly.

'Perhaps that's the kind of secretary I need.'

Molly giggled. 'Put it out of your mind,' she said. 'Which were those two names?'

'Oh God,' Keith said, 'I hope I'm right.'

CHAPTER 11

Keith's sister Elsie had been informed by greetings telegram of the nuptials, because Keith had not felt up to a sustained telephone conversation on the subject. However, he could not postpone contact with his sister indefinitely, and when he could no longer put off phoning her to compare diaries and gather messages she was so plaintively insistent on meeting Molly, who had previously been only a voice on the phone to her, there was nothing for it but to promise a visit.

It happened that circumstances were drawing Keith northward again. He had still to complete his business rounds, he had some questions to ask, and he wanted to revisit the site of his confrontation with Johnny the Intermediary and the unfortunate Paisley. The latter, in addition, was being held in connection with the events leading up to the thumping of Constable Murchy, and although the police had Keith's written statement they were anxious to meet him in person.

So, *en route,* a visit was made to Elsie, and while the two ladies exchanged confidences Keith was glad of the chance to unload some surplus weight from the van into the *pied-à-terre* that he maintained in two rooms of the rambling farmhouse. The sudden acquisition of a wife, another dog, Molly's luggage and the extra food and water required to feed two extra mouths had taken the van beyond the loading that Keith considered safe, and he removed several guns and a large collection of duplicated tools into the house. Later, he was to be very glad that he had done so.

Keith was forced to haul the van all the way to Inverness to give evidence at a sheriff court appearance of Paisley which turned out to be a non-event. He grumbled at the cost of his fuel, although he sold the Dickson Round Action there for a price that made Molly's eyes pop.

A profitable visit to an old client soon took them back into the area of Loch Lochy, and they spent the morning at the quarry with music from the van all around them. Molly's exposure to music had been limited to the 'pops' on the radio played as a soft background to housework, and her vague sense that 'there must be something better' had been justified when she took to Keith's collection like a fish to a fly. She had spent a whole day whistling the pastoral theme from what Keith persisted in referring to as 'Rossini's overture to the *Lone Ranger*', and had laughed aloud at Schumann's *Carnival*. It had all given them a renewed sense of mutual satisfaction, and had bored their friends to near tears.

The wrecked car had been removed, although bits of it still lay around. In the quarry itself, Keith was glad to recover his tow-rope. To satisfy Molly's fascinated curiosity he relived the events of his last day there, playing for her benefit all the parts in turn although he drew the line at hurling himself into the remains of the blackthorn. Then they went down into the thorns and brambles in the bottom of the quarry to search for the shoes that Keith had thrown there. With the aid of the dogs they recovered three, and after a late lunch in the van they sat down to examine their trophies.

'Go ahead,' Molly said. 'Do a Sherlock for me. I'll be Watson.'

'No,' said Keith, 'you do it and I'll stand back and admire.'

'But it's a man's shoe,' Molly objected.

'Women notice things about a man. I'll do it when we find a woman's shoe.'

'I bet. All right,' said Molly, 'I'll try.' She picked up Paisley's grey casual. 'We don't need to know any more about this one. I mean, the police have him and they know where he comes from.'

'Try it anyway.'

'All right.' Molly studied the shoe. 'This man walks with a limp.'

'For God's sake, how can you tell that from one shoe?'

'Of course he does,' Molly said firmly. 'If you pulled him out of a tree and up a cliff by one leg . . .'

Keith tried not to laugh. 'And he has a flat top to his head where I dropped him on it. And he's covered with half-healed scratches. Fair enough. Now, seriously, what can you tell from the shoe?'

'All right,' she said. 'It's a cheap, casual shoe, chosen with a mind to price and comfort and quietness, perm any two from three. Comfort mostly, I think, because he has trouble with his feet. He's got arch supports stuck in, and you can see a wee bulge where he has a bunion. He shuffles a bit. Walks with the feet turned out – this foot at least. It's a dirty old shoe, so he's short either of money or pride. Will that do?'

'I can't see anything else,' Keith admitted. 'What about Johnny?'

'The Gingerbread Man,' Molly said reflectively. 'What do we know about him already?'

'Almost nothing. I hear that the Strathclyde police had had some whispers about him but no positive identification at all. He's obviously very careful – the odds and ends I took out of his pockets were so anonymous that it was ridiculous. Money. A few keys. Handkerchief. And four different driving licences, all stolen.'

'He's careful about his things, too,' Molly said. 'These shoes aren't new, but they've been well looked after. They were expensive. He has a short, broad foot, so he had these made, but there's no name in them. They're light and comfortable, but with a very hard toe-cap.'

'For fighting,' Keith said.

'If you say so.'

'Which makes him a hard man.'

'Not as hard as you, seemingly. He came out with polished shoes, but he's been in some sort of mud – the welts are still packed with it. Would he have got that while looking for you?'

'I shouldn't think so,' Keith said slowly. 'There's nowhere I could have taken the van that he couldn't take a car.'

'Perhaps he got out of the car to ask somebody if he'd seen you.'

'Or perhaps he got out to speak to his client. We'd better look at the car if we can find it.' Keith leaned across and felt the soles of the shoes.

'What are you looking for?'

'I was wondering if they were sticky, as if he'd visited a factory with a sticky floor, but they aren't. The soles are clean, as if he walked on wet grass or something after going through the mud.'

Molly spread a piece of paper on the table and picked up one of the shoes. 'Your knife?'

'I'll do it,' Keith said. 'You put on some coffee. I know a geologist who can probably tell me where it came from.' He started scraping.

Molly produced an envelope and a pen. 'Name and address? I'll post it in Fort William this afternoon.'

As they drank their coffee, they studied the little pile of grit.

'It's pink,' Keith said.

'Red,' said Molly. 'Reddish brown.'

'Pink as your knickers,' Keith said firmly. He put a hand on her leg under the table, and then forgot about it and left it there. 'It's like quarry dust, but I don't think it is. A quarry would make sense, though. It's a little like pink Aberdeenshire granite, Peterhead maybe, but I'll swear it's not granite.'

'Do any other quarries produce a pink stone?'

'Oh yes. But when I look at this I'm sure I've seen it before, and I seem to see a whole hill of it. And that doesn't make sense.'

'Leave it to your geologist friend,' Molly said.

The wrecked car was easily tracked down in the custody of a local garage, but the proprietor had no authority to let them touch it. All that they could do was to peer in through the windows and see traces of the reddish grit on both the front carpets.

They slept that night at a favourite place of Keith's, between the main road and Loch Linnhe.

Just before dawn, Keith stretched out a fore-finger and prodded Molly where it pleased him to prod her. 'I'm going rabbiting,' he said.

She sat up. 'Hold on. I'm coming too.'

'It's too dark for photography.'

'Always darkest before dawn, or something.'

'All right. But you'll have to be quiet, and leave the dogs behind. Rabbiting at dawn means pussyfooting along and waiting to see what bolts.'

They dressed quickly in front of the hissing heater.

'You should have ferrets,' Molly said.

'In a van?'

Molly said nothing, but she filed the comment away in her mind. When the time came to put down roots, the keeping of ferrets might prove a useful inducement.

When they stepped outside, Keith sniffed the air. 'It'll snow when the wind drops,' he said.

Darkness was ebbing away as they followed a track through the gorse towards the loch. Suddenly, Keith stopped dead. 'Ploughed,' he said.

'What?' said Molly. She was still half-asleep.

'Ploughed. All this agriculture's the curse of the country-side. Bloody farmers leaving crops and animals all over an otherwise perfect landscape. Some bastard's ploughed up the whole area. It used to be alive with bunnies.'

'They'll still be around somewhere.'

'But where? That's where all the buries were.' He pointed into a prairie of ploughland. 'We'll try the whins.'

They paced slowly through the gorse and broom, but not a rabbit bolted. So, being who they were, they sat down beside the loch, close together despite the encumbering gun and cameras, and watched the dawn grow into a cold, colourless light that promised snow to come. Small divers bobbed in the advancing tide, and further out a fish jumped.

Suddenly Keith stood up. 'Duck,' he said.

Obediently, Molly ducked.

Keith swung his gun up and fired. High overhead a lone

146

mallard staggered and died. As its wings folded the wind caught it.

'Damnation!' Keith said with feeling. 'It's in the water.'

'Shall I run for the dogs?'

'Too late. The wind's taking it out. By the time they got here it'd be too dangerous.'

'I'll go.'

The phrase had no meaning for Keith, who was watching his duck drift away. He was very fond of a roasted mallard. Then Molly ran into the water, splashing white droplets into the air. She had stripped to a couple of scraps of white nylon, and Keith thought she was the most beautiful thing that he had ever seen.

'For Christ's sake be careful,' he called.

'You don't want to lose me?'

'I'd rather lose the duck.'

'Much rather?'

'Much rather.'

'That's good. Brrr.'

She waded and then swam, arching her back to keep her hair out of the water so that her buttocks made twin islands that came and went. She reached the duck and turned. Keith felt his breath come again as she dog-paddled back.

When she was only knee-deep, he picked up one of her cameras. 'A good retriever carries the bird in her mouth,' he said.

Molly giggled between her shivers, but she took the neck of the bird between her jaws.

'Now retrieve it properly to hand, and I'll try to warm you up again,' Keith said. He took off his quilted jacket.

Five minutes later, arm-in-arm, they were heading back to the van. Their thoughts were on bacon and eggs and toast and coffee and walking the dogs, and, in Molly's case, dry underwear.

From the very moment that they crested the last rise and saw the van below them it was obvious that something was wrong.

It may be that Keith's life was saved by his habit of never unloading his gun until the very last moment permitted by the etiquette of safety. He had been caught out too often by that inspired bird that waits until all the guns are empty and then takes off to live and die another day. Be that as it may, Keith walked with his gun open but with cartridges in the chambers.

Beside the big van there was a man's figure, and stealth was written in his every movement. When they first saw him, he was putting down a square four-gallon drum, very gently, about ten yards from the van. Then he walked, easing his weight slowly onto each foot in turn, towards the van, feeling in his pockets as he went.

'Try to get a shot of him,' Keith said urgently. Then, as he realised the man's intentions, he broke into a run. He tried to shout but his vocal chords seemed to have turned to wool. Then it was too late. He saw a match leave the man's hand, a tiny spark that curved through the air. As it touched down, the ground under and around the van erupted with a soft explosion that was followed by a roar of flame towering up, the only splash of colour in the white light of that day. An area around the van's door had received particular treatment, for there the flames bulged out and roared higher into the great billows of black smoke that formed above.

Keith's recollection of the next few seconds was to remain forever patchy. He remembered running and trying to shout, and he remembered the figure, black against the flames in the shadow of the smoke, turning with something in its hands. He remembered the man staggering and falling into the edge of the flames just as the van's petrol tank blew up. Of the firing of shots he had no recollection at all. He just remembered standing, weeping, where the heat of the blaze kept him back, hearing the roar as his possessions went up and the screaming of the two dogs.

CHAPTER 12

It was very late that night before Mr Enterkin reached Inverness, and later still before he was admitted to the office of Superintendent Mellish. In that austere room he found his client confronting, with a certain exhausted truculence, no less than four senior police officers plus a sergeant who was staring gloomily at a nearly empty shorthand book.

Mr Enterkin had had a long day. So had the others. But the solicitor bounced into the room with a twinkle and a cheerful nod to each of the tired faces. 'Good evening,' he said. 'Let me introduce myself. My name is Enterkin and I represent Mr Calder.'

'Now perhaps we can get on,' said a voice, and Enterkin looked again and recognised Munro's long face.

'You got my message, then?' said Mellish.

'No. It's probably waiting at my office. I had a phone call from my client's wife and set off at once. I'm sorry to have taken so long. I could have flown from Turnhouse, but I thought it better to come by car and visit the scene before coming here, and there's snow on the high ground just to make things difficult. The ploughs are out.'

'Where's Molly?' Keith asked. 'Is she all right?'

'Right as rain, my boy, and waiting downstairs. You've a good girl there. She seems to have kept her head admirably while, if I may say so, all about her were losing theirs and most women would have been running round in hysterical little circles. And who are all these gentlemen? Acting Chief Inspector Munro I know, of course.'

The man in the uniform of a superintendent, standing behind the paper-stacked desk, smiled and nodded. 'I'm Mellish. Local. You say you know Chief Inspector Munro,' and in his voice there was the faintest possible suggestion that this might not be wholly a privilege. He indicated the two men in plain clothes, and his manner suggested a degree of professional respect. 'Superintendent Gilchrist and Chief Inspector Turner are from the Serious Crimes Squad in Strathclyde. They only preceded you by a few minutes.' Mellish was a big man, grey and square as a lump of granite. His accent was Aberdeenshire, the pure Doric of the farms of Buchan, tempered slightly by years of exposure to other tongues, although his words were correct and precise.

'And what serious crime brings them all this way?' Enterkin asked.

'That will no doubt be revealed to us in due course,' said Mellish, and the words sat so oddly on his accent that Enterkin nearly smiled. 'It can hardly be that an isolated death out here would fetch them this distance. They're here to observe for the moment – as is Chief Inspector Munro,' he added firmly.

Superintendent Gilchrist, a slim man, ramrod-straight which gave him a military look, smiled faintly. 'At the moment, I'm afraid I know as little as you do,' he said.

'Less,' said Enterkin. 'Much less.' He sat down beside Keith and there was a general rumble of chairs. 'I've agreed to act for you in this one matter.'

'That's understood,' said Keith.

'Have you seen a doctor?'

'Several,' Keith said. 'There was a doctor came out with the ambulance. He put a patch on me. Then I was taken to the local station, and they called another doctor who replaced the bandage and examined me for shock. He said I'd do. Then they took me to Fort William and did it all over again. And then I was brought through here and they called yet another doctor, and he said that I had been shocked and needed a rest, so they made me lie down in a cell for most of the afternoon.' Keith sounded indignant. There were smiles.

'Good,' said Enterkin. 'Now, what have you said so far?'

'Very little,' Keith said. 'I was trying to tell Mr Mellish all about it when Munro arrived. He wanted me cautioned, and when Mr Mellish said that there was no call for that just yet awhile Munro cautioned me himself.'

Munro turned a dull red.

'Aye,' said Mellish. 'Well. I was just wanting to find out what happened. Time enough for cautions before taking a proper statement.'

'Let's assume,' said Enterkin smoothly, 'that Chief Inspector Munro felt that a caution was in your best interests.'

'Maybe,' said Keith. 'After that, I said that I was saying nothing until you were here.'

'Very wise. But you can tell your story now.'

'Don't you want to hear it first?'

'Not in the least.'

Keith shrugged. 'I already referred Mr Mellish to my earlier statement, and he's got it there.'

'Perhaps,' said Enterkin, 'the two gentlemen from Strathclyde might be permitted to read it while we talk, but just give us a brief summary of it.'

'It says how I was present at the shoot when Ronald McLure died, for which my brother-in-law (as he is now) was arrested. McLure was found burned but there was a bullet in him, and I was asked by the defence, being a gunsmith, to investigate. And I was investigating. And two men came and offered me money to leave it alone, and when I wouldn't they started to beat me up. And I knocked seven colours of shit out of them,' Keith added reflectively. 'You've still got one of them in custody – that's the man Paisley. The other got away and went down to Newton Lauder, where he beat up a constable. He was trying to get at my wife, either to intimidate her or possibly to snatch her. I caught up with him and thumped him again.'

Gilchrist looked up from the copy of Keith's earlier statement. 'And was that the same who set fire to your van this morning?' he asked.

'I don't know,' Keith said helplessly. 'How could I tell, in that light? But it would make sense – either as revenge, or because it would wreck his reputation to fail, or even because his client still wanted me to stop. He meant to burn Molly and me alive. He listened outside the van, and he heard the breathing of the two dogs . . .'

'Just tell us what happened,' Enterkin said.

'We were coming back from an early morning walk.' Keith rubbed his face.

151

'Are you all right?' Enterkin asked. He produced a large hip-flask.

Keith waved it away. 'I'll do for a bit yet. I'd shot a duck. I wonder what ever happened to that duck.'

'Molly was most concerned about it,' Enterkin said. 'She thought a fox had probably carried it off from where you dropped it. She wanted to go back again and look for it. She said you'd be wanting that duck.'

'It was a good fat one. It weighed like a ton. I was carrying it and my gun as we walked back to the van.'

'Was the gun loaded?' Mellish asked.

'It was open for safety, but there were cartridges in it. If you unload before you have to, sure as hell you'll have birds around your head like midges and rabbits running between your feet.' Somebody gave a short chuckle. 'Anyway, as soon as we could see the van, at about sixty yards, we could see a fellow at it and he seemed to be moving about on tip-toe, so I knew that he was up to no good.'

'Do you remember what you said to your wife?' asked Enterkin.

'No,' said Keith. 'Probably something that'd not bear repeating.'

'Oh, it would bear repeating all right, but not just yet. Go on.'

'I knew something was far wrong. Maybe it was just the way he was acting, but I'd seen him put down a can and the wind was towards me, so maybe I smelled the petrol or maybe that was later. I started to run. I meant to shout but my voice would only make a croak. He threw a match and – Boom! – the whole caboodle went roaring up in flames.'

'Tell us about the exchange of shots,' Mellish said gently.

Keith rubbed his mouth. 'The only way I know that I fired at him is because I found that one of my cartridges was spent. And I know that he shot at me because I've two holes in my jacket and a groove in the flesh under my left armpit, but I never felt it at the time. I just don't remember anything about it – my mind was too taken up with the horror of it all. I'd taken years to build up my business and the van, and I could hear the dogs yelling. But I can tell you this – I'd not have shot unless he shot first. I'm often asked to give safety instructions to young pupils, or to speak to clubs about it. I seem to spend half my life impressing on people that you must never ever let a gun be pointed at anybody, loaded or not. It'd be against my nature.'

'Then how would you not remember doing such a thing?' Munro asked.

'I don't know that I did,' Keith said. 'But if I did, then I could easily not remember. Everybody knows how patchy your memory can get in an emergency. It's as if your mind's too taken up with doing the right thing to spare any time for recording it.'

'Do you have to concentrate, to shoot straight?' Enterkin asked.

'No more than you would, to kick a ball. After all these years it's as instinctive to me as knocking in a nail is to a joiner.'

'But,' said Munro, 'you can't swear from your own memory that you didn't shoot first?'

Mellish looked quickly at Enterkin, but the solicitor shrugged. 'That question's already covered by Mr Calder's earlier remarks, so he may as well answer it.'

'No,' Keith said. 'I can't swear it from my memory. I just know that it can't be so.'

'It seems to me,' Munro began, looking at Mellish, 'that you have no option – '

'And it seems to me,' Mellish broke in, 'that it is not for you to tell me what options are open to me.'

'Gentlemen,' Enterkin said quickly into the crackling silence, 'if you'll bear with me for a few minutes I think I can clarify this aspect of the case.'

'Very well,' said Mellish.

'Thank you,' Enterkin said, beaming. 'You will recall that I asked Mr Calder what he said to his wife when they first saw the man at the vehicle, and he didn't remember. He might have been forgiven if he had uttered some expletive, or an expression of surprise, or even called upon his maker. But instead, with rare presence of mind, he said "Try to get a shot of him". So his wife assures me. In this context, of course, the word "shot" was used to mean a photograph.'

'And did she?' asked Gilchrist quickly.

'She photographed the whole series of events, and very good they are too. This, I must admit, surprised me. At the risk of being called a male chauvinist, which perhaps I am, I'll say that in my experience a woman's instinct in an emergency is to freeze – which instinct, in that half of the human race that is more likely to be "minding the baby", is probably the right one. But Mrs Calder explained this to me. She said that when she first took up wildlife photography she missed a number of unrepeatable shots because she was too interested in watching the event to pay attention to her photography. So she trained herself so that, whatever the fascination of the subject – be it a fight between robins, a mating of deer or a rabbit hypnotising a stoat (or possibly the other way around, for I know little of these matters) – she has learned to concentrate her mind on her camera. And this self-training took over, with the result that we have an excellent record of those few seconds.

'Very sensibly, after telephoning me on her husband's behalf, she took herself into Fort William, and by the time when, by arrangement, I picked her up there, she had persuaded a local photographer to develop and print her shots.'

In a dead silence, Enterkin produced a box bearing the label of a much-used photographic manufacturer, and opened it.

'While much credit goes to Mrs Calder for her discipline and photographic ability, it must be admitted that luck was with her. This first shot shows Mr Calder already running. You can see that his gun is still open, but he has dropped the duck which you can see on the track behind him. The man by the van is in the act of turning and he has something in his hands which could be a Sten gun. Was there a Sten found near the body?'

'Never mind asking questions,' Munro said.

'I think,' said Mellish, 'that Mr Enterkin is entitled to know the answer. Yes, a Sten was recovered.'

'It could have come out of Calder's van when it blew up,' Munro said.

'I never had a Sten,' said Keith.

'In any case,' Mellish said, 'the floor of the van was metal and remained more or less in one piece. The gun clearly arrived from outside.' He studied the photograph through a glass. 'Without prejudice, I'm prepared to accept for the moment that this is the same gun or similar.'

'This,' said Enterkin, 'is also the only photograph with any kind of a picture of the man's face, so here is a greater enlargement of that part of it. A poor but recognisable likeness, I think you'll find.' He passed the second print to Keith.

'That's him,' Keith said. 'The intermediary. The man with all the names.'

'May I?' Gilchrist stretched out and took the print.

'The third print, from the second negative,' said Enterkin, 'shows Mr Calder about ten yards nearer to the van. It has actually caught a muzzle-flash from the Sten, which is pointed almost in the direction of the camera. It's almost a miracle that Mrs Calder wasn't hit.' Keith drew in his breath at that. 'You'll see that Mr Calder still hasn't closed his own gun.' He passed the photograph across the desk.

'In the fourth print, from the third negative, the Sten has swung past Mr Calder, who is another ten yards forward, still running, and perhaps thirty to forty yards from the other man. The tear in Mr Calder's jacket is visible, so he had already been hit. And he has closed his gun and is aiming from the hip – indeed, the gun is somewhat blurred compared to the rest of the photograph, so I think we have caught the gun in the moment of recoiling. The last print shows the man falling backwards into the flames.'

Mellish lined up the four photographs on his desk. 'Mrs Calder is to be congratulated,' he said. 'It would be next to impossible to get a conviction for culpable homicide in the face of these.'

'With all due respect,' Munro said bitterly, 'you have to hold him. It may prove to be justifiable homicide at the end of the day. It's not a matter that the fiscal has power to settle or to recommend bail. A man's died in a shooting.'

Mellish looked at him coldly. 'You hold the egg this way, Granny,' he said softly.

Munro turned red, and his mouth twisted. Gilchrist chuckled. 'I'm afraid you asked for that,' he said. 'However,

Mr Calder's future is no direct concern of ours, so perhaps you could let us conduct our bit of business and get on our way?'

Mellish nodded.

'Thank you. Mr Calder, your future may not be my direct concern, as I said, but *if*,' and Gilchrist emphasised the word, 'you killed this man in the photograph then the world contains one wicked bastard less. We wanted him in connection with our investigations into a network of corruption that makes all other recent cases look like games in a pre-school playgroup. He was the contact man and the intimidator, and there's little doubt that he's killed on occasions. In fact, if we knew where to look, we could dig up at least five from under the Glasgow motorways. We owe you a favour.'

'Perhaps,' Enterkin said, 'Mr Calder might call on you in connection with his investigations into another matter?'

Gilchrist smiled. 'I don't see why not. I'm about to consult him about them.'

'Before you start,' Mellish said, 'perhaps I should say that one of the corpse's hands was under the body, and was relatively unburned. I sent the prints back to Inverness immediately, with instructions that they be compared with the few prints that we found in the car that Mr Calder wrecked during the incident at the quarry, and if the same they were to be put out on the wire, with a description of the man from Mr Calder's previous statement, to all other forces. Answers have been coming back all evening. He was wanted in London for extortion and perjury, in Leeds for corruption, interfering with witnesses and grievous bodily harm, in Birmingham and in Manchester for conspiring to pervert the course of justice, Bristol the same plus G.B.H., and so on and so forth.'

'Ah,' said Gilchrist. 'We thought as much.' For ten minutes, he questioned Keith. It was a masterly performance. At the end of that short time he knew everything that anyone had said to Keith about McLure and corruption, and every word that had been said by Paisley and by the late intermediary. When he had finished, he stood up. 'Come and see me as soon as you can,' he said, 'and we'll dot the i's and cross the t's. I don't think it'll be very long.' And he winked.

'One moment, Superintendent,' said Munro. 'I have a question. Who do you think he was working for, this intermediary? Somebody in back of McLure and his corruption in the building industry?'

'Or McLure's real murderer?' Enterkin put in.

'I've got his real murderer in custody,' said Munro.

'The hell you have,' Keith said.

'The truth is,' said Gilchrist, 'I don't know. I don't suppose we'll ever know all the truth. But from what we know of the man, either would be perfectly in character.'

'But you'll let me know,' Munro persisted, 'if you come across any kind of lead as to who he was working for?'

'I'll let you all know,' Gilchrist said firmly.

With the departure of the two plain-clothes men the room seemed larger and colder. Mellish got up and switched on an electric fire. 'The heating went off an hour ago,' he said. 'I think we could do with some coffee and sandwiches. Sergeant, could you fix it?'

'Before I get any more coffee,' Keith said, 'I need to pay a call.'

'I also,' said Enterkin.

The telephone rang. 'Second on the right,' Mellish said, picking up the instrument. 'He's in your custody, Enterkin.'

When the two men were alone in the echoing toilet and in process of making themselves comfortable, Keith said, 'Am I going up the river?'

'Not in the teeth of that evidence,' Enterkin said. 'It depends on how I do my stuff, plus a little bit of luck. The danger is that they may feel obliged to hold you in custody pending a trial for culpable homicide. I could argue that you're a businessman to whom time is money – which may not wash, since your business has just been wiped out – and that you're on your honeymoon, and that you're investigating for the defence in a murder enquiry, which is probably the best argument of the lot. I can threaten to sue for improper or malicious arrest, which isn't the kind of card I'd like to play. Or I can threaten to ask the High Court to sist your brother-in-law's trial – '

'Sist?' Keith asked. 'What's that?'

'Postpone,' said Mr Enterkin irritably. 'Delay. Defer. Postpone. Put off. Where the hell was I?'

'Threatening the High Court, I think.'

'To *ask* the High Court to sist the trial on the grounds that my investigator's being kept out of circulation, and ask for bail. Bail's unusual in a murder case, but it's not unknown. That might get Munro to change his tune, but might not have much influence with Mellish. In fact, I suspect that anything that annoys the hell out of Munro would seem like a good idea to Mellish at the moment. You just keep a smile on your face and your big mouth shut, while I walk like Agag for the next few minutes.'

'Right,' said Keith.

'Speak when spoken to,' said Enterkin, 'and that means when spoken to by me.'

They took their time, and when they rejoined the policemen coffee and meat sandwiches were already on the desk. Mellish had finished his phone call and was making notes.

Enterkin sugared his coffee thoughtfully, sipped it and made a face. 'I hadn't quite finished my analysis of the photographs,' he said.

'All right,' said Mellish. 'Let's finish that phase of the discussion.'

'I'm laying all our cards on the table,' Enterkin said, 'because my client's services are essential to the defence in the forthcoming murder trial. This in spite of the fact that I find in myself no little talent as a detective.'

'Now is your chance to show it,' said Mellish.

'Let's go back to the second-last print, from the third negative. You'll notice that it seems a bit spotty, unlike all the others.'

'Dust on the negative?' suggested Mellish.

'That would account for the white spots, but not for the dark ones. You'll notice, if you study the photograph carefully, that the spots are all elongated, which is an effect that occurs with rapidly-moving objects on a photograph, and they appear to be radiating out from two centres. The dark spots on the right of the picture, I suggest, are fragments of gorse flying from the top of the bush which Mr Calder

158

had just run past. You'll also notice that the topmost sprig of the bush which is visible in the previous two photographs has now disappeared, and I conclude that a bullet from the Sten has recently passed that way.

'The lighter spots mostly show in front of the dark figure of the other man. And at his feet can be seen a scar in the gravel track which, again, does not show on either of the preceding photographs but shows again on the last one.

'To look at me now you might well suppose that I was always fat and, let's say, middle-aged; but in my youth I served through the war as a private in the King's Own Scottish Borderers. Mr Calder, how often have you fired a shotgun from the hip?'

'Almost never.'

'You're attempting to do so in this shot. During my army career, if it can be called a career, I was taught to shoot a rifle. I was trained to shoot accurately standing or lying down, from the hip or from the shoulder, standing, walking or running forwards or backwards. And one thing which I remember is that most men shooting from the hip for the first time, especially when running, shoot low. If you look at the gun in the photograph, and the scar on the ground, and the marks in the air which I suggest are pebbles flying up from the gravel, I think that you will agree with me that that's what happened. And if you look at the last photograph, you'll see that the posture of the figure strongly suggests a person stepping back and tripping, rather than falling after being shot. I suggest that any court would conclude, as I do, that the man was spattered with flying gravel, stepped back possibly thinking erroneously that he had been peppered, caught his heel and fell into the flames.'

'But that would amount to the same thing,' Munro said. 'He fired and a man died.'

'It raises a number of interesting points,' Enterkin said, 'but I think that a judge would decide differently. He would hold that, in the circumstances proved by these photographs, it was not unreasonable for Mr Calder to fire back in the direction of the other man without hitting him, and that the spattering of gravel, the man stepping back and falling were not the foreseeable consequences for which my client would be liable.'

'But he meant to hit him,' said Munro.

'You don't know that. My client has already stated that he had no recollection of firing. Do you think that any court would hold that it had been proved, beyond reasonable doubt, that my client intended to shoot to kill? Unlikely. But if it did, it would also find the act justifiable.'

'And that's all your evidence?' Mellish asked.

'As far as I know, but it's possible that time will furnish a little more. Firstly, as soon as I saw the photographs – in Fort William – I realised the implications. And with a rapidity of foresight of which I had not believed myself capable, I returned to the scene. Your constable was still guarding the cooling debris, more to forfend against gypsies removing the remains of the firearms than anything else, I think. I persuaded the good man to dig up the scarred gravel into a fertiliser bag and seal it. It may or may not contain shot.'

'Probably not,' said Keith. 'It would ricochet all over the place.'

'Do me the favour,' said Enterkin, 'of repeating aloud the advice which I gave you when we visited the gentlemen's ablutions.'

Keith sighed. 'Speak when spoken to, and that meant spoken to by you.'

'Excellent advice,' said Mellish. 'Why don't you take it?'

'In other words,' Enterkin said, 'don't interrupt when the grown-ups are speaking. Now, whether or not that sample produces any shot is irrelevant. But I suggest that the acid test is whether the body produces any, and I venture to predict that it will not.'

'Prediction,' said Mellish, 'implies something that lies in the future, but I'm already able to answer that question. You're not the only one with foresight, Enterkin. When I saw the scene and heard the first reports, I could see the urgency of knowing whether there was shot in the body or not, so as soon as the on-the-spot work was finished I packed him off by ambulance to the forensic scientists in Glasgow. It'll take days for a p.m. result to come through, so I asked them to pass him under the X-ray camera on receipt, and let me know the result immediately. That was the phone call that I had just now.' He paused. 'No shot.'

Keith and Mr Enterkin breathed again, but Munro bristled. 'That doesn't mean a thing,' he said. 'The body was badly burned. If the skin and the subcutaneous fat were burned away, any pellets in that layer would have fallen to the ground. They could still be found.'

Mellish grunted. 'In view of the other evidence, it's my belief that a prosecution would not be successful anyway, so that the considerable expense in time and travelling would not be justified. Of course, the procurator fiscal may take a different view.'

'You'll put it to him, then?'

'I'll mention it, but not as a probability. I'll see the fiscal first thing in the morning – which isn't long away now. If he agrees with my view of the matter, he'll probably bring it before the sheriff immediately with a view to bail. But he may feel that even that's unnecessary and deal with it by a fiscal enquiry. Either way, we should be able to see Mr Calder on the road by noon.'

'How did you come up?' Keith asked Mr Enterkin. 'Hired car?'

'And driver.'

'Would you wait, and take us to Aberfeldy on the way back?'

'I don't see why not. You're paying for it.'

That shut Keith up again.

Munro was not pleased. He knew better than to protest further, but his bolt was not yet shot. 'I think we're entitled to see the other photographs on the same film,' he said. 'After all, we may have been shown a selection of shots because they support one view of the matter. . . .'

'Superintendent Mellish is entitled to see them,' Enterkin said. 'I doubt if you are.'

'Do you have the negatives with you?' Mellish asked.

'No, they're in the custody of the photographer who developed them. I had intended to have him introduce them as evidence, if necessary. But they are, of course, open to you for inspection.'

'Do you have a full set of prints there?' Munro asked.

'Yes.'

'Can we see them?'

'Why,' asked Enterkin, 'are you so determined to have my client out of circulation?'

'I don't like amateurs confusing witnesses and tampering with evidence.'

'I think,' Keith said, 'that it's because I told him that if he'd had a sister she'd've been ugly.' Enterkin looked at him. 'Sorry,' Keith added.

'Your comment may have arisen from a sincere belief,' said Enterkin, 'but this is not a propitious moment for uttering it.'

Mellish stretched and yawned. 'Why don't you just show us the photographs? Then we can try to get a few hours' sleep.'

'I'll do so, but under protest,' Enterkin said. His lips were compressed, but whether from anger or because he was suppressing a smile Keith could not guess.

Enterkin spread the remaining photographs on the desk. There were a number of shots of Keith, both candid and posed, an excellent portrait of a hovering kestrel with the sun behind it glowing through every feather, a hare in its form. The last enlargement was of Molly with the duck in her mouth.

There was a moment of appreciative silence.

'I bet I can get that on the cover of *Shooting World*,' Keith said.

'You could get it on the cover of *Penthouse*,' said Enterkin.

The sergeant was grinning. Superintendent Mellish tried to keep a straight face, but between the comedy in the photograph and Munro's indignant expression he broke down and laughed until tears danced in his eyes.

Munro got to his feet. 'I am obliged to you, Superintendent, for your patience,' he said formally. He paused beside Enterkin. 'I shall be wanting a word with your client, about a certain rifle,' he said.

'Any time,' said Enterkin, but Keith felt his bowels congeal.

Munro marched out, with dignity.

'If that concludes our immediate business,' Enterkin said, 'I think I should hurry down and reassure my client's wife. And perhaps someone would phone on my behalf and see whether there are hotel rooms to be had for the rest of the night, for the three of us.'

'Two. Mr Calder stays here.'

'Three. The driver must sleep too.'

'If I'm footing the bill,' said Keith, 'I'd prefer a cell.'

Mellish smiled. 'Tell the desk sergeant from me to try the Ganymede for you. They've had a late function on, so the staff should still be up. I'll bring Mr Calder down to see his wife in a minute.'

Enterkin thanked him, and bustled out.

'Well, Angus,' Keith said. How's that Dickson suiting you?'

'Grand,' Mellish said. 'Just grand. Throws a lovely pattern. I won a shield at the clay pigeons last weekend. But Keith, man, I only hope to God that Marie never learns what I paid you for it.'

CHAPTER 13

Superintendent Mellish was as good as his word and by noon the next day Keith was released on his own recognizances, and Enterkin's hired car set off for Aberfeldy with the solicitor sitting beside the driver and making a show of not looking round. The snow had stopped and the ploughs were working, but it was a slow journey.

With the driver sitting in front and grumbling eternally at being so far from home on such bad roads and without adequate sleep, discussion was impossible; but when they stopped for a meal at the holiday centre in Aviemore they found a corner table in a big dining-room. Those skiers who had already over-stretched themselves on the new snow were comparing damage in the other half of the room, the driver had isolated himself in a visible aura of disgruntlement, and the three had privacy at last.

'Who *was* he working for?' Molly asked. 'Johnny the Gingerbread Man, I mean.'

Keith yawned hugely. He was used to surviving on a ration of sleep that not even a soldier in battle would have tolerated, but he was near the end of his resources. 'The murderer,' he said shortly.

'Not necessarily,' said Enterkin. 'Not necessarily at all. The services of such a man would be expensive. That kind of money belongs more in the area of corruption. And you heard the list of offences that he was wanted for. His name would be known among those in the web of corruption that McLure span around himself. A lone murderer would be less likely to have the money or the contact available.'

'A reasonably well-heeled murderer might easily think the money well-spent,' Keith said, 'and there's no saying that he doesn't have a contact in those sort of circles. More to the point, I've hardly scratched the surface of the corruption scene.'

164

'Somebody might well have wished to make sure that you never did scratch it. You've asked enough questions.'

'But the only hints I've had to the corruption thing have come from discussion with individuals who couldn't be part of the network.'

'But people talk,' Enterkin said. 'And don't forget the secretary. Miss Thing.'

'Scobie,' Molly said.

'Miss Scobie. God alone knows what contacts she may still have. She told you very little, remember, and even that remains unsubstantiated. She may have tried a little blackmail on her own account.'

'You surely can't believe that he made his second visit on behalf of a different client from the first one.'

'True. Look at it another way. Some Mr Big in the world of sweeteners may prefer that Mr Fiddler takes the blame, because if he – Fiddler – is exonerated there may be another and fuller investigation into McLure's activities which might really set the cat among the pigeons.'

'Could it be,' Molly said slowly, 'that Inspector Munro was told to find another – what do they call it? – another patsy in a hurry?'

There was silence. The waiter was collecting soup plates and delivering the roast beef and Yorkshire pudding, but there would have been a silence anyway.

'I don't like it,' Keith said when the waiter had gone. 'It would explain his hostility to me and his absolute determination not to consider for a moment the possibility that anyone other than Ronnie might be guilty, but it's asking a little too much of coincidence. There's no reason that I can see why an inspector of police in a rural force should already be on the payroll of a city-based, building industry, bribery network. So that suggests that somebody approached the officer already in charge of a murder case, intending to offer him a bribe. That may not be as dangerous as approaching a bear and offering to scratch its tummy, but it must come a close second.'

'If there were enough money in it,' Enterkin said, 'and in this case there would be, it would be safe enough given proper precautions.'

'Like what?' said Molly with her mouth full.

'As, for instance, making preliminary contact by telephone after first checking up on how Munro was placed financially.'

Molly swallowed urgently. 'And how *is* he fixed for money?' she asked.

'Well, since he has three children and a wife recently stricken by polio, I think we may take it that he could use money.'

'The poor man!' Molly said, suddenly melted.

'Poor sod,' echoed Keith. 'How do we investigate that aspect?'

'We sleep on it.'

'That superintendent from Strathclyde said that we'd probably never know it all.'

'He was probably right,' said Enterkin. 'But I'll look into his life-style, and, if nothing more, we may at least dig up some material that counsel can use in cross-examination.'

Over the sweet course – a production-line *crème caramel* – Molly asked, 'But who did kill Mr McLure?'

'One of two,' Keith said. 'I'd like to make a case against the mannie Hook – '

'Because of what you were told up at Invergordon by – what was his name? Tough?'

'Hardy.'

'Same thing,' said Enterkin. 'Yes, the motive's all there. A chief executive or something with a local authority, possibilities of corruption with McLure over building contracts, worried to death before McLure's death and suddenly relieved after it.'

'But it won't work,' said Keith peevishly. 'I've been over and over it in my mind. Physically, he just could not have been there to do it, and I can't see any way that he could have helped in a conspiracy.'

'Who – ?' Molly began again.

'Payne or McNeill,' Keith said. 'It must be one of those two. They were walking each side of McLure. Then there was me, and I know I didn't do it, and Derek Weatherby didn't come past me. On the other side there was Hamish, but Janet saw him out in the field chasing a runner just before it happened, and anyway Andrew Payne would have had him in sight all the time. One of those two must have had cause to kill him. It could have been Payne, because of the arbitration thing.'

'I thought,' Molly said slowly, 'that arbitration was to do with strikes and things.'

'It can be,' said Enterkin. 'But if you think of it as being a law suit taking place outside the courts with the judge chosen by the parties or appointed by somebody chosen by them, with the full authority of the courts to enforce his judgement, then you'll see its significance.'

'But setting motive aside for the moment,' Keith said, 'either of those two would be capable of loading up a special cartridge.'

Enterkin snapped his fingers and pulled from his pocket a piece of paper half-covered by writing in pencil by an unformed hand. 'I brought along Fiddler's list of people who bought carcasses from the estate. I meant to give it to you the last time that we met, but you were somewhat preoccupied. Both Payne and McNeill figure on the list.'

'There you are. I've often found a relatively undamaged bullet when I've been cutting up a carcass, and it's the kind of thing that a man sometimes puts up on a shelf as a keepsake. And then when he wants a bullet that can't be traced back to him, it's there.

'Then,' Keith went on, 'he may have made overtures to get himself and McLure out on the same shoot –'

'Yes,' Molly broke in, 'and he may have tried it before, for other shoots.'

'Good girl. Of course, Sir Peter's was the first of the season except for grouse and partridges, which are more open-country scenes and not so suitable.'

'But he could have asked *before* about getting on another one *later*,' she persisted.

Keith thought for a moment. 'True, and worth following up if we get the chance. Anyway, he succeeded in getting on this particular shoot along with McLure. Of course, if it was Payne he's a syndicate member anyway, but Sir Peter thought that it was Hook who suggested McNeill.

'All three had dogs and were in good physical condition,

so they could be expected to be set to walk through the woods together. In fact, I think that each of them had walked alongside McLure once already before it happened. Either the opportunity didn't arise or, just possibly, whoever-it-was was waiting for the other one to be on his other side.'

'Why?' Enterkin asked.

'It's a long shot, but suppose either that they were accomplices or that the murderer knew that the other one had a motive and wanted to leave himself an "out".'

'Lay grounds for "reasonable doubt", you mean?' said Enterkin. 'You're right, it is a long shot. And presupposes a very long-sighted murderer.'

Molly had been sitting quiet, nibbling pensively on cheese straws. 'Were you thinking,' she asked suddenly, 'that that particular bullet might have been used to deliberately implicate Ronnie?'

'Not necessarily,' Keith said. 'Why?'

'Well, it couldn't have been. He couldn't have known that you were going to panic and hide the rifle in the first place that you came to.'

Keith choked on his coffee.

'Now you've got it all over your clothes,' Molly said reproachfully.

'What makes you say that?' Enterkin asked.

'Oh, I figured that out some time ago. The police made their minds up that Ronnie had the rifle, so they didn't think any more about it. But I knew Ronnie didn't have it. If he was doing anything illegal, he always told me so that I wouldn't put my foot in it without knowing. So who else would it have been but Keith? And I knew that he'd told you, Mr Enterkin, because why else would you be getting him to get another gunsmith to give the evidence? And if Keith had shot Mr McLure and left the gun in our wash-house to involve Ronnie he wouldn't have told you. So I just had to decide who I'd rather have in prison, my brother or my husband. That was easy,' she added.

The two men looked at each other with their mouths hanging open.

Arriving back at the farm near Aberfeldy, Keith slept for

168

twelve hours and Molly for ten. They spent the best part of a week with Elsie and her husband. At first, the telephone was in constant use as Keith tried to rebuild his shattered business. His insurance policies, by good luck and thanks to Elsie's tireless prodding, were ample and fully paid; and the company promised early settlement, by which, Keith was given to understand, was meant not more than a few months provided that no loophole was found. So it was equally fortunate that Keith's wallet, fat with his day-to-day working capital, had been in his pocket at the time of the disaster. His bank-balance, too, was less unhealthy than had on occasions been known.

Their joint attempts to find another retired mobile bank, or a similar large vehicle suitable for conversion, were entirely unsuccessful. Whether or not this was because Keith left most of the telephoning to Molly we shall never know. There are points beyond which even a bride is not to be trusted.

So when Sunday came around and they sat down to the traditional heavy farmhouse lunch, Keith talked of emigrating.

'Now, Keith,' Elsie said. 'You're just a bittie depressed.'

'You're probably right,' Keith said. 'The Scottish Sabbath always gets me down. Everything I enjoy doing is illegal on a Sunday.'

'Most of them's illegal the rest of the week,' said his brother-in-law.

'That's true.'

'What you want,' said Molly, 'is another dog.'

'And wait a year while I train a pup? Or pay a couple of hundred quid for a good trained dog?'

That night as they lay in bed, warm and comfortable, Molly returned to the subject. 'Do you really want to go abroad? We will, if you do.'

Keith sighed. 'You don't want to, you'd hate it. And tired as I am of this over-governed, tax-ridden, maternalistic country it's the place where I'm happy. We'll talk about it again when Ronnie's free – when that happens I may really want to get out of the country. Meantime I have a score to settle with someone.'

169

'He's dead,' Molly said sleepily.

'He was working for somebody else who sent him to burn us alive. Or blow us up. Did you hear the bang when those tins of Nobel Eighty went up?'

Molly was asleep.

But in the morning a new day dawned, and with it hope. The loss of Keith's van and contents had, for some reason, been missed by the daily papers but had featured in the Sundays. And the phone began to ring.

There were offers of all kinds. Offers of sympathy, of fresh work, of a job. An offer to forget about a gun which had been lost in the fire. Offers to lend transport, offers of equipment for a new van, offers of machinery and tools at bargain prices and offers of a bed for the night at any time. There was even the offer of an overdraft.

Keith was moved. 'I never knew I had so many friends,' he said.

Elsie knew his circle of acquaintances at least as well as he did. 'Some of them's friends,' she said. 'The rest are just plain relieved.'

'At my van getting burned?'

'Don't be daft,' said his sister. 'Those are the ones that have daughters or sisters.'

'Or aunts or cousins or grannies,' said Molly, who had few illusions about Keith. 'Now that you're no longer in general circulation, they don't mind knowing you again.'

'Yon bank mannie now,' Elsie persisted. 'He's got two daughters and he'll not want them served until after they're married.' Elsie and her husband had always taken an agricultural view of Keith's amours, treating them as they would the news of a bull that had got into the wrong field.

Keith said that he wished they wouldn't talk like that, but he tackled his problems with new heart.

Pending the replacement of the big van, some form of transport was obviously essential. Among the many offers had been one from a Tayside acquaintance and occasional client, whom Keith had cured of a master-eye problem and coached into the prize-winning class. Keith begged a lift into Dundee to inspect the large estate car that was on offer at a very modest price, and bought it on the spot. On impulse, he drove straight into the city centre and treated himself to a high-quality radio-cassette-player and installed it in the car with a little help from a garage. He also bought a large carton of blank cassettes. One part of his life at least could be rebuilt.

As soon as Keith was back at Aberfeldy and the car, its paintwork and the longevity of its M.O.T. certificate had been properly admired, Keith begged the use of his sister's music-centre and set Molly to transcribing his own modest collection of records onto the cassettes while he dealt with a number of messages. These included word from Joe Quaich that his preliminary report was ready and in general agreement with Keith's conclusions.

Before settling down to work on the claim forms, Keith read with interest a note which had come by the same post from his friend the geologist. Omitting the friendly insults with which it started and the ribald enquiries after Keith's married life with which it concluded, the body of the letter read:

The grit which you sent me contained small amounts of unidentifiable earths and clays, but most of it was red (burnt) shale left over from the deceased Scottish shale-oil industry. It therefore originated in the general area between Bathgate and the Calders. I could have placed it more accurately, except that the sulphate and other solubles have been washed out of the sample. This suggests that the material may have come from the surface of a bing, but you must remember that burnt shale is used for road bottoming etc, and also for temporary car-parks and the like. The sample also contained a tiny fragment of pitch.

'Not really a lot of help,' said Molly. 'There's all sorts of farm roads and things made up with shale.'

'I knew I'd seen whole hills of it,' Keith said absently. 'But pitch, now. Why does that remind me of something?'

A telephone call from Sir Peter Hay broke off what might have been a revealing discussion. 'How soon can you come and see me?' he asked.

171

'What about?'

'I'd rather tell you down here. I want to suggest something. Make it soon before the impulse leaves me.'

Keith did one of his instant appraisals. 'We'd have to be down there soon anyway. Ronnie's coming up before the sheriff for trying to knock my block off in the police station.'

'Don't wait that long. I think I should speak to you before you commit yourself to something else.'

'All right,' Keith said. 'We'll be down tomorrow, but it may be late afternoon before we arrive. Could we ask you to get someone to go down to Molly's cottage and light fires? There's coal and sticks and everything there.'

'No need for that. Come and spend a night or two with me, the pair of you. My wife's away on a pre-Christmas shopping safari,' he added as an extra inducement.

'I think we'd both like that,' Keith said. 'Thank you. One other thing. You were going to find out who mentioned whose name in connection with your guest list for that shoot that McLure died on.'

'I'll get on with that, and let you know when I see you.'

They disconnected, and Keith phoned Mrs McLure.

For the rest of the day, Molly patiently transcribed records while Keith loaded the estate car. For no better reason than that he was accustomed to have his tools and his stock with him and that the back of the car was an empty shell, Keith loaded the spare guns and tools, together with such clothes as they could muster between them.

They left early on the following day and made good time on the long run south. After the Forth Bridge, Keith turned to enter Edinburgh.

'I want to make a short visit,' he said. 'Do you want a few minutes – a very few minutes – at the shops?'

Molly considered. 'No, I'll get what I want in Newton Lauder tomorrow.'

'You're not very smart for visiting the Hall.'

'Lady H. won't be there, and Sir Peter won't notice. Anyway, there's not a mark on this dress. I can't think why Elsie gave it to me.'

'I can. Elsie's a red-head. That colour would look all

right on a blonde, which you're not. Elsie's stouter than you are, and it was too loose on her. And she's twenty years older than you are.'

'It'll do for tonight. I'll wait in the car.'

Keith parked outside McLure's house and walked up to the door. By daylight, the perfection of the garden was even more obtrusive. He was shown into the immaculate front room where the chilly widow was browsing through the week's supply of glossy magazines. She gestured with a copy of *Scottish Field*. 'Is this your article on dog training?' she asked.

Keith said that it was.

'You write well. Not enough to make me want to work on this bastard, but well.'

'She's still the same, is she?'

'Never looks up. Except, oddly enough, when I shut my cigarette case. I don't think she approves of women smoking. Old-fashioned bitch.' She poked the springer spaniel with her toe.

Keith had the clue that he wanted. 'And I can have her?'

'Take her away with my blessing. I was going to have her put down anyway.'

Keith excused himself for a moment and went out to the estate car. He opened the back. Molly was playing a cassette. 'Stravinsky?' Keith said, surprised. 'Where did you get that?'

'Among your records.'

'I didn't mean you to copy that stuff.'

'You didn't say so.'

'No harm done. Shan't be long,' he added. 'I only came out to get a gun.'

'If it's to shoot that blonde I could see you talking to in the front room, go ahead.'

Back in the house, Keith watched through the crack of the door as he closed the gun with a snap. Instantly, the springer bitch was on her feet, eyes alight and undocked tail sweeping like a broom. As Keith came round the door she ran to him, stood up against his knee and barked.

'Well, I'll be damned,' said the widow.

'For a hundred generations she was bred to do certain

work. Your husband represented the leader of the pack, but when he died she also lost the chance to go out and do the only things in which she felt truly fulfilled . . .'

Mrs McLure looked at him through half-closed eyes. Keith thought that she was weighing the enhanced value of the dog against the risk of his spreading the story that she had welshed on a deal. In the end, she sighed. 'I said you could have her and you can have her,' she said.

'Right. One last thing. Who knew that your husband intended to emigrate?'

'Almost nobody,' she said promptly. 'It was supposed to be a deathly secret, but when he first mentioned it he didn't say so. Then, the same day, while he was out, somebody phoned and wanted me to write something into his diary for some weeks ahead and I said that he might have left the country for keeps by then. I was just hanging up the phone when my husband walked in at the door. That's when he said on no account to let anybody else know.'

'Who was the caller?' Keith stooped and fondled the anxious bitch.

She frowned. 'I think it was one of the people you asked about last time you were here. Yes, I remember. It wasn't the one with the nose and not much else – the chinless wonder. Another one.'

'Payne?'

'I think so. I've no memory for names at all. Won't you have a drink before you run along?'

'Better not,' Keith said. 'My wife's waiting for me in the car.'

Mrs McLure did not ask him to invite Molly to join them, but coldly showed him out. Tanya stuck close to his heel, except for a short detour around Mrs McLure.

While Molly and Tanya exchanged courtesies, Keith set off for Newton Lauder in a hurry. He wanted to consolidate the springer's return to activity. They bowled up to the Hall as the sun was getting low, and Keith managed to compress his explanations and excuses to his host into little more than a dozen words before they set off, accompanied by the intrigued Sir Peter, for the woods below the Hall.

174

Pigeon were determined to come in to roost in the dusk, but in the very difficult conditions Keith only got four for nine shots, well below his normal performance. Tanya, whose behaviour had been exemplary, looked at him doubtfully but decided to accept him. Sir Peter, whose own dogs were unruly and hard-mouthed, was filled with envy and admiration. Molly, who loved Tanya for herself, was also pleased to point out that liver-and-white photographs much better than plain black.

It was a contented party that sat down to a dinner which, though modest by Mr Enterkin's standards, Molly found impressive. It was served in a gloomy cavern of a dining-room amid heavy, dark oak furniture and a number of draughts. The only redeeming feature in the room was a large oil-painting hung over the fireplace. It was a glowing portrait of a plain woman with a very kindly face.

'My mother,' Sir Peter said in explanation. 'She died shortly after that was painted, so that's just how I remember her. I think that's the only thing I'd rush to save if this damn place did catch fire. I should be so lucky,' he added with a sigh.

'Oh, but Sir Peter,' Molly said, 'it's a fine house. So grand!'

'Too damn grand,' Sir Peter retorted kindly. 'It was built when it was considered more important to be grand. with the aid of twenty or more servants, than to be comfortable. Even speaking about it depresses me. Let's talk about something else.'

'We could talk about why you wanted us down here,' Keith suggested.

'Be patient a little longer; there's something I want to show you in the morning. In the meantime, I can answer your questions about my guest list. Who did you want to know about?'

Keith gathered his thoughts together. 'Andrew Payne was there as a member of the syndicate you said?'

'That's right.'

'And David McNeill?'

'Was suggested by Bill Hook.'

'And Hook himself?'

Sir Peter referred to the back of an envelope on which was drawn what appeared to be a family tree rife with illegitimacy. 'He was suggested by Andrew Payne.'

'And McLure?'

'Hook again.'

'There's food for thought,' Keith said.

CHAPTER 14

They slept that night in a huge, cold room and in a damp four-poster with musty hangings. Molly said that she began to see what Sir Peter meant.

After breakfast Molly and Sir Peter were obliged to kick their heels while Keith held a brief training session on the lawn, but at last they piled into Sir Peter's car and drove the mile down the hill to park in the square.

Sir Peter sat looking out through the windscreen at some children playing on the Town Hall steps. 'The reason I wanted you down here,' he said at last, 'is that I have a proposition to put to you, and I wanted you to consider it on the spot and not harden your attitudes in the abstract, as it were. A tenant of mine died recently, and the business was sold up. You've lost your van and all its equipment. You've just got married. Maybe this is the time to settle down. So come and see what I have to offer.'

They followed him meekly along the square.

The shop, Georgian in style with a bow-window, looked charming even in the cold light of mid-winter. It still bore, in elegant gold script on the black sign-board, the name of the defunct jeweller and silversmith.

'Sorry to sound like an estate agent,' Sir Peter went on, 'but you'll notice that the position's good and there's parking nearby. There's a flat upstairs and a bit of garden at the back. Because it was a jeweller's, it's got all the grilles and things. There's a small strong-room, and the back shop where they did the watch-repairs would probably do for your workshop.' Sir Peter paused and coughed. 'I took the liberty of having a quiet word with the chief constable. I knew him when neither of us had a seat to our breeks. About licences or permits or whatever you gun-chaps need. He said he'd rather have you in one place where he can keep an eye on you.

'Now, I don't want to stampede you. Anyway, I've got to go and look at a leaky roof. I'll leave you to look around, and pick you up again in about an hour.' A bell over the door jingled as he made his exit.

Tanya preceded them, tail waving. 'Anyway, Tanya likes it,' said Molly.

The shop, Keith admitted, was good. The cupboards and showcases had been left in place, and would display sporting gear as effectively as they had done watches and challenge-cups. The workshop was serviceable and had a three-phase electrical supply. To Keith's satisfaction, there was a basement.

'Is that important?' Molly asked.

'Testing guns,' Keith said shortly.

The flat was large enough and well windowed, but dingy. Molly said, 'We could redecorate it ourselves.'

'We?'

'I'll paper if you paint.'

'H'm,' Keith said.

The garden, though small, was larger than might have been expected and held some good rose-bushes and an apple tree which, Keith said, was due for pruning. The slope was to the south and open to the sun, and Molly pointed out the best place where a hutch of ferrets might be stood.

On Sir Peter's return they adjourned by tacit agreement to the inn on the other side of the square and settled them-selves, with a round of modest drinks which Sir Peter insisted, as host, on buying, in a bay window from which, by only a slight craning of the neck, the shopfront could be seen. Tanya, who would not now be denied from accom-panying Keith wherever he went, had been in such places before, for she settled herself immediately in the one place from which an intelligent dog soon learns that it will be bribed away with potato crisps, the base-line in front of the dart-board.

'Well,' Keith said at last, 'I know Molly's keen. She hasn't said so, but she's quivering like a pup waiting to be sent for the dummy.'

'But what about yourself?' Molly asked anxiously.

178

'Before you decide,' said Sir Peter, 'let me say a little more. If you want to have a go, I'll give you a starting shove. You can have three months rent-free – it'd probably take that long to find a new tenant anyway – and nine months at half-rent. And if you need some kind of security for a bank-loan, I'll see what can be arranged.'

'That's very handsome, Sir Peter,' Keith said slowly. 'But why should you bother?'

Sir Peter laughed. 'Partly because I like you both, but also to suit myself. I'd like to have you, or somebody like you, here. At the moment, if I want a trout fly or a pair of waders, I have to go ten miles. For a box of the commonest cartridges, fifteen. If I want some tuition, or if a guest turns up wanting anything other than twelve-bore ammunition, or needing his gun repaired, it's into Edinburgh. And there are several other estates and a number of shoots all in the same position. God alone knows how many farmers do most of their shopping here. You're between two prime fishing rivers. And there's both a clay pigeon club and a major rough-shooting club locally. So I'm not alone in thinking that it's high time that we had a shop and a gun-smith around here. I'm damned sure there's the trade to support it.'

'A lot of my business is in boys' guns. I've been the only specialist in that. It means personal fitting, and it's scattered all over the country.'

'No boy needs his gun refitted more than once a year,' Sir Peter said firmly. 'A single tour in the summer would be quite enough. And most of your customers would be quite happy to give the pair of you a bed for the night. But if you're not prepared to settle and put down roots, just say so.'

'I've done it before and I can do it again,' Keith said. 'Shall we discuss details?'

'Like rent and repairs? Discuss them with Enterkin. He attends to all that sort of thing. Let's consider it provisionally settled.'

Molly dabbed quickly at her eyes, and then leaned across and kissed both men on the nearest cheek. 'God bless my soul,' said Sir Peter.

The barman came over with a second drink for Keith, and when he looked round a stranger in a grey suit raised his glass in salute.

'I don't know him, do I?' he asked Molly.

She looked round. 'It's Mr Murchy,' she said, and gave a little wave.

'The Bobby who was supposed to be guarding you?'

'And got knocked on the head.'

'I'd like a word with him. Will you both excuse me a minute?'

'I've got to meet the builder in a few minutes,' Sir Peter said. 'I'll see you back at the Hall.'

'And I want to visit Ronnie,' Molly said, 'and then go to the cottage and light fires and see what clothes I have left. And probably go shopping for something that doesn't make me look like an elderly bag dressed in cast-offs.'

'You look charming,' Sir Peter said.

Keith hesitated. 'I'd like to be with you when you choose new clothes.'

'You'd have me turned out like a tart.'

Keith snorted with laughter. 'All right. How much do you need?'

'Um. . . . Fifty?' she asked tentatively.

Keith looked at Sir Peter, who raised his eyebrows and said, 'Rock-bottom minimum in my experience.'

Keith sighed and took out his wallet.

'And can I have the key of the shop?' Molly asked. 'I'd like to measure for curtains. You just stay here.'

'I'll probably get plastered.'

'You've earned it,' Molly said.

'Probably do you good,' said Sir Peter, 'but don't be late back for lunch.'

Keith carried his pint over to Constable Murchy and raised it in salute. 'How's the head?' he asked.

The constable smiled. He was a quiet, nondescript man. Promotion had passed him by without in any way spoiling his calm enjoyment of life. 'Solid as ever,' he said, 'and by God you gave him better than I got. I never saw anybody take such a thumping. If we'd caught him he could have had you charged, except that I'd have sworn he did it himself tripping over a loose shoelace. Mind, I do owe him for a week's sick leave.'

'I hope you used it well.'

'I got the garden dug, which it was sorely needing.'

'It's an ill wind,' said Keith.

'Very true,' said Murchy. He looked around the empty bar, and lowered his voice. 'That fellow that knocked me out . . . Is it true that you killed him?'

While his mind rapidly explored the possible permutations of the situation, Keith asked, 'You wouldn't be asking on behalf of Inspector Munro, would you?'

Murchy looked hurt. 'I'm off duty, and I'm asking on behalf of Constable Murchy. That beggar did me a lot of no good. Put on to guard a wee girl and got myself clobbered by the very man I was there to guard her against. Made me a laughing-stock. Hard to live down, a thing like that.'

So Keith recounted the incident, taking care to say nothing that was not already known to Inspector Munro. Murchy listened intently. When the tale was done he blew out his cheeks. 'You live an adventurous life, don't you?' he said wistfully.

'Not when I can help it, but this business with my brother-in-law seems to have pushed me into it. You'll have the other half?'

'Just the one, then – I'm on duty later.' As the second pint went down, Murchy's manner continued to warm. The discretion of his training prevented him from congratulating Keith openly, but there was no doubt that he had come to regard the younger man as a favourite nephew.

Keith wondered how far he dared press his luck. 'I saw two dogs having a fight this morning,' he said. 'Lots of noise, but they didn't hurt each other.'

'Funny how often they don't. You do a bit of training, don't you?'

'A bit. Of course, sometimes you get a real fight, especially with dogs like terriers that are bred for fighting, but usually if one dog's prepared to back down it comes to nothing. It's as if there's a sort of ritual, just like there used to be for duelling in the old days, so that honour's satisfied but nobody gets hurt. Grouse are the same. Very territorial birds, and if one of them doesn't back down the blood and feathers can fly; but if one of them knows he's boss, then it's just a ritual to protect the boundaries.'

'Aye. I've noticed the same with robins in the garden,' Murchy said. 'Funny. I just got a Christmas card this morning with two robins sitting on a branch, and I said to the wife, "If you ever see two robins that close there'll be murder done". But, as you say, unless they're both determined it stops at ritual.'

'You'll be giving evidence against my brother-in-law, when he comes up for that scrap we had when you pulled us apart?'

'I suppose so.'

Keith looked him in the eye. 'If Ronnie's counsel asks you whether you could swear, on your oath, that Ronnie's attack on me wasn't just ritual, with no real harm meant, what will you say?'

Murchy frowned, and considered the matter for the duration of a long pull at his pint. 'I don't know that I could swear to that, I suppose. Except that I could see your face, and you didn't think it was just ritual.'

'What I thought isn't in your evidence,' Keith said. 'And you shouldn't have been looking at my face.'

'It's important?'

'They've charged Ronnie with everything up to attempted murder. The worse he's convicted for, the worse it'll look when the other matter comes to trial.'

'Aye, that's right.' Murchy looked around again, but the bar was empty except for an old man doing his pools in the far corner and the barman listening to the radio. 'I never thought of it before,' he said, 'but you're right, there's two sorts of fights. Either they're really trying to down each other, or they've got to make a display of aggression but they're both being careful not to hurt in case it gets out of hand and turns into the other sort. Mind you, Munro won't love me if I say that.'

'Does he love you now?'

Murchy raised an eyebrow. 'Not a lot, no,' he said. 'And I couldn't swear, on my oath, that I loved him a hell of a lot either. But I'll have to think about it.'

'You do,' said Keith. 'Entirely between you and me, off the record and behind closed doors, what's Munro really like?'

Murchy pondered again. 'A stickler,' he said at last. 'He's neither the friendliest man to deal with nor the cleverest, but there's nothing about him that you could put your finger on and say that it made him a bad officer, except that he's maybe a bit slow to change his mind once he's made it up.'

'And there's never been a hint that he's been on the take?'

Murchy's expression of surprise was utterly convincing. 'Not him,' he said. 'No way! There's always some word goes around. And he's the one man to get hot under the collar if there's the least suspicion that there's been the least kind of a gift taken. For instance, if he thought, just for the sake of the example, that I'd accepted a couple of brace of pheasants from someone – '

'I was just going to say that I had a couple of brace in the car if you'd like them,' Keith said quickly.

'That's very kind of you. Shall I come out?'

'I'll drop them in to you,' said Keith, who hadn't poached them yet.

Once Keith had made up his mind to a course of action, it was in his nature to move with a speed which others might consider precipitate. Moreover, if he had taken to himself an extravagant wife then the sooner he was back in business the better. As soon as lunch was over, he hurried down to see Mr Enterkin.

Details such as the rent and rates, responsibilities for maintenance and custody of the resident cat were soon settled, if not wholly to the satisfaction of both; but, as Mr Enterkin pointed out, Keith would still have haggled in the face of a thief's bargain with cash discount and green stamps, and Keith said that Enterkin, on Sir Peter's behalf, was fit to pluck a pheasant in frosty weather and sell the feathers back to it. This exchange of insults past, they shook hands on the deal.

'How are you getting on in the matter of your brother-in-law?'

'I've been set back a bit, no doubt about it,' Keith said, 'but I'll make it up.'

'Not long now.'

'No. But, I'll tell you something, I'm learning a lot about McLure. Did you know that I've got his dog?'

'To replace Hebe? No, I didn't.'

'Amazing what a dog can tell you about its master. In McLure's case, it's his inconsistency. The bitch is having to learn that I always mean exactly the order I give, no more and no less. Dogs appreciate that, but McLure didn't. And he was sentimental about his dog, possibly ashamed of that affection, but I think the dog was the only creature he felt at ease with. She likes to come up into my lap, and as long as she's not muddy I don't mind. But as soon as someone else comes into the room she'll jump down.'

They spent some minutes in discussing the tactics to be used at Ronnie Fiddler's trial for assault, and the implications of Keith's talk with Constable Murchy. On the whole, Enterkin was optimistic.

Just before they parted, Enterkin asked, 'And how do you find married life?'

'Fine, just fine.'

'I seem to detect a certain lack of enthusiasm. Is the shoe rubbing? You can tell me, if only that I can be warned if I should ever be rash enough to contemplate matrimony on my own account.'

'It's only a little thing.'

'My boy,' said Enterkin severely, 'don't try to tempt me into indulging in rude and schoolboyish humour. I shall resist the bait. What's the problem?'

'At first, we seemed to have everything in common.'

'How ominous that sounds!'

'Even our tastes in music. After the van burned, I got Molly to copy my records onto cassettes for me. Do you have any records?'

'All of Mozart and some Haydn. But get on with the sad story.'

'I'll borrow them off you some time, if I may. Anyway, Molly found and copied some odd stuff of Stravinsky and Bartók.'

'Oh dear!'

'Worse follows. Last night after dinner she found that Lady H. has quite a collection of records, and there's some good audio equipment up at the Hall. She settled down to do some taping while Sir Peter and I talked about guns and things. And she came across a whole lot of avente-garde –' there was a pause while Keith sought for the *mot juste* '– camel droppings by Schönberg and Stockhausen and Thea Musgrave and similar nut cases. Believe it or not, she *liked* them!'

'My poor boy,' said Enterkin, 'what have I done to you?'

The next few days were among the busiest that Keith had ever known. On top of making arrangements for collecting the various tools and appliances and stock that had been offered to him and preparing to open the shop for business and getting the flat ready for occupation and talking to Ronnie Fiddler's lawyers, he was still trying to pursue his investigations. Between times, while fighting to put more and more hours into the operating day, he asked questions and revisited the scene and sat and pondered and asked more questions, without ever feeling that he was approaching any closer to the truth.

In the midst of this activity, most of a day was lost when Ronnie faced the various charges arising from his assault on Keith. The time lost would have been longer but that the weather entered a period of bitter frost, with which the sheriff court's outdated heating system was quite unable to cope, the result being that all concerned seemed anxious to get the business over as expeditiously as possible.

Ronnie's advocate, who looked astonishingly young even for junior counsel, had been well briefed. By good luck Murchy was the first of the two constables called to give evidence, and after a penetrating cross-examination and a great show of resistance he allowed himself to admit that the attack might have been no more than a display of ritual aggression with no intent to cause harm. The second officer stuck doggedly to the facts and refused to speculate as to the thoughts in Ronnie's mind at the time.

It was left to Keith to conclude the evidence for the

prosecution, and he stated positively that the attack had been a parody of a real fight, and that he had hardly felt the hands laid on him.

The procurator fiscal let the point go. 'What,' he asked, 'was the reason for the attack.'

'There wasn't what you'd call a real reason,' Keith said.

'What, then, provoked the attack?'

'It was all very foolish. Perhaps the court may care to know that I married the accused's sister a few days after the incident –'

There was muted laughter in the court and the sheriff leaned forward. 'I trust that you are not referring to your marriage as foolish?'

'No, my Lord,' Keith said quickly. 'I'm sorry. I don't always have the knack of saying just what I mean.'

The sheriff was an elderly man with a lively sense of humour. Keith had overhauled his Browning for him, and had coached him more than once. 'I think you owe it to us to be more careful,' he said. 'Both to the court and to Mrs Calder.'

'I'll try, my Lord. I was going to say that I was tired and upset, and so was the accused. We were both irritable, and I let myself be provoked by something that he said into making a quite unpardonable remark that he may well have taken as being a reflection on his sister. I may even have given him grounds for believing that I had no intention of marrying at all. I have since apologised for what I said, and I consider that I got off lightly. If anyone had spoken to me like that about my sister – '

'I think that you had better stop at that point, Mr Calder,' said the sheriff.

Questions finished and arguments began. As the sun left the windows of the court and the temperature dropped, the procurator fiscal, and after him Ronnie's counsel, shortened their arguments and accelerated their modes of speech. The sheriff, in summing up and giving judgement, was almost gabbling. He found Ronnie Fiddler guilty of only the most minor of the charges and decided that, in view of all the circumstances, an admonition would be sufficient.

Ronnie Fiddler rose to be taken below. He had brooded

silently throughout the proceedings. The defence had not called on him to testify, despite the inference that might be drawn from this omission, just in case his hasty temper might lead to his downfall; and Keith, when testifying that the attack on him had been as gentle as a baby's play, had been sure that Ronnie was going to leap in with an indignant denial. But as he left the court Ronnie winked at his brother-in-law. It was a tiny gesture, but a big step forward.

Just when Keith was becoming despondent about making further progress with his investigations and was beginning to have bad dreams of the whole truth about the rifle being dragged out in open court, it was time for another expedition.

Keith had a long-standing engagement to speak to an audience of naturalists, wildlife conservationists and shooting men in the Edinburgh area, and overnight hospitality had been offered by one of the organisers who lived almost opposite the hotel which was to house the event. A fresh letter extended the invitation to include Molly, who was more than ready for a break from endless decorating, so the pair set off, with the inescapable Tanya. Defiantly, Keith adhered to Mozart the whole way, while Molly exuded an air of maternal superiority.

The evening was a success from the start. Since he was to sleep within walking distance Keith could abandon his usual caution and indulge his enjoyment of a few good drams. Thus seasoned, he spoke with more than his usual wit, fluency and point. His subject – *Field Sports and Ecology* – was a pet study of his, and his views, which were moderate and balanced, had matured out of years of observation, reading and much pondering during his long hours at the wheel.

He was well received, and was able to answer nearly all the questions put to him; and those that he could not were answered by others, with Molly chipping in twice from the back of the hall. The different groups ceased or at least suspended disagreement, and mutual respect was cemented by a wildlife quiz between two picked teams.

At the end of the quiz, honours were even between the

naturalists and the shooting men, and the chairman asked for a tie-breaker from the audience.

The thin man with glasses stood up at the bar end of the room. He was swaying slightly from side to side, and his voice had the rounded fruitiness that can sometimes be heard when the speaker is about one third of the way to falling on his face. His question, however, was clear. 'The period of quarantine for most mammals is six months,' he said. 'There is an exception. For one mammal the period is life. Tell me which one. The prize is not getting a dose of rabies.'

Keith's hand shot up and the chairman nodded. 'The vampire bat,' Keith said, 'because of its very high status as a spreader of rabies.'

'Correct,' said the thin man. 'Give the gentleman an inoculation. And may I conclude by reminding you that rabies is an incurable disease and a ghastly death. It must not get loose in this country. Thank you very much.' He folded in the middle and sat down.

The meeting closed a few minutes later. Keith managed to obtain drinks from the crowded bar, where an air of bonhomie and pre-Christmas festivity was evident, and took them to the table where Molly was sitting. From under the table, Tanya's tail protruded, flicking from side to side whenever Keith or Molly spoke.

They were soon joined by the thin man with the hydrophobia phobia. He was bearing another round of drinks and the light flashed from his glasses. Keith was later to be wakened at night by the realisation of how nearly he had snubbed and sent packing the one man present who could tell him much of what he wanted to know ...

'Enjoyed your talk,' the thin man said, sitting down uninvited in his odd folding-up way. 'Jolly good evening all round. Always valuable to let them see that shooting men are usually naturalists and conservationists too. An' I was glad of the chance to get that question in. I'm the contact man on rabies between the M.A.F.F. and the clubs, and I like to remind people of the dangers as often as I can. The holiday season will be back with us all too soon, and a lot of bloody fools will be smuggling pets into the country,

188

closing their stupid minds to the fact that dear little Bonzo may be importing one of the world's foulest diseases.'

'You're preaching to the converted,' Keith said.

The thin man stared at him glassily. 'Happens all the time, though. You can't keep people motivated. Makes me sick.'

'Me too. We'll just have to keep the fox population at a low level.'

The thin man went straight on without seeming to hear. His speech was passing from the fruity stage to the slurred. 'They forget. Take my boss, now. Back in the summer, I had him almost prepared to carry a banner. Was going to speak to the tourist board and hold meetings and things. Suddenly dropped the subject. Like I said, they forget.'

'Don't they just?' said Molly. She pointed at Keith. 'He forgets all the time. At least, he forgets me. Don't you, Lover?'

'All the time, Fat Bum,' Keith said. He pulled her glass out of reach. 'I think you've had enough.'

'Who is your boss?' Molly asked the thin man. 'Is he here?'

'No. Couldn't come. 'S Andrew Payne. Think you know him,' he said to Keith. 'He was on that shoot when whatsit got killed. McLure. I'm a legal eagle by training, but I'm his office manager. Payne's, not McLure's,' he added in explanation.

Keith tried to do a quick-think, but the ramifications were too complex for his fuddled mind. To give himself time he excused himself and fetched another round and some sandwiches. He made the stranger's drink a double.

When he came back, Molly gave him a meaning look. 'Just fancy,' she said. 'Tom Sinclair, here, knows almost all the men who were on that shoot.'

Sinclair made an airy gesture that almost knocked the tray out of Keith's hands. 'Partly the rabies job,' he said, 'and I used to work for a game farm. But I knew McLure and McNeill from Mr Payne's business. We had an arbitration going.'

'That,' Keith said carefully, 'would be David McNeill with his Lothian Floorings hat on?'

'Tha's right. He has a lot of interests, but Lothian Floorings is far the biggest. McNeil was on the other side and McLure was to hear it. It was a blow when he was killed, 'cause we were on the way to winning.'

Keith laughed. It sounded strained to his own ears. 'If both parties didn't think that, there wouldn't be any arbitrations or court cases at all.'

'No doubt about that. But we'd had a premilinary –' Sinclair stopped and shook his head ' – prelim'nary meeting an' a short hearing on a question of time-bar, an' each time McLure made a great show of being fair but you could tell from his questions that he favoured our arguments. He was going to award our way, all right.'

'How nice for Mr Payne,' said Molly. She had repossessed the drink which Keith had moved away from her and poured it into the new one, and she was keeping her glass out of Keith's reach. 'What a pity that it didn't work out that way,' she said carefully.

'Abbleslutely true,' said Sinclair, pronouncing each syllable with the precision required by his condition. 'I'm glad I've no money in the firm. If he loses, I reckon he's wiped out. But he was chirpy as a crippet from late summer right up to – oh – about a week before McLure was killed. Then he started to get worried again. I can tell. Looks worried all the time, but that's just his face. I can tell when it's real. He was worried all right, though I'd've known if there'd've been any new moves.'

Keith's mind was still in low gear. To gain time, he asked, 'Was it worry over the arbitration that made him lose interest in the rabies thing?'

Sinclair tried to focus his eyes, but abandoned the effort. Instead, he scratched his head, and brightened a little when he found that there was at least one task that he could accomplish successfully. 'Dunno,' he said. 'I heard that someone he knew had smuggled a dog in on a yacht. I told the boss. What I expected was that he'd at least have a word and warn him that if he didn't put the dog into quarantine he'd blow the gaff. Marrafac', I thought he'd hit the ceiling. But he just sat quiet for a minute, an' then gave half a laugh an' told me to forget it.'

For a second there was an island of silence in the babble of the bar.

'That wouldn't by any chance have been Mr McLure would it?' Molly asked.

'Marrafac' it was.' Sinclair let one of his hands dangle. Tanya licked it and he patted her head.

Keith swallowed a lump out of his throat. 'Did Payne ever hear that McLure was going to emigrate for keeps?' he asked.

'Not that I know of,' said Sinclair. He looked up at the ceiling for a moment. 'He did ask me once, said it was just a hyposethis, what the legal position would be if the arbiter resigned or died or emigrated. I tol' him that if the arbiter died you just got a new one, he couldn't resign, but if he went abroad the whole thing'd probably go into the deep-freeze.'

'Would that matter to Mr Payne?' Molly asked.

'God, yes. We're still owed thousands an' thousands for a flooring job that went all to pot.'

'When was that?' asked Keith.

'When was what?'

'When was it that he asked those questions?'

'Oh. Late in September, I think.'

'About a week before McLure died?'

Sinclair nodded.

'About the same time that Payne started to act worried again?'

There was no answer.

'If you think it over in the morn's sober light,' Keith said, 'I think you'll see the wisdom of not telling anyone about our little chat. For a legal eagle, you haven't been very discreet.'

Sinclair frowned and tried to focus. 'What've I said that isn't public knowledge?' he asked truculently.

Keith hesitated, but only for a second. It was important, he thought, to prevent Sinclair confessing his garrulity to Andrew Payne. 'You shouldn't have said anything about the faking of that letter,' he said. From his own experience,

Keith guessed that Sinclair would be far from certain that he had not, in fact, said anything of the sort.

When they left Sinclair was sitting, staring at nothing across the room. Something was upsetting him, but it might only have been his stomach. He seemed not to notice the springer bitch that shadowed them out of the room.

CHAPTER 15

They waited in the hall of the hotel for their host to finish a beery argument with a couple of friends.

'By golly,' Keith said. 'Now I know it's nearly Christmas. That wasn't just a legal drunk, it was Santa Claus.'

'What about poor Tanya, though?'

'Her six months must be about up, but I'll find a vet I can trust and get his advice. Meantime, don't let her lick you; and if she behaves oddly get the hell out of range quickly.' Keith snapped his fingers. '*That* must have been what Joe was talking about when he said he didn't want to make trouble for a widow.'

'The rest of it . . . is it good or bad? I mean, don't we now have two main suspects instead of one?'

It was dark before they reached Newton Lauder the following evening, and the municipal Christmas tree sparkled brightly in the centre of the square. There was still a light in Enterkin's office, so Keith went up.

'Come in and sit down,' Enterkin said. 'Fiddler's getting impatient. I'm surprised it didn't happen before, but some people can sit still and some can't. He says he doesn't give a tinker's something-I-won't-repeat about Christmas, but if he misses Hogmanay he'll have your guts for galluses. His words. He added "Just as long as that's understood", so he probably meant it.'

'Knowing him, he probably did. But I am making some progress.'

'You'd better,' Enterkin said grimly. 'I think I should tell you, at the risk of spoiling your Christmas, that counsel are expressing doubts about getting him off with what you've got so far – or, at least, they're not so confident as to be prepared to miss out on any bits of evidence. Unless something more conclusive turns up, we'll have to bring out the whole history of the rifle. Which, at best, might mean your new shop being confined to selling fishing tackle and football boots and, at worst, your wife running it for you. But let's hope it doesn't come to that.'

'Yes, lets,' said Keith. His voice sounded hollow.

'And Fiddler also says you didn't get *him* a dog.'

'Tell him all right I'll get him a bloody dog too.'

'Don't get excited. You came to report progress?'

Keith breathed deeply for a few seconds. 'Some,' he said at last. 'Molly thinks it's a step in the wrong direction, but I'm not so sure. It may be the right line.' He recounted the revelations of the night before. 'So now we have strong motives for the men on both sides of him.

'McNeill was one party to the arbitration McLure was hearing, and was still waiting for a lot of the money that should have come to him for the original job on the factory. He was also liable for a lot of damages, as I gather, for the making good and for loss of profits and so on. The other party was Payne, whose business had suffered a bundle when the floor went wrong.

'Now, let's look at things in chronological order. Payne was worried. My informant, who was drunk out of his mind or he wouldn't have been so forthcoming, reckons that if Payne loses in the arbitration he's bust. Then he's told that McLure smuggled a dog into the country. The penalties for that are severe, and they include the destruction of the animal. McLure could have paid quite a bit for a trained dog, and it seems to have been the only creature that he had a real fondness for. And the courts are getting tough about evasion of quarantine. Payne could've been expected to hit the ceiling, but instead he says to forget it, and he becomes what my informant called "chirpy as a crippet". I think he meant cricket, but never mind.'

'Blackmail, you think?'

'Well, what do you think? Suddenly McLure's dealing with the arbitration in a way that makes it clear that he's going to come down in favour of A. Payne & Co. And then Payne learns that his tame arbiter has a firm intention of going abroad before dealing with the matter, and also learns that that's the one thing that could hang the whole

194

thing up for years. His attitude to that would depend on the balance between his need to get his damages for the dud job and a possible wish to postpone the risk of getting soaked for the work plus the cost of the arbitration. And, of course, he would have to weigh the chances of winning or losing with a different arbiter who might not lay himself so open to having his arm twisted. But at that point we learn that he started worrying again, so we must presume that he can't afford to delay any longer the chance of getting his hands on the money he thinks is due him.'

'A cash-flow problem,' said Enterkin. 'That can happen to the best of businessmen, although they don't all kill for it.'

'But they could?'

'Oh yes, they could.'

'And only a week or so later, down goes McLure.'

'He'd have to be very short of working cash, not to prefer a delay.'

'Maybe he was. Perhaps you could find out – I wouldn't know how. But let's look at it from McNeill's viewpoint. He feels badly let down, he's laying out a hell of a lot of money, and suddenly the arbiter is letting it be seen that he prefers the arguments put by the other side. As far as we can tell, he doesn't know that McLure's going abroad; but I don't think that it matters. He might be just as perturbed over the whole thing going into limbo as he would be by a hostile arbiter.'

Enterkin protruded his lips, as if for a monstrous kiss, while he thought. 'It would be nice to hypothesise a conspiracy between the two of them,' he said, 'but it would never work. Between them, they've lost so much money over the defective floor that one of them has to go to the wall. And I don't envisage either of them accepting that role.'

'Better to live in hope than to accept the not inevitable?'

'Yes. And what now?'

'More research. We came back by way of Lanark today. Joe Quaich gave us the names of the two farms that McNeill rents the shooting of, and we went to take a look at them. Usual sort of thing, a bit of moor above, some woods with a few wild pheasants, a pond that looked as if it might be good for duck-flighting – it had some hides beside it. The lower arable land was all overlooked by farm-houses, cottages, a railway and a couple of roads, which made it pretty unlikely that he'd have done any testing down there. So we went up to the moor. The farmer'd only go up there once in a blue moon, so McNeill'd only have to say "I'm going to see if I can knock off a few foxes" and nobody'd think anything of hearing shots from the moor except to bless the man who was killing foxes and reducing losses at lambing time.

'It was as cold as chastity up there, and just as uninteresting. Not a bad moor, but the heather needs regular burning if he's going to make the most of the grouse.'

'Never mind the shooting prospects,' Enterkin said.

'Sorry. Habit of thinking. It's mostly pretty flat and featureless, which isn't what you'd choose for the purpose, but there were a couple of very suitable gullies. And I couldn't find a damn thing.'

'Would you have found it, if it had been there?'

'Probably,' Keith said, after a pause.

'So what do you do next?'

'Sir Peter's invited McNeill to the Boxing Day shoot, and Payne'll almost certainly be there as a syndicate member. I want to chat to both of them. I haven't been able to get a line on any close friend of either of them, so the next step might be to break into their houses and do a search.'

'Have you gone off your chump?' Enterkin demanded, his voice risen to a protesting squeak. He cleared his throat. 'If you get yourself caught, I won't act for you.'

'Yes you will and you know it. And don't forget that I've got about a sixty-forty chance of getting jugged anyway if I can't prove something against one of them in about the next three weeks.'

The ensuing weekend immediately preceded Christmas. Everyone who might have 'assisted Keith in his enquiries' seemed to have gone to the moon, with the annoying exception of the two suspects. Each of whom answered the telephone to a wrong-number call from Keith.

196

On the Saturday evening, Keith drove across country to Berwick-upon-Tweed, to visit a vet with whom he had, in younger days, hunted geese and girls around the northern estuaries. The vet listened to Tanya's history, examined her thoroughly and dispelled Keith's fears. 'After all,' he said, 'if she'd been in quarantine she'd have come out of it several weeks ago. So there's no point making a song and dance about it now. You didn't need me to tell you that.' The rest of their conversation, while still biological, was not related to veterinary practice.

Thereafter, Mr and Mrs Calder spent their time in a final assault on the flat. The Monday, which doubled as Christmas Eve, was first marked by Elsie's husband, driving a borrowed lorry and bringing the remainder of Keith's possessions from the farm, some of the promised bargains in stock and equipment, and a number of items of surplus furniture on permanent loan. That evening they moved into their new home.

'After all,' Molly said, 'Ronnie might get out at any time, and he won't want us under his feet.'

'I wouldn't want me to be under his feet either,' said Keith. Privately, he thought that there was more than a chance that when Ronnie came out Keith would replace him.

Despite a number of improvements waiting for another day, their living-room at least was cheerful with its new paper and a blazing fire. Somehow Molly had found time to obtain a token Christmas tree and to put up some decorations. The radio played carols. They left it on.

'I thought,' Keith said, 'that it was the bride that was supposed to have something old, something new . . .'

Molly laughed and took his hand. 'The old's the furniture, and the new's the carpets and curtains.'

'The borrowed is most of it.'

'And,' said Molly, 'the blue is what you said when Tanya got under your feet while you were carrying your record-player.' The spaniel looked up from the special place she had adopted under the coffee table and before the fire, and thumped her tail.

For years past, Keith had been alone at Christmas. Companionship brought a new meaning to the festival. 'Would you like to go to the midnight carol service?' he asked.

So they went to the service. Keith prayed for the soul of Johnny the Intermediary, and then for his own. He wondered if it would be irreverent to put in a word for Hebe.

Boxing Day was always the last and best major event on the syndicate shoot, all that followed being a cocks-only day for the workers on farm and estate. It was therefore treated as a social as much as a sporting occasion. This year the weather remained frosty, which was a relief to some of the less eager walkers, but the sun and the dryness of the air made for comfort.

By the time the whole party foregathered at the Hall in the late dusk for what Lady Hay erroneously believed to be sporting fare, satisfaction was general. Birds had flown high and fast. The bag was satisfactory, but there were enough hen pheasants left on the ground for the nesting season to come. Sir Peter had pulled off several magnificent (for him) right-and-lefts with the refitted Holland and Holland, and was demanding a pack of Keith's new business cards in order to distribute them throughout his vast circle of acquaintances. Keith himself had missed disgracefully on several occasions and nobody had noticed. It had been a splendid day out.

For this one day, every available farm-worker plus the guns' wives, relations and friends had been conscripted for beating and other duties. Molly was present as a picker-up and as official photographer. Even the gloomy interior of and big dining-room seemed cheerful as a background to the babble of cheerful voices, and the presence of nearly thirty bodies brought the temperature up to a tolerable level for much of its area.

All day, fate had thwarted any attempt by Keith to isolate either Payne or McNeill for a casual-seeming chat. He had waited until both had entered the Hall in order to search both their cars, without any useful result, and had asked Molly to slip out and search the coat of either of them if Keith should at last manage to get him alone. But a friend among the beaters had monopolised Keith while the buffet was eaten, picking his brains endlessly on the subject of portable hides, and it was only as the guests began to circulate with their drinks that he found himself free to seek out his men.

As soon as he approached McNeill, however, the tall man rounded on him and backed him into a corner.

Keith had described McNeill as 'the tall man with the face like a parrot', and seeing again the thin face with the big nose and bright colouring he felt that the description was apt; but he had forgotten the harshness of McNeill's voice, the closeness of the eyes under the shaggy eyebrows and the air of angry superiority.

McNeill was certainly angry. The harsh voice that had been authoritative was now hectoring. 'What the hell were you up to on my shoot on Friday?' he demanded.

'Calm down,' Keith said. 'I just took a walk with my wife.'

'Walking be buggered. I know you for a bloody poacher. And do you know what I think of poaching? Armed robbery, neither more nor less.'

'You may be right,' Keith said, 'but I wasn't carrying.'

'What d'you mean, carrying?'

'I wasn't carrying a gun.'

'Well, what were you carrying then? Sulphur?'

Keith laughed at that. 'What the hell would I be doing with sulphur on a moor?' he asked.

McNeill's colour heightened further. 'Jam jars, then. Or raisins and whisky? Or the makings for dunces' caps? I know all about you poachers, so don't try to kid on with me.'

'Right,' Keith thought, 'for that I'm going to clean you right out before next season.' But aloud he said, 'I wasn't poaching at all. We just walked.'

'Stay off my bit of shooting, or there'll be trouble.'

'Look,' Keith said reasonably, 'we did no damage and caused no trouble. There's no law of trespass in Scotland, you know.'

McNeill's voice had been rising, and it had a penetrating quality. Keith was sure that it was audible across the room over all the hubbub. Sure enough, Sir Peter appeared beside them, and McNeill bit off his last remark and fell back a pace in deference to his host.

'Come now,' said Sir Peter. 'Can't have a lot of squabbles going on, to spoil a good day out. You'll oblige me by keeping your voice down. What's the trouble?'

'Mr McNeill is telling me that I mustn't take my wife for a walk on the farms where he rents the shooting.'

'I think the bastard was poaching me rotten,' said McNeill.

'I just went for a walk, using my eyes.'

Sir Peter caught on. 'Mr Calder is handling a matter for me,' said Sir Peter. 'Was it that, Keith?' Keith nodded. 'He's enquiring into the death of McLure on behalf of myself and Ronnie Fiddler.'

'Who you know,' Keith added, 'from buying deer carcasses off him.'

If the allusion meant anything to McNeill, he was too poker-faced to show it. 'I know Fiddler, but I don't see – '

'I'm looking for the place where the murderer tested out his method before he used it, and the traces he must have left there, and also for anyone who gets angry about it.'

He watched McNeill's face as he spoke, but it showed only exasperation. 'Are you, for God's sake, accusing me of killing McLure, despite the fact that Fiddler's awaiting trial for it?'

'I'm not accusing anybody yet,' Keith said. 'I'm looking around, which the law allows me to do.'

'You'll have to be quick,' said McNeill contemptuously, and then his patience broke again. 'Blast your bloody impertinence, sniffing around trying to stir – '

'That's enough!' Sir Peter spoke quietly, but McNeill stopped dead. 'While you're my guest you'll please behave yourself. And, incidentally, criticism of Mr Calder's behaviour is criticising mine. If you can't contain your temper, you'd better leave.'

McNeill pulled himself together. 'You're quite right, Sir Peter, and I beg your pardon. You just stay away from me,' he added to Keith, and to Sir Peter again, 'Thank you for your hospitality. I hope I see you again.'

'It seems unlikely,' said Sir Peter.

McNeill took two paces towards the door, hesitated and then strode out.

A dozen conversations suddenly restarted.

'I wonder,' said Sir Peter, 'why he said you'd have to be quick.'

'Probably because the trial's coming so close. I'm more interested in why he didn't ask me what I was looking for and whether I'd found it. I must try and have a chat with Payne. I'll try not to set off any more explosions.'

Sir Peter smiled wryly. 'You wouldn't succeed if you tried. He doesn't enter quarrels easily, although I suspect a hard and resolute core somewhere. But, God, I hope it isn't Andrew that you're after. I wouldn't call him a close friend, but I know him well enough to have golfed and shot and fished with him a number of times.'

Keith placed himself close to Payne in the crowd, so that at the next shuffle of conversation-partners they were bound to find themselves chatting together. Soon they were exchanging pleasantries about the day, the shoot, the company and the hospitality.

Payne was, as Keith had described him to Inspector Munro, tallish, bald and well-dressed. His height was less than McNeill's, but Keith still found himself looking up. Apart from his clothes, which were perfection in tweed, his most notable features were a high, domed forehead which, because of his baldness, seemed to continue forever, giving him a look of inhuman super-intelligence, and his perpetually worried expression. Yet his voice, which was slightly hoarse, and his face both suggested a certain shyness and his conversation seemed modest and unassuming considering his status in the business world.

'I believe you're a member of the syndicate?' Keith said.

Payne smiled shyly. 'For the moment,' he said. 'But I'm thinking of giving it up next season. Pressure of business, you know, both timeous and financial. I don't get out often enough to justify what is, after all, a fairly expensive hobby. I can get by with a little coastal wildfowling and busting some clay pigeons on Sundays. And I can probably count on occasional invitations.'

'I expect you can,' said Keith. 'Let's hope that better times come round again.'

'I'll drink to that! There's plenty of business about, but money's in short supply, so other firms put off settling their accounts for as long as possible. But you're in business for yourself, too. Don't you find that people are slow to settle?'

Keith, who dealt almost entirely in cash, made an evasive answer and Payne turned the conversation towards the wild-fowling scene. They were still discussing the prospects for geese on the Tay when a hard-looking woman came up, captured Payne's attention and bore him off.

Keith thought that, behind a placid and shy front and a face that looked worried in repose like that of a blood-hound, Payne showed tiny signs of genuine stress; but whether these stemmed from his cash-flow problems or from knowledge of Sinclair's indiscretions Keith had no idea. But of one thing he was sure. If, as Enterkin suspected, Payne had faked a letter as evidence in the arbitration, Sinclair would have said nothing. But if he had not, then Sinclair would have spoken and Payne would certainly not have been so friendly.

CHAPTER 16

Keith and Molly returned home with the tired contentment that follows a good day in the open. Keith kindled a fire while Molly fetched beer. They sat down each side of the fire, in chintz-covered wing-chairs that belonged in Aberfeldy. The radio played Grieg.

'Did you get anything in their coats?' Keith asked.

Molly nodded. She rooted in her bag and produced two cartridges. 'The Grand Prix was from Payne's pocket and the Impax from McNeill's.'

'Good.' Keith examined the bases carefully. 'So McNeill's was a reload and Payne's not. Yet we knew that Payne bought loading materials.'

'Maybe he only loads one size and buys the rest.'

'That's right,' Keith said. 'He said something about clay pigeons. You use far more cartridges at that than you do in most ordinary shooting, and it's a damned nuisance keeping two different sizes of shot. Anything else?'

'They both had a whole lot of spent cartridges in the poachers' pockets.'

'That again suggests that they both reload, but it may just be good behaviour. Keep Britain Tidy.'

'There was one other thing. Among the spent cartridges in Mr Payne's pocket was this one.' Molly passed it over. 'It's been closed up again.'

'It was McNeill who complained to Hamish about one barrel misfiring,' Keith said thoughtfully. 'But whoever shot McLure must have been functioning on one barrel until he got his chance. He could have closed up a case and had it handy so that he could show it to someone and complain of misfiring, but he'd be a bloody fool to leave it in his pocket. Anyway, it doesn't mean a lot. Closing up the crimp on an empty cartridge is just the kind of thing that a nervous man like Payne might do while talking to somebody.'

'So we're no further on?'

'Not a lot. We'll have to get moving tomorrow. We'll start with Joe Quaich.'

Fortunately Molly did not ask what the programme would be after Portobello. It was Keith's intention to inspect the outsides of the houses of both his suspects, with a view to nocturnal entry whether the houses were empty or not. And it was also his intention to postpone explaining this to Molly until the very last moment.

Molly, however, had another worry on her mind. 'Keith, after all the business with Johnny the Gingerbread Man, whatever his name was, weren't you nervous about going shooting with those men? After all, one of them sent Johnny after you before, and all the questions you're asking must still be getting back to him. Weren't you afraid that he might be thinking of another kind of shooting accident?'

Keith felt his innards turn over. He had never given a moment's thought to such a possibility. 'I decided that he wouldn't do that,' he said glibly. 'Another shooting accident in the same place and much the same company'd be too much of a coincidence.'

'I hope you're right. You will be careful?'

'I'll be careful.'

Hot-water-bottles were needed before the estate car could be opened in the morning. The temperature had dropped fur-
engine warmed they were soon on the road, and they were
using hot keys, aerosols and a variety of other expedients on their recalcitrant doors. Once the car was open and the engine warmed, they were soon on the road, and they were in Portobello by mid-morning.

The gun-shop was busy, the day being a holiday for many, but Joe Quaich took them down into the basement where he had his workshop and a small testing range. Molly was persuaded into the one comfortable chair, while the two men perched against the bench.

Men who work with guns and trade in them tend to become practised witnesses, and Joe's precognition, drafted in his clear, small handwriting, was a model of all that a precognition should be – a concise statement of the facts, expressing all the answers that would be made to the questions that counsel would ask. Keith suggested one or two minor amplifications, which Joe inserted carefully between the lines.

'That's fine,' Keith said. 'I'll take it with me and get Enterkin's office to type it up.'

'And I'll be called when?'

'About three weeks.'

'That sounds all right. Is that all?'

'One other thing, Joe. Where did you do your testing?'

'In the garden.'

'Your neighbours didn't object?'

'They never do, as long as I choose a reasonable time. Why?'

Keith picked up a dismantled target-pistol from the bench and looked through the barrel towards the light. 'Joe, imagine that you're a private citizen and you're going to kill somebody in the way we've been discussing. You have to get it right first time, because if you pull the trigger and he isn't killed you're over the ears in trouble, right?'

'Right.'

'So you've got to do some testing. You wouldn't just wander out onto the foreshore or into a field?'

Joe Quaich snorted with amusement. 'No way! You'd have to have a private place where you could take enough shots to see what size of group you were getting and whether you had a dangerous percentage of duds. And just in case somebody – some nosy-parker like you – rumbled the method, you wouldn't want there to be any chance of being connected later with the sound of a lot of shots that you couldn't explain. And you certainly wouldn't do it at home, just in case you left traces.'

'Where would you go, then?'

Joe scratched his head. 'I'd probably go to a clay pigeon ground. Most of them get used for coaching or practice at odd times, so that the sound of shots wouldn't bring any curious spectators or suspicious farmers or gamekeepers.'

'Now there's a thought,' Keith said. 'But which one?'

'Depends on how far he'd be prepared to travel.'

'I don't think he'd go too far afield. But there are very few within, say, fifty miles around Edinburgh; and those are overlooked from roads and houses. Not very closely, but you never know who may have a pair of binoculars on you. Where do you do your coaching, Joe?'

'I used to have the use of an old quarry, but somebody built a house beside it and I had to stop. For the last couple of years I've been going to the ground by Polbeth.'

'I haven't been to that one. What's it like?'

'Quite good. The local club have put up a tower for high birds, made out of the bottom half of an electric pylon, and built some trap-houses. They're going to have to move, though. In fact, I believe the members are coming in on Sunday to take away the tower and the barrels and stuff that they set up there. You see, it's an old shale-bing. It was worked for years, but then a railway spur was run into another bing and it was cheaper to take the stuff away for road-making from there. But now the other bing's run out, and they're re-opening this one.' He sighed. 'I'll have to find somewhere else again.'

'You'll have to be quick,' said Molly.

'That's right,' Joe said. 'I believe they'd've had the machines in by now but for the frost.'

'Red shale,' Keith said suddenly. 'And there's pitch in clay pigeons. Once he had a private place, he might well use it for secret meetings as well. And it would explain why McNeill said I'd have to be quick,' he added.

'That's what I just *said*.'

They threaded around Edinburgh and left it by way of Juniper Green, where Keith left the main road for long enough to park for a few minutes outside Payne's house. They saw a modestly luxurious modern home of red pantiles and cedar and stone.

'Too many neighbours,' Keith said. 'He'd never dare to do his testing here.'

'Do you think we might ever have a house like that?' Molly asked.

'Give me five years.' The words were unhappily apt, in view of Keith's thoughts. The front door had panels, but their removal would probably be noisy. The windows looked solid and well-made, which suggested sound ironmongery. but the glass seemed to have been fixed with beads from the outside. Keith could see no sign of a kennel in the garden, and since Payne's dog was fat and spoiled he supposed that it lived in the house and had the run of it at night. Then he thought that the house was unlikely to contain a workshop, but there was a large shed in the garden, too large and too good to be for the garden tools. Keith had a little bet with himself that Payne did his reloading there. It was very visible from the road.

'Why are we sitting here?' Molly asked.

'Just weighing up the man and his financial position. There's a lot of money showing there. I wonder how much is at the back of it.'

'Not a lot, from what that man Sinclair said.'

They drove out, westward. After a few miles the Enigma Variations coming over the radio finished. The announcer's voice promised a piece by Stockhausen. Molly leaned forward and switched off the radio.

'I thought you liked that sort of thing,' Keith said.

'I thought I did too,' Molly said in a small voice. She took out a cassette and put it into the player but without pressing it home. 'Or I thought I would. And I read an article that said that enjoyment wasn't the point. I wanted to improve my mind. Don't laugh.'

'I'm not.'

'But I got talking to Sir Peter at the buffet yesterday. He was awfully sweet. He said that music was for enjoying and if you didn't then there *wasn't* any point. And he said my mind didn't need any improvement. He said I had a lovely mind. Do you think my mind needs improvement? Don't answer that. And I said that Lady Hay listened to that sort of music, and he laughed that laugh of his, the one that sounds like a horse that's just dropped its rider in the pond, and said that any music that she liked was played on the lute, spinet and virginals, whatever they are. He said that she only keeps that other stuff around to impress what he called the longhairs that she likes to cultivate.'

She pressed in the cassette, and sat back fondling Tanya's head. A Rossini overture spilled out.

Keith was saved from the need to reply. He had been watching the hill above the road, and now saw what he took to be McNeill's house. He parked where a hedge gave them some concealment, and got out binoculars from the glove compartment. 'In the country, but still too near his neighbours,' he said. The house was old-fashioned, with sash-and-case windows that a knife would open in a matter of seconds. The dog had an outdoor kennel and run. It was not, Keith knew, a noisy dog.

They drove on again. Keith put his arm around Molly. but took it away again when a police car appeared in the mirror. He wondered what he could do to repay Sir Peter for his unwarrantable and probably unconscious interference. Dear, feudal Molly would never have accepted such retrograde advice from anyone else, but in her eyes the folk up at the Hall could never be wrong.

Guided by Molly from Joe's written notes, Keith found his way to a shale access-road and parked at the end. The sloping wall of red shale, doted with weeds, rose up before them. Steps had been cut up the face, reinforced with timber, and well trodden.

Tanya came out of the car with them. 'Shall we take her?'

'Bring her along,' Keith said. 'She'll howl the place down if we don't.' He put two fur-covered dummies into his game-bag, after a moment's thought added a handful of clay pigeons and a hand-thrower and took his gun out of its sleeve.

'What d'you want that thing for?'

'This is the one occasion when I'd look odd without one. Anybody who sees us will think I'm giving you some coaching.'

'Or the other way around.'

Seeing the gun, Tanya danced ahead of them up the steps. As they climbed, the trap-house on top of the tower emerged, looking like a guard-tower in a prison-camp film.

At the top, Keith turned and looked back over a field and then roof-tops. 'From those houses you could see the car, but not somebody up here if he kept away from the edge, he said.

'If you find the traces you're looking for, are you any better off?'

'At least if we know where he did his experimenting we can try to connect somebody with the place. Someone in those houses might have noticed the car. Or empty cartridge-cases; firing-pin marks are as distinctive as fingerprints. Well, almost.'

The top of the bing seemed to stretch forever in each direction. It was generally flat, but stepped and contoured as the machines had left it. The tower stood near the middle of the most level area, and round it a number of trap-houses had been built, like miniature bunkers half sunk in the ground, roofed with concrete slabs. Oil-drums and wooden barrels full of shale were dotted around throwing long shadows in the bright sunlight.

'Why barrels?' Molly asked.

'Presumably for hooking ropes onto for controlling spectators and other competitors. They've had some major events here.'

'I mean why wooden barrels, not just oil-drums? Barrels are expensive aren't they?'

Keith kicked an oil-drum. Half the side fell out, spilling shale. 'That's why. Shale's pretty corrosive stuff.'

'I just wanted to know.'

Keith was looking around. 'I can't think why I haven't been here before. It's a good layout. They can give almost every combination of sporting birds.'

'Well, good for them! Where do we start?'

Keith gave her hair a friendly tug. 'That's what I've been trying to work out while you've been yapping away. If I was testing up here, I'd go down to one of the lower levels and shoot towards the face of the next level up. That way I could both see what size of a group I was making and I could make a pretty good guess whether I'd got enough velocity from the recoil and by the way the shale flew when the slugs hit the bank.'

'If he did it up here, against the back of one of the trap-houses, we're sunk.' Molly pointed to the litter of wads and broken clays that spattered the ground around the tower.

'I don't think he would. The bullets would leave more traces here than the wads would anywhere else.'

'He only had to pick up some used wads here and you'd never have got off the ground.'

'Fortunately he wasn't that clever. What scares me is that the wad he used with the bullet that killed McLure may have been the *only* new one that he used. Let's go down to the lowest level and work back up. We're looking for plastic wads that don't have the imprint of shot in them, and scraps of bog-paper, newspaper, anything that he might have tried out as wadding. If we find anything like that near the bottom of an embankment, we'll go further out and look for cartridge-cases, in the hope that he was really careless.'

They went down to the bottom level and began to follow each embankment. Fortunately the shale had been removed in deep bites leaving high banks and few of them; otherwise the task would have been endless.

It was a cold and tedious business, but Keith relieved the monotony by decreeing a few minutes' break each half-hour, for dog-training and photography or a little clay-pigeon practice. Then it was back to pacing slowly along, six feet apart and scanning the bare shale. Tanya, puzzled but ever-willing, worked a zig-zag path ahead of them, searching for she knew not what.

By noon the top of the tower was again in sight. Half an hour later, when most of its height was poking up over the last step in the shale, Molly said suddenly, 'I think there's someone in the high trap-house.'

'Don't look again,' Keith said urgently. 'Carry on searching, but if you see anything don't pick it up. Did you let him know you'd seen him?'

'I'm sure I didn't. I just straightened my back because I was getting a crick, and I thought I saw somebody duck down out of sight. You know how you see movement out of the corner of your eye. I never turned my head at all.'

'Good girl! Keep it that way.'

They paced along slowly for a few minutes, eyes on the ground.

'Keith, I'm scared.'

Keith, who was not feeling very courageous himself, tried to laugh. 'If he had a rifle with him and was going to knock us off, he'd have done it by now. Anyway, he's got no call to do anything unless he sees us finding something. Hey, cheer up! I'm the man, I'll do the worrying.'

Molly laughed shakily. 'Somehow that isn't an awful lot of comfort just now. What are we going to do?'

'Keep him treed up there. We'll take another break in a minute. You go down towards the car. Then run and find a phone. Get the local police if you must, but it'd be better if you can get Munro or one of his boys to come. Whoever it is, tell him that it's important he arrives in civvies or he'll probably get us all killed, and he'll need some support. Got it?'

'I've got it.'

'You need an excuse, and I need my lunch. Bring the sandwiches back with you, if you've got the guts to come back.'

'I have,' said Molly shortly. 'Be careful.'

'I'm a devout coward. I don't want you to lose me.'

'He won't shoot me when I start to walk away?'

'He'd be nuts if he did.'

Molly looked at Keith. Her face was calm but very white. 'You don't think he is nuts?'

'He's been pretty logical so far.'

Molly nodded and trotted off. Any wobble in her knees might have been blamed on the uneven surface. Keith, careful not to face the tower directly, passed a few minutes in training exercises with Tanya. He went through the whole repertoire of training, with dummies and shots and whistles and hand-signals in what he hoped was a convincing illustration of an unworried man indulging in his hobby, but he felt that it would not have convinced himself. Like Molly he felt his knees loose and a knot in his stomach, and the unnatural red landscape, from being a familiar industrial by-product, seemed extra-terrestrial and hostile. Keith shivered. Tanya put her whole enthusiasm into the exercises, but Keith was less enthusiastic. Soon he resumed his slow pacing along the embankment, dreading that he might come across some clue too obvious to pass by.

He had finished the length of the last embankment by the time that Molly returned carrying their lunch. 'I had to go miles to get water for Tanya,' she called. She was smiling quite naturally, and Keith's heart went to her in admiration.

They sat down together on the roof-slab of a trap-house about sixty yards from the tower and ate their sandwiches. The ceremony of eating was less festive than usual. 'Eat slowly,' Keith said. 'We don't want him to start wondering why we're still hanging around.'

'I'm wondering that,' Molly said lightly.

'Keep your voice down. If you're scared, sit down on the ground with your back to the trap-house.'

She shook her head. 'No, if you're going to get shot I don't want to be left behind.'

'You just can't stand the idea of me getting something you can't have,' Keith said gloomily. He usually liked egg-and-tomato sandwiches, but these seemed to have no taste although Molly was tackling them avidly. 'I believe you're enjoying this,' he said.

Molly smiled the smile that always made his heart lift. 'I believe I am. I think this is our day. Nothing exciting ever happened to me before, except the day the van got burned and that was awful. But here we are and it's all going our way for the first time. The man who did it's up in that tower thing – at least I suppose he is and not some tramp taking shelter. And I think we're going to prove our case and get Ronnie out and live happily ever after.'

'And the annoying thing about that is that if you're wrong I won't be able to say "I told you so". There's whisky in the flask if you want some Dutch courage. Is Munro or somebody coming?'

Molly took out the flask. 'I don't need the courage, but it's awful cold up here. I phoned Newton Lauder, and there was a long pause, and then they told me that Chief Inspector Munro was in Edinburgh for a meeting and they got him on the radio and gave him my message just as he was getting back into his car, so he should be here shortly. Do you want some?' She shook the flask.

'I'm driving.'

'If you're so lucky. How did he – whoever he is – come to be up in the tower?'

'That's easy. At the Hall yesterday, McNeill lost his rag with me, about going onto his shoot. I had to give some explanation. I was talking to McNeill, but the room was quiet. I think everybody must have heard me saying that I was going round looking for the place that the murderer had tried out his method. Stupid of me saying it, I should have kept my trap shut and let McNeill shout his head off, but there it is. So if either of them didn't already know that that's what we're looking for, they do now. He might just have come over to make sure that he hadn't left any evidence, but I don't think so. I think he wanted to watch and see whether we found anything. He could easily have found out when we set off, or slipped a fiver to somebody in one of those houses to phone him if our car turned up.'

'There's no other car parked near ours.'

'He could have walked up from the other side while we were down at the low level.'

They sat in silence for a while, looking at the view and feeling eyes on their spines.

Molly finished her sandwiches and took a pull from Keith's flask. 'If he's watching from the tower,' she said, 'it must be because the place can be seen from there. Isn't it bloody maddening. If we knew where it was we could go away and come back later for the evidence.'

'I do know where it was, and we can't.'

'Where and why, then?'

'After you went to the phone, I scouted along the last bit of bank. I didn't see any wads, but I spotted a place where there's a conspicuous white stone that would make a good aiming-mark, and the shale all around it's chewed up. I bet there's a dozen or more bullets buried in behind it.'

'So why don't we just go away and dig them up later?'

'Because they might not tell us anything.'

Molly frowned, and sipped again from the flask. 'He couldn't have got enough of other people's bullets to do all his testing. So he must have fired them first out of his own rifle. Or borrowed one, but that could also be traced. So the rifling-marks would give him away, wouldn't they?'

'If the police co-operated, which is far from certain, and if he didn't get his bullets by pulling them out of cartridges instead of firing them. No, while we've got him treed we hang on and see if he can explain what he's doing here – with a rifle, if he's got one.'

As they spoke, Molly was snatching occasional glances at the tower using Keith's flask as a mirror. 'Any movement?' Keith asked.

'None at all. Just an occasional pale shadow of a face. Shall we do something to make his eyes pop out?'

Keith looked at her sharply. She was flushed, probably from the effect of the neat spirit. Molly was a modest girl, Keith knew, but sometimes – and particularly when, as now, she had taken an unaccustomed dram of whisky – a rare wildness came over her. Keith sympathised, for he was subject to such moods himself, but this was not the time for madness. 'Don't throw your knickers over the windmill just now,' he said sternly. 'We may be joined by a dozen Bobbies any minute.'

Molly sighed whisky fumes into Keith's face. 'You're not the fun that you used to be any more,' she said. 'Never mind. Which of them do you think it is, up in the tower?'

'I'll tell you,' Keith said slowly. 'I think McNeill has the stronger motive. But McNeill has his own bit of shooting and Payne would be more likely to come and do his testing here. And Payne had the closed-up cartridge in his pocket. McNeill told me I'd have to be quick. And McNeill was inside the wood.'

'In other words, you don't know?'

'No, I don't bloody know,' Keith said irritably. 'I think it's McNeill, but I think I think that because I don't like him.'

Molly was cold. She sipped from the flask again. 'I think it's somebody quite, quite else,' she said.

'*What*?'

'*You* keep *your* voice down. You know it's one of those two?'

'Yes.'

'That's exactly the situation you'd get in a thriller, and

then he'd come down the ladder or get unmasked by the great detective, and he'd turn out to be Sir Peter, or Mr Enterkin, or Inspector Munro or that Miss Thingie in Dunfermline.'

'And where, may I ask, were they hiding from the dogs when the line of guns went by?'

'Hiding up a tree?'

'I thought of that,' Keith said untruthfully. He paused. 'The trees are small conifers around there, about eight or nine feet tall. Not much up to hide. The only taller trees are deciduous, bare as a cobweb and about sixty yards further on from where it happened. And if he's in his car on the way here, it can't be Chief Inspector Munro.'

'Somebody taking my name in vain?' said a voice behind them.

CHAPTER 17

They swung round. Inspector Munro was standing, feet astride. He was in uniform, the silver sparkling bright in the low, wintry sunlight. One hand was behind his back, but in the other he held a portable radio unit. He was looking up at the tower.

For a long moment, Keith was stunned. The impact of Munro's presence coinciding with his own words left his mind distorted. Munro had been in the tower, and had crept down behind them. Munro had insisted on prosecuting an innocent man. Munro had hampered his every attempt to prove Ronnie innocent. Munro with his radio could have answered as if from Edinburgh. Munro. . . .

The illusion was shattered by the first shot from the tower, which smashed the radio set to a tangle of wires and a scattering of plastic, and cost the inspector the tip of his little finger. They argued later as to whether the bullet was meant for the inspector or for his radio. Munro and Molly were sure that the murderer's first concern was to prevent them communicating with the local police; Keith swore that, against the sun, no man could have been sure of that shot over open sights. The murderer was in no position to elucidate.

That nobody was killed in those first seconds was due to the speed of reaction of the men present. The acting detective chief inspector was down behind the nearest barrel before the last transistor had hit the ground. Molly lifted a camera, but Keith grabbed her round the waist and swung her over and down and the two of them rolled together in through the open front of the trap-house. They dropped three feet to the muddy floor, Keith underneath and winded, Molly on top and, incredibly, showing every sign of considering the whole episode a delightful romp.

'You swept me off my feet,' she said. 'Again.'

216

'Gerroff me,' said Keith. 'I nearly shot that bugger Munro. And now I wish I had. Get off,' he repeated.

'When I say that to you, you never do.'

'You never really mean it. I do.' He rolled her off him, and they sat up.

During their hasty retreat into cover one or two shots – they were never sure how many – had been fired. Now they heard a bullet hit the barrel that sheltered the inspector, and another smacked in through the open front and hit the back of the trap-house a hammer-blow, followed later by the sound of the shot.

Molly raised herself to peer over the edge.

'Careful,' Keith said. 'He's trying to pin us down while he waits to see if Munro brought reinforcements.'

'I don't think he can see us in here, against the sun. But just in case . . .' Molly loosened her hair, and with her fingers combed it down over her face.

'You look like something out of the jungle,' Keith said. He scraped some dark mud off the floor and darkened his face and the backs of his hands. They heard more shots.

'They say married couples come to resemble each other,' Molly said. 'I say, he doesn't seem to be short of ammunition. How much have we got?'

Keith opened his gun. At the sound, Tanya came and looked curiously in at them. 'Out,' Keith said briefly. 'Chase 'em up. I've got one in the gun and three in my pocket. Where's the game-bag?'

'It's still up on the roof. Could you get Tanya to fetch it, do you think?'

'I probably could. But he'd guess why, and he'd shoot her.'

'Would he?'

'It's what I'd do.' Keith picked up the spent bullet. 'Two-four-three,' he said.

Cautiously, they raised their heads. The soles of the inspector's feet were about five yards away. 'What a most unattractive bum he's got.' Keith said.

The inspector twisted round. 'For Christ's sake do something,' he said. He shook blood from his hand.

217

'I've only got four rounds left,' said Keith. 'And I'm saving one of those to put right up your arse from here. I suppose you didn't bring anybody with you?'

'No.'

'Or tell the local Bobbies that you'd be here?'

'No. I don't take my orders from the likes of you.'

'Ah. But do you wish you had?' There was no answer. 'Acting Detective Chief Inspector Munro, you're an idiot. What are you?'

Again there was no answer, but Munro's backside expressed injured dignity.

'We're out-gunned, aren't we?' Molly asked.

'Not necessarily. But he's beyond the range of ordinary shot.' Keith squatted down and took the knife from his belt. He began carefully to cut round each of his four cartridge-cases, about an inch from the brass base. Two more bullets smashed into the back wall above his head.

'Why doesn't he run for it?' Molly asked.

Keith spoke absently, concentrating on his task. 'Better ask him. But firstly he might be seen and identified, and secondly he doesn't know yet what armament I've got here. I might have my drilling with me – I don't suppose he could tell the difference at that distance. Even if I had a few BB cartridges with me I could tickle him up a bit . . .'

Keith became aware that Molly had raised herself and was busily photographing the scene outside. She had muddied the backs of her hands.

'For God's sake, are you nuts?' he demanded, pulling her down beside him. 'Suppose he sees the brightwork of that camera!'

Molly was laughing excitedly. 'Do you realise what the pop press pays for this kind of on-the-spot photography?

Keith had to admit to himself that she had an argument, but felt impelled to give warning. 'The last bullet that I got through me still hurts,' he said.

The shooting from the tower had stopped for the moment. 'What's he waiting for?' the inspector's voice asked anxiously.

Keith peered cautiously over the lip of the trap-house. 'At

a guess,' he said, 'he now knows that there's no immediate help coming for us. He's wondering whether there's any way out for him except by killing all three of us, and he'll probably decide not. And he'll wait for a cloud to come over the sun, because then he'll be able to see in here. Take a look around. Any clouds near the sun?'

The inspector screwed himself round again for a look at the sky. 'One or two small ones,' he said. 'Not very close.'

'He'll also work out that he has to knock you off first. He'd have a job making us keep our heads down in two different places, but with both you and the sun gone we couldn't risk looking out and he'd have time to get down the ladder and either rush us or make a run for it.'

'I'm bleeding to death already,' the inspector said plaintively.

'You've got a week or two left.' Keith raised his voice. 'Drop the rifle and come down, Payne. We can wait longer than you can.'

There was no answer from the tower.

Tanya wandered over to the inspector. She looked at him for a moment, puzzled, and then started to lick his face. The inspector told her where to go.

'Get away before you catch something,' Keith said. 'Like stupidity.'

'Why are you so sure that it's Payne?' Molly asked.

'It isn't. It's McNeill. It has his kind of ruthlessness. But if he thinks we think it's somebody else, it may confuse his thinking.'

The murderer's logic, however, must have run closely parallel to Keith's. He opened up with a series of aimed shots at the barrel. Keith and Molly, looking out of their bunker but prepared to duck on the instant, could see the barrel of a rifle, a pair of hands, a dark and shapeless hat and a fragment of a face.

'I've got binoculars in the game-bag too,' Keith said. 'At this distance I'm damned if I can make out which one of them it is.'

'I still think you're wrong,' Molly said conversationally. 'McLure was a lad for the girls, and he wouldn't have known a moral scruple if it had jumped up and down in front of him wiggling its ears. Suppose that he was messing about with Weatherby's daughter. Suppose he'd put her in the club or something. Either of them could have let you go by and then come round behind you.'

'But according to Janet – ' Keith stopped in mid-sentence.

'Exactly,' said Molly. She put down her camera and cupped her hands for a shout. 'You don't have to shoot me, Mr Weatherby. I don't know who you are.'

Keith ground his teeth. 'You'd better give me my flask back.'

'It's in the game-bag, too.'

A bullet hit the top hoop of the barrel. The hoop sprang apart and the staves opened slightly, allowing a trickle of shale to fall on the inspector's head. Tanya wandered over to inspect the damage. The murderer held his fire.

'Not Weatherby,' Keith said. 'He doesn't give a damn about dogs.'

'Will you two stop chattering like old wives at a *ceilidh* and do something about the situation,' said Munro. His words were meant to be authoritative, but his voice was shaking.

'You made the situation,' Keith said. 'You do something about it.'

'I call on you – '

'Under what section of what act?'

Tanya had lost interest and wandered away. The murderer's next shot hit the middle hoop of the barrel.

'I don't think Payne could shoot that well,' Keith said.

The barrel began to open like a flower as the weight within it forced open the bottom hoop. The inspector, venting a stream of Gaelic in a very high voice, seemed to be trying to burrow under the flowing mound of shale.

Keith lifted his gun and fired. The front half of the cartridge, holding together more than an ounce of shot and travelling close to the speed of a rifle-bullet, hit the upper corner of the trap-house on the tower and exploded. The trap-house was built to protect the trapper against stray pellets, but its double thickness of corrugated metal might have been paper against such a projectile. The upper corner ceased to exist, and the interior was filled for an instant with tiny, buzzing hornets.

Keith kept his aim on the place where he had last seen the man with the rifle, and waited. 'Throw down your rifle, McNeill,' he shouted. 'The next one comes up through the floor.'

The staves of the barrel collapsed suddenly, leaving the inspector prone behind a low pyramid of shale that was still flattening as it sought its own angle of repose.

'Keep your bum down, Inspector,' said Molly.

Munro was afraid to lift his head, but he turned his face. One eye glared at them frantically. 'Shoot the *mhuc* now,' he said.

Molly brandished her camera. Her face was alight with unholy glee. 'Don't,' she said. 'Don't. That man's been persecuting you and Ronnie for the last three months.'

'Just in the way of duty,' Munro said shrilly. 'Over now. Satisfied – '

'Inspector,' said Keith, 'you're an *amadan*, a bloody fool. What are you?'

'I'm a bloody fool. Now will you shoot him?'

'Cartridges are expensive.'

'I'll pay for it. I'll *pay* for it.'

Molly was still photographing. 'These shots are worth hundreds,' she said. 'But just imagine what a photographic record of the murder of an acting detective chief inspector would be worth. Thousands!'

'You can't get away with inciting your husband to let me be killed,' Munro bleated. 'I'll make a complaint.'

'You won't be around,' said Molly.

The sun began to fade as the rim of a distant cloud touched it. At the same moment, a pale blur reared up in the trap-house on the tower, two pale hands fumbling with a dark rifle. Keith fired at a point a foot below the hands, and saw a hole the size of a hen's egg appear in the metal. The figure vanished, and there were sounds from within the trap-house.

They waited a full minute before moving forward. Molly trotted behind the two men, photographing with one hand while hunting in her camera-bag for a flash with the other.

Keith went first up the ladder, the reloaded gun in one hand, gripping precariously with the other. He paused and listened, and then, quickly, looked in over the top.

But Andrew Payne was quite dead.

CHAPTER 18

Both Keith Calder and Ronnie Fiddler appeared before the sheriff the next morning, and statements were made by Acting Detective Chief Inspector Munro and by the procurator fiscal. The charges against Ronnie were formally withdrawn, and although reference would still have to be made to the High Court it was found possible to free him immediately on a nominal bail. Into Keith's shooting of Andrew Payne a fiscal's enquiry would be necessary; but Munro stated, on oath, that the shooting was carried out on his orders and to save his life, and Keith also was freed.

Keith and Molly met Ronnie, by appointment, as he emerged an hour later from the side door of the sheriff court building. He stood filling the doorway for a moment, blinking at them. Then he came down the steps uncertainly, seeming to taste the pavement with his feet, and gave Keith his hand. 'I have to thank you,' he said simply.

Keith avoided a direct reply for, to be honest, Ronnie had three months in prison to thank him for. Instead he said, 'You don't mind about Molly and me?'

'Have her and welcome. I never realised what a damned bad cook she was until they put me inside and I found that I was eating better.'

'Keith and I are going to get married again,' Molly said, 'properly, in church. We want you to give the bride away.'

'I thought I just did.'

'But you'll come to the church?'

'Aye. But I'll not wear a black coat an' stripey breeks. 'Long as that's understood.'

'Yon wife of yours,' said Chief Inspector Munro. 'Would she really have had you leave me to be shot?'

'I don't think so,' Keith said. 'I'd filled her with whisky to keep her courage up.'

'It was just the whisky talking? I hope so, I'd not like to be thinking that I was misliked as much as that.' Munro's long highland face was mournful, but he brightened. 'But still, when the time came you did what had to be done. I'm obliged to you for that. And whatever you may think of my handling of the case, my rank's been confirmed. So all's well that ends well.'

Keith did not think that Munro's promotion was a well ending. 'It's all over, then?' he said.

'Aye, barring two fiscals' enquiries and a High Court appearance by that brother-in-law of yours. And barring a few words that I want to say to you.' Munro looked around his barren office without seeming to see it. 'I was doing my duty as I saw fit, and I'll not say that I'm sorry for it. But it was the help you gave those laddies from Strathclyde that got me my promotion, so I owe you a wee bit of something – no more than that.

'That rifle, now. The one that was the cause of all the trouble. It'll just be destroyed, and no more said about it. And,' he added sternly, 'there'll be no need for you to make another like it, as your pal Jock Hendry's got his certificate back. No need to work so hard at not looking surprised. I'm not altogether a bloody fool, whatever I may have said while I was under pressure.' He smiled grimly.

'From now on,' Keith said, 'I'm a respectable business-man.'

And on that note, perhaps, we should leave him. We may discard as a coincidence the uncomfortable fact that McNeill's ground was cleared of every bird a few days later.

Another coincidence was that, before January was out, the Hall burned to the ground. Sir Peter and his lady were at Dawnapool at the time and the servants away. It appeared that the house had been burgled before, accidentally or deliberately, being set on fire. The only article recovered was the portrait of Sir Peter's mother, which turned up in the Left Luggage department of the local railway station.

The fire brigade was seriously hampered in its efforts to save the Hall by a sheet of ice covering the steep driveway. It was as though a land-drain had overflowed, but all the land-drains were frozen at the time.